D1535604

AGGIE MORTON
MYSTERY QUEEN

AGGIE MORTON
MYSTERY QUEEN

THE BODY
UNDER THE PIANO

MARTHE JOCELYN

WITH ILLUSTRATIONS BY ISABELLE FOLLATH

tundra

Tundra Books, an imprint of Penguin Random House Canada Young Readers, a
Penguin Random House Company

Library and Archives Canada Cataloguing in Publication

Title: The body under the piano / Marthe Jocelyn.
Names: Jocelyn, Marthe, author.
Description: Series statement: Aggie Morton, mystery queen ; 1
Identifiers: Canadiana (print) 20190099070 | Canadiana (ebook)
20190099291 | ISBN 9780735265462
   (hardcover) | ISBN 9780735265479 (EPUB)
Classification: LCC PS8569.O254 B63 2020 | DDC jC813/.54—dc23

Published simultaneously in the United States of America by Tundra Books
of Northern New York, an imprint of Penguin Random House Canada Young
Readers, a Penguin Random House Company

Library of Congress Control Number: 2019907433

Edited by Tara Walker with assistance from Margot Blankier
Designed by John Martz
The text was set in Plantin MT Pro.

Printed and bound in Canada

www.penguinrandomhouse.ca

1   2   3   4   5   24   23   22   21   20

Penguin
Random House
tundra | TUNDRA BOOKS

FOR TARA

Aggie Morton

Hector Perot

Grannie Jane

Mummy

Tony

Augustus Fibbley

Charlotte Graves

Constable Beck

Irma Eversham

Marianne Eversham

Rose Eversham

Roderick Fusswell

Inspector Locke

Leonard Cable

Florence Fusswell

Lavinia Paine

CHAPTER 1

AN UNUSUAL FRIEND

I WILL TELL FIRST about making a new friend and save the dead body for later. This follows the traditional rules of storytelling—lull the reader with pleasant scenery and lively dialogue, introduce a few appealing characters, and then—*aha!*—discover a corpse!

The friend I found was not a nice young lady introduced by Mummy or Grannie Jane. He was a boy! A *foreign* boy. He was, to be truthful, a bit peculiar. But I determined to be open-minded, as potential friends did not often come my way. Except of the made-up sort. I had a whole school-room full of imagined girls and their fictional endeavors to occupy my solitary hours. I named them and clothed them, worried about their spats, and rejoiced in their reunions. But they did not ever think of me.

A real person my own age was quite out of the ordinary. After my dance lesson late on a Saturday morning in October, I went into Mr. Dillon's sweet shop downstairs from the Mermaid Dance Room on Union Street. Just as always, I took a moment to scratch the ears of Frostypaws, the shop cat. Just as always, Charlotte was with me. When would Mummy understand that a person of already-turned-twelve can get through an hour of life without a nursemaid?

Charlotte and I lingered as the other girls from my dance class paid for their violet pastilles and buttermints and went home with their own unwanted nursemaids to their lunches. I preferred to make my selection in a con-sidered manner, without needing to speak in front of anyone listening. An audience caused in me a dizzying panic. Mummy said that being shy was temporary, that someday I'd speak as easily to unfamiliar grown-ups as I did to Tony, my dog. But each time the words caught in my throat, *someday* felt further away.

Because Charlotte was the one who carried the tuppence that Mummy allowed for sweets, she waited patiently for my decision—as she must, since it was her job to do so, and sometimes to wait *on* me, to keep me safe and to explain things that needed explaining.

My sister, Marjorie, had gone to proper schools, but by the time it was my turn, seven years later, Mummy had developed certain notions about the education of children not like those of other parents. Children should roam free, she felt, though always close to home and under the steadily watchful eye of a nursemaid. Free-roaming bodies and brains would result in greater wisdom and well-being. This meant no school, no governess and no friends.

I learned history and literature from Mummy and from books in Papa's library. For natural science, I explored the garden. Going to All Saints Church every Sunday was for Bible stories and religious studies. I practiced dance with Miss Marianne, in the Mermaid Room, and played the piano and the mandolin with other lady teachers. Papa had been the one to teach me mathematics, but my skills in that area had faltered since last November when he died. I did not miss arithmetic, but I missed Papa with every breath. The Morton family, with all of England, had mourned Queen Victoria's demise nearly two years earlier, but since then we'd learned the truth in our own house. Grief was a story with endless forlorn endings.

None of my lessons, nor any of the books I'd read, had yet explained how the smallest occurrence might cause a tremendous impact on the universe. If I had chosen chocolate buds on that Saturday, as I usually did, instead of strawberry drops (in the jar on a higher shelf, reached only by using a stool) . . . And if Frostypaws had picked a different moment to pounce on her master's bootlaces (dangling so temptingly from atop the stool) . . . And if the bell on the shop door did not announce customers with such a strident jangle (causing Mr. Dillon to twist around in surprise) . . . Hector Perot would not have walked through the door into the mayhem of shattered glass and scattered sweets, and we would have had no reason to speak to each other.

At the time, I did not see that a sequence was unfolding. One never does. Afterward, it was clear how the moments piled up, each leading naturally to the next, quietly altering the course of things. At the time, however, in Dillon's Sweets & Sundries shortly after noon, poor Frostypaws squawked like a chicken and fled behind the barrel of demerara sugar. Mr. Dillon had landed on his large behind, but waved us off as he struggled without success to regain a vertical position. Charlotte and I crept closer, using the toes of our boots to push shards of broken glass and cracked strawberry drops into a pile. The bell-jangling newcomer stood just inside the door.

"May I be of assistance?" he asked.

He had an accent that chopped his words with precision. His skin was near as pale as milk. Black hair was slicked flat on a head that seemed a bit large for his skinny body. He was tidily dressed in a navy blue sailor suit with an impeccably clean white collar.

He was not as handsome as Leonard, the boy who worked in our garden and looked like a matinee hero on stage at the Royal Arms Theatre. But this boy's eyes were very green and very bright, bringing to mind a glass of lime cordial.

Eyes like lime cordial? Agatha Caroline Morton, can you not do better than that? *Glittering emeralds? A new spring leaf? The tail feather of a peacock?*

"Give me a hand, will you, boy?" Mr. Dillon's bottom was still planted on the floor amidst the glass splinters.

The boy hurried over. I approached more slowly, worried that Mr. Dillon mightn't like being seen this way. I should be mortified if it were I, stuck like a fat beetle not able to clamber up onto my own two feet. Though if I were a beetle, I'd have six feet and perhaps better balance.

"I shall find a gentleman to help us," said Charlotte. She set the bell a-jingle as she scurried into the street.

But the boy was already gripping Mr. Dillon's left wrist and elbow, attempting to heave him upright. I quickly seized the right arm and anchored my foot against the confectioner's.

"One. Two. Three!" I cried. "Pull!"

"Un. Deux. Trois!" said the boy. "Tirez!"

And up came Mr. Dillon, red-faced, whiskers quivering, his shop apron twisted and sweets crunching beneath his boots.

"Well, now, I thank you." Mr. Dillon straightened his apron and withdrew a handkerchief from its pocket.

He patted his forehead and removed his spectacles to wipe moist eyes.

Charlotte burst back through the door, leading a tall young man in uniform.

"Oh!" she said. "We've come too late." Flushed and breathless, she hastened to apologize to her recruit. "Mr. Dillon was on the ground when I went out to seek assistance, and I . . . It was the stool, you see. And the cat. I'm afraid I have bothered you for nothing, constable."

"It's never nothing, miss." Apart from a pink tinge to his cheeks, the constable was unruffled, and very kindly with Mr. Dillon. He made certain there were no broken bones and gave us his hearty congratulations for successfully rescuing the old fellow from the floor.

"My name"—he appeared to be speaking to a jar of barley sugar on the counter—"is Constable Morris Beck. Should you require my services in the future."

Charlotte blushed and made a slight curtsy. "Thank you, sir. I am Miss Charlotte Graves, and this is my charge, Miss Agatha Morton."

I nodded hello.

Constable Beck touched his helmet. "Pleased, I'm sure." His face and Charlotte's both were now the color of raspberry pudding. *Poached salmon. Crousse peonies. Flamingo feathers.*

I glanced over at the strange boy. He raised one finely

shaped black eyebrow. We were agreed! Never before had I been present during an interlude of Love at First Sight, but with that eyebrow, the boy appeared to indicate that we were witnessing exactly that.

"Allow me also to introduce myself," he said. "I am Hector Perot." He bent stiffly forward from the waist in a little bow. I managed not to giggle. Certainly foreign! But likeable nonetheless.

"Aggie Morton," I said, and curtsied.

The policeman muttered something about returning to his beat and bumbled his way backward to the door, making the bell ring yet again. Charlotte pretended not to watch his departure.

"Well, now," said Mr. Dillon. "I believe my rescuers deserve a reward." He handed each of us an empty cone of paper. "Go on, fill them up," he urged. "Choose whatever you like."

Strawberry drops, crushed to smithereens and swept into the bin, were no longer of interest. I picked caramels and chocolate buds and a small lump of fudge. Hector filled his paper to the top with black licorice pastilles.

"Might I have a small box instead of the cone, monsieur?" he said.

When Mr. Dillon produced one, Hector carefully placed his sweets in straight rows along the bottom.

"You win now a loyal new customer," he assured Mr. Dillon. "I am being here again, this I promise."

I was reluctant that another encounter with this boy be left to chance alone.

"I am always here on Saturdays," I said, with unusual vigor. I did not look at Charlotte. "At this same time."

"We shall meet then, upon another Saturday."

"We shall," I said. "And perhaps we can devise a new method of attracting the police. What do you think, Charlotte? Without having anyone topple over?"

CHAPTER 2

A FLURRY OF PREPARATIONS

I MIGHT HAVE SPENT the week yearning for Saturday to come again, hoping for renewed acquaintance with Hector Perot, but first there was Friday to fret about. Miss Marianne was hosting a concert in the Mermaid Dance Room. The name of the evening, and its intention, was Befriend the Foreigners. I had written a poetical tribute that I was meant to read aloud. All week I wished that Friday evening should never arrive, or else should be over and done. And yet here I was, with an hour to go, spinning around and around on the piano stool.

Miss Marianne had given firm instructions as to how we should arrange the studio. I had already placed six sturdy crates along one side of the room, with Charlotte trailing close behind in case I stubbed a thumb or some other calamity. Our audience members this evening were to fill these containers with cast-off clothes and other useful items, later to be sorted and distributed to needy refugees and immigrants who had recently arrived here in Torquay.

There seemed to be many reasons for people to travel far from home, some with only a small bundle of belongings. Several families had fled religious persecution or starvation in Russia, caused by the cruel neglect of their Tsar. A number of Belgians were here to avoid brewing turmoil under the dastardly King Leopold, and a few destitute lascar seaman awaited berths on ships back home to India.

I had never yet seen a refugee, but the town simmered with talk, if a person stood about in the right places to hear it. Shops were ideal for eavesdropping, or the church vestibule, and certainly our own kitchen at Groveland, where Cook and Sally gathered endless tidbits from tradesmen and the servants from other households. It was generally discussed that visitors from other lands were frequently remiss in their bathing habits, and that they wore clothing incompatible with our English sense of fashion. Some liked spicy food and considered bread pudding and haddock to be inedible. As I, myself, was not enthralled by haddock, we perhaps shared a place to begin.

"Miss Aggie?" Charlotte beckoned me over to assist in arranging chairs for the audience. When those were set, Miss Marianne provided festive cloths to drape over the piano and the piano stool. We put a plainer covering on the table where refreshments would be laid upon arrival from the Royal Victoria Hotel. The hotel had generously donated all the treats to be served, thanks to Florence Fusswell's father being the general manager. This was only one of the reasons that Florence Fusswell thought she was queen of the evening. Another was her abundant yellow hair and pink skin and what she herself referred to as her *rosebud lips*. She busied herself straightening the chairs that Charlotte and I had already set out in perfectly tidy rows. Lavinia Paine, best friend and loyal follower of Florence Fusswell, stood next to the mirror, counting as she touched her fingertips to her toes fifteen times. Her dark plaits dangled and swayed like two scrawny cow's tails switching away flies.

I returned to the piano stool and began again to swivel.

A large ladleful of my confidence drained away in the presence of girls so certain of themselves. I was perfectly able to utter my own opinion at home with my family or any of the servants. Or with intriguing foreign boys in sweet shops. But these prattling girls my own age made my words dry up. It was not the same as being shy with adults. I simply did not have a knack for silly chatter. I wished to know what people chose *not* to say aloud, what dark secrets simmered, and what might happen next. I sometimes took a certain pleasure in imagining misfortunes that might rain down upon Lavinia Paine or Florence Fusswell.

I stopped spinning.

What if the chair Florence was lifting at this moment were to fall and crush her toe? Would there be a gush of blood? Or might it be better that she suffer a clean fracture? The story possibilities flowered before me . . .

Yes, to begin a tale of horror, I'd use a broken bone.

The injured girl howled as her foot swelled and throbbed. She was driven in a rickety and bouncing cart to the Torquay Hospital where the surgeon declared that the toe—no, the whole foot—must be cut off! Incoherent with distress, Florence begged for mercy. As the surgeon lifted his knife, a nurse helped the trembling girl to escape. (The unnecessary amputation of an extremity seemed a bit cruel, even in a fiction created for revenge.) *But the nurse, whose name was Ethelwin Smirke, concealed a dark intent. After forcing Florence to hobble, despite her injury, down two flights of crumbling stairs, Nurse Smirke imprisoned the sobbing girl in a cellar inhabited by a great number of hairy gray spiders, more than thirty, who had grown rather bigger than usual, due to their consumption of the rank and oily substance dripping from the rusted pipe that runs along the ceiling . . .*

Shrill laughter interrupted my pleasant daydream. Florence and Lavinia were falling over themselves to assist a young man edging his way through the door. He hauled in one large floral bouquet, and then another, and set down the ornate vases on either side of the piano. He tugged off his cap to reveal a mop of chestnut hair and dark eyes. Girls like Florence and Lavinia would not normally deign to look at a delivery boy, but this was Leonard—especially handsome, and almost eighteen. As he was employed by my mother, the prestige of knowing him was rather more mine than theirs, was it not? He slept in the grounds-keeper's shed at Groveland in exchange for helping in the garden and the hothouse. I saw him every day, so let Florence and Lavinia try to shift the heavy pots into the most suitable position. What did I care?

Miss Marianne soon stepped in to scold them away. "Please allow the young man to perform his task. There are fifty-five programs, my dears. I hope I can trust you to fold them precisely?"

"Hello, Leonard," I said.

"Miss Agatha!"

"Your arrangements are lovely."

"Yes, miss. From your own greenhouse. Pretty as anything."

The Groveland gardens, neglected since Papa's death, had quite revived under Leonard's care this past summer. He'd assembled the bouquets for my sister Marjorie's wedding last month, only weeks after he'd arrived in Torquay and moved into the shed behind the kitchen vegetable plot.

"All for a good cause, eh, miss? You've got a soft heart for creatures in need, haven't you? Animals and humans."

"We all do!" Florence had crept closer again. "That's why we're here, isn't it, Lavinia? *Very* soft hearts, we've got."

Lavinia clutched a sheaf of programs and nodded in ardent agreement. "No one softer," she said.

Soft in the head, I thought. How easily they peeved me! Leonard smiled as if he'd read my thoughts.

"We're dancing tonight," said Florence. She pushed a program into his hand and pointed:

A Graceful Moment
Music by FRÉDÉRIC CHOPIN
Interpretation by MISS MARIANNE EVERSHAM
Movement by FLORENCE FUSSWELL
and LAVINIA PAINE

Florence whispered, "Maybe he can't read."

Lavinia ignored her. "My name is only second because the listing is alphabetical," she said.

But Leonard's finger had moved down the page.

"And you, Miss Agatha? You're saying a poem?"

A shiver tingled up my neck. I'd got this far in the day by avoiding thoughts of what was coming at the end of it. A recitation that waited like a jowled monster to gobble me up. I managed a bit of a nod and stared hard at Leonard's scuffed boots. One of his laces had been broken and re-knotted in at least three places.

"*She's* the one who wrote the verse," said Florence. "It's not by a real poet, not Tennyson or anyone."

"That makes it better then, doesn't it?" said Leonard. "Writ special for these new strangers come to town."

My heart about burst with gratitude. I glanced up to bestow an appreciative smile, but he was turning to nod at Miss Marianne.

"You'll be back in the morning, Mr. Cable?" said Miss Marianne. "To collect these up again?"

Leonard nodded. "If you're sure, ma'am, that you don't want to keep them? Till the flowers aren't so fresh?"

Miss Marianne smiled at him. "You're a kind lad to offer, but no. Return them to Mrs. Morton. We need to dance in here!"

Leonard slid his cap back on and touched its brim in a salute. The door opened as he reached it, and all at once the entrance was congested with quite a crowd.

Rose Eversham was first, with her mother a step behind. The Evershams lived next door to Mummy and me, in a villa named EverMore. Wasn't that a divine name for a house? Miss Marianne lived there too, being Rose's aunt, and with no family of her own.

Following the ladies was Florence's brother, Mr. Roddy Fusswell, from the Royal Victoria Hotel, holding aloft an

15

enormous platter of macaroons and tiny fruit tarts. On his head was a gray top hat. His hands were sheathed in yellow leather gloves. He wore a frock coat and a billowy cravat, as if our recital were occurring at the Royal Albert Hall in London and not above a shop on Union Street. His two assistants each carried a plate of dainty sandwiches.

A chittering hum started up, all of us thrumming with excitement to be near Rose Eversham, starring subject of gossip flying about town this past week. Stories claimed that she'd been seen in the company of more than one young man at the roller rink on the pier, laughing and twirling without a care who noticed. Further whispers said that her mother had scolded her sharply on the high street, only to have Rose *turn and walk away*, as rude as can be!

(One of the young men was Roddy Fusswell, another was Charlie Trotter, the butcher's son. Rose had also been seen kissing a sailor, but it was Lavinia who made that claim, so we could safely dismiss it.)

And here she was, sailing through the door like a queen on the prow of a ship. Leonard ducked his head as if caught in a glaring beam of sunlight. He slid to one side, allowing the parade to enter.

Rose waved at Miss Marianne. "Darling Auntie M.! You see? Not a minute past five o'clock. I vowed not to be late and I'm as good as my word. And! With *Mother*."

Had her eyes performed the slightest of rolls? And was that an answering flicker in Miss Marianne's? It seemed there was a conspiracy of niece and aunt. Everyone— truly, everyone—knew Rose's mother to be a trial. Our maid, Sally, called Mrs. Eversham a prickly old cow. Though we were neighbors, I rarely had the opportunity to examine her so closely as this.

Mrs. Irma Eversham had the face of a grumpy dog. She paused on the threshold, looking about as if she'd caught a whiff of something rotten. Roddy Fusswell, holding his tray of treats, was only half a step behind. He now met her back with a *thunk*. For a terrible moment the pastries threatened to shower down upon her head (as he was tall and she was squat), but Mr. Fusswell managed an agile twist and kept the tray aloft. A solitary jam tart slid over the rim and landed on the crown of Irma Eversham's hat. Rose and Miss Marianne both lunged forward to offer aid. Roddy Fusswell plucked at the tart from above, knocking Leonard's shoulder with his elbow. Mrs. Eversham became a spitting cat, turning her head so abruptly that the tart flew off and was nimbly caught by Miss Marianne.

"Keep away from me!" Mrs. Eversham shook off all assistance. Miss Marianne stepped back, pressing Leonard into the door frame. Roddy Fusswell hovered too closely but could not move in the knot of people. Mrs. Eversham's indignation made the room vibrate.

"And furthermore," she said, "keep away from my daughter."

"Mother!" Rose switched her valise from one hand to the other, making a great show of its contents being heavy. "Let us think about the needy," she said, quickly and loudly. "I've gone through my wardrobe and had a good clean out. I shall have to order new things very soon, unless you want to see my unmentionables!"

"Rose!" scolded Mrs. Eversham. "Such brazen talk!"

"Will you come and sit down, Mrs. Eversham?" Charlotte's calm voice and steady hand reached through the mayhem. "We have reserved you a place here in the front row."

"Yes, Mother, please sit," said Rose. "I will make you a cup of tea. And a biscuit? You love a sugary biscuit."

"I will not sit," said Mrs. Eversham. "And I will not stay. I did not want to be here and the present company confirms that. Do not *fuss*, Rose! I can certainly get my own self home."

Rose made no further effort to convince a change of mind. Lavinia stifled a giggle. Leonard had been creeping toward the exit but froze when Mrs. Eversham turned to leave. I slid behind Charlotte as Roddy Fusswell put down his platter and offered to escort Mrs. Eversham to the street. She refused with a brusque flap of her hand, as if he were a hornet. He put a hand under her elbow and again she swatted him. This time he retreated, treading on poor Leonard's toe.

Mrs. Eversham continued calling, even as she descended the stairs. "I'll see to it that any young man who approaches my daughter will be imprisoned on a charge of attempting to assault her. Does everyone hear me?"

I was not the only person waiting to exhale when we heard the door below slam shut. My palms itched to applaud. It had been ten minutes of jolly good theater, better than a Christmas pantomime!

A phlegmy noise in Roddy Fusswell's throat set the room back in motion. Leonard finally made his exit, though I imagined that he opened the street door with great caution, in case Mrs. Eversham had not yet trundled off. Rose lifted the lid of her valise and dumped the contents into one of the crates.

"How do you bear it, Rose?" asked Roddy. "She is insufferable. She should not be tolerated a single day longer!"

"Life would certainly be smoother," said Miss Marianne, "if she were not in Torquay."

"Sadly true," said Rose. "At least once a day, I find myself wishing that she were dead."

CHAPTER 3

A DELIGHTFUL EVENING

OUR AUDIENCE WOULD be here any minute. We madly folded the remaining stack of programs, except for Florence, who preferred to shadow her brother. Roddy Fusswell was precise in directing his helpers as to where the trays should go, the angle at which to place the dainty serviettes, and where the milk jug and sugar bowl must stand in proximity to the tea urn.

"Go *away!*" he whispered to Florence, which Lavinia seemed to think was hilarious. Florence swiped a lemon tart and crammed it into her mouth before Roddy could stop her. He clamped his fingers around her wrist as she chewed, squeezing so tightly that she began to splutter crumbs.

"Oww!" She tugged, but her brother held on. "Let me

go!" she said. Then, "Oh dear." More loudly. "What *is* that on your face?"

Roddy Fusswell glared at Florence as if she were a slug on a plate of biscuits. He released his grip and one of his hands slid upward to check.

"Oh!" she said. "I thought it was a fuzzy yellow millipede but now I see! It's your attempt to grow a mustache!"

Lavinia snorted. Roddy looked as if he might tip the tea urn over his sister's head. But Miss Marianne put a hand on Florence's shoulder.

"This evening is about befriending," she said. "Have we not heard enough harsh words for one night? I am at the end of my tether with unpleasant relations."

Coming in now was the Reverend Mr. Teasdale, vicar of All Saints Church, accompanied by his dour wife. Mr. Teasdale would shepherd donations from the Mermaid Room to the needy families. Indeed, he ceremoniously placed his own contribution—a woolly red cardigan— on top of the offerings from Rose's drawers. He and Mrs. Teasdale took up positions nearby to direct further gifts. Lavinia and Florence were to give each family a program. Mummy arrived, looking very smart. Despite being still in mourning for Papa, she'd put a blue feather in her hat, exactly the color of her eyes. She brought me a set of new pencils as a good luck present, wrapped with a velvet ribbon.

The minutes until my recitation were whirling past at a dreadful speed. One moment we all waited in place, worried that no audience would appear. The next moment, the room and donation boxes were half-filled and the platters of tea cakes half-empty. Only a few moments more and every chair was occupied. The boxes overflowed with a most peculiar collection of items for the about-to-be-befriended immigrants and refugees. Would someone fleeing a turbulent homeland need a veiled hat covered with coral-colored chrysanthemums? Or a pair of tasseled patent leather pumps? Fortunately, there were also heaps of warm jumpers and knitted stockings, sturdy flannel trousers and tweed skirts. Dozens of the needy poor would have a warmer winter thanks to our concert.

Miss Marianne gave us the signal to duck behind the curtain that hid the narrow pantry from the main studio. I squinted through the opening to keep watch. Miss Marianne turned down the gas lamps on the audience side of the room, leaving the empty stage bathed in a bright, expectant glow.

A slim young man in a brown suit opened the door from the hallway with too much force, just as the chatter subsided. Everyone jumped a bit, turning to stare at the stranger. He raised his hands in apology, snatched off his hat, and took a place against the back wall.

The girls beside me shivered in their dance tunics, breathing sugary breaths. Miss Marianne had forbidden fancy costumes, despite Florence Fusswell's protests, as this was a charitable performance, not a time to be frivolous or vain. The rehearsal tunics were the color of porridge. Mummy had agreed, as ten months had passed since Papa's death, that I might put aside my mourning clothes and wear last year's Sunday dress, grass-green silk with a pleated skirt. It was a bit worn at the elbows, but I'd be facing forward, wouldn't I? Charlotte had assured me that no one would notice. I held my poetry notebook and wished the evening done with, imagined my dress on its hanger and myself beneath the covers of my bed.

"Good evening, my friends." Miss Marianne stood with Rose next to her. "Thank you for joining us for this special gathering." She gestured toward the impressive assortment of donations. "Together we have made life better for our new neighbors."

Gentle applause rippled through the room.

"I believe that friendly foreigners have much to offer our community," said Miss Marianne. "The determination and endurance of immigrants seeking a new home is inspiring to those of us who are fighting for a woman's right to have a say in the quality of her home as well."

"Not this again," said Florence.

Miss Marianne's favorite topic, Votes for Women.

"The day will come, before these girls are grown, when they will have a voice their mothers and aunts do not. That voice is called the vote!"

"My father will make noise," said Lavinia. "He says the ideal woman is a mute."

On cue, a loud harrumphing in the audience came from Mr. Paine.

"Auntie?" said Rose.

"Get on with it," said Mr. Paine, rather more loudly than was polite. "Let's have the dancing girls." Lavinia's eyes were squeezed shut.

Miss Marianne put an arm around Rose's shoulder and summoned a cheerful smile. "I shall leave the preaching to Mr. Teasdale henceforth," she said. "May I introduce my favorite niece—"

"Your only niece!" said Rose.

"And my star pupil, Miss Rose Eversham."

People clapped, and Mr. Roddy Fusswell whooped in the vulgar manner of a football fan.

"Rose," said Miss Marianne, "will introduce the girls who follow in her footsteps."

"Thank you all for being here," said Rose. "Let us show appreciation for the gracious contribution of flowers from Mrs. Morton's greenhouse, and the delicious treats provided by the Royal Victoria Hotel."

Another smattering of applause.

"Most of you knew and remember my father," Rose said, "Captain Giles Eversham, may he rest in peace. He taught me that an important step in becoming an adult is learning to give instead of to receive."

A sympathetic murmur ran through the audience. Mr. Teasdale nodded so vigorously that I expected to see his head topple off. Now *that* would be a colorful detail in a story, would it not?

Wrenched from its perch, the dislodged cranium rolled to a stop next to Mrs. Teasdale's tightly laced boots. A geyser of blood erupted from the reverend's stiff white collar and spurted heavenward.

Rose waved a hand at the brimming donation boxes. "My father would be proud of us tonight."

The listeners began again to clap, but Rose held up a hand. "Please save your applause for the artistes. As you see in your program, my aunt has arranged a dance to complement the music of Chopin."

I pulled aside the curtain to let the dancers pass, and held my breath as Miss Marianne sat upon the piano stool and began to play. The girls swayed on the stage like knobby saplings in a gusty breeze. The tip of Florence's tongue stuck out at the corner of her mouth. Lavinia perspired like a glass of iced lemonade on a summer day. I had an inkling that what was taught in the Mermaid Dance Room was more rewarding for the dancers than for the audience. But applause came, whether deserved or not. Florence and Lavinia hurtled into the pantry. The dreaded moment had arrived. My stomach seemed to be full of walnut shells.

"Your turn, go on!" Florence gave me a hefty shove.

I was next to the piano, my mouth as dry as talcum powder.

"And now . . ." Rose smiled in a futile effort to bolster my courage. "We will hear a poem written especially for this occasion. Please welcome Miss Agatha Morton."

The audience waited for me to begin, rows of kindly faces, all eyes on me. The ability to move my lips departed altogether. My fingers clenched my notebook so tightly that its cover was slightly damp. Mummy beamed in the second row, with Charlotte next to her. Miss Marianne nodded from the side of the room, and the slim bespectacled stranger at the back was writing in a notebook of his own.

But *chuh, chuh, chuh* . . . a familiar pulsing in my ears confirmed that I would not be reading aloud this evening. I was icy cold and burning hot in alternating shivers. Mummy's smile faltered and Charlotte's was gone altogether. Silently, I implored Rose to save me. And so she did. Rose, whom I now would love forever, stepped close and slid an arm about my shoulder. She gently extracted the notebook from my hand.

"Change of plan," she said. "*I* shall have the honor of delivering the world's first reading of a poem entitled . . ."

I mutely shook my head. I had failed to name the poem!

". . . of a new work by Agatha Morton!"

I tiptoed over to stand near Miss Marianne, my eyes prickling with hot tears. She put a soothing hand on my shoulder as we listened.

"You've left your troubled home behind," Rose began,

"to seek new shelter far away.
May strangers on the road be kind,
And faith your guide along the way.
Bravely, you sailed landward, ho!
Facing peril with each tide,
Your heart steadfast, your eyes aglow.
We here await with arms held wide."

Rose shot me a pleased grin and dramatically flung open her arms as the room rattled with applause. She put the notebook on top of the piano and held out both hands to me. I walked as gracefully as my wobbling legs could manage to join Rose and the dancers at center stage, willing myself not to faint. My ears buzzed through the final ovation, through Rose's affectionate pat and Miss Marianne's warm embrace, through Mummy's hug and Charlotte bringing me a cup of fruit punch.

"All you had to do was read, for goodness' sake," whispered Florence.

"Next time," I mumbled, praying that it be true.

Florence glared and slurped her tea.

The crowd was rapidly dispersing. Lavinia departed with her parents. Rose put the few remaining cakes and Uneeda biscuits into a tin from the pantry. Florence slumped, pouting, in a chair, waiting for her brother to finish his duties.

Mr. Roddy Fusswell stacked the cups and saucers, rinsed the creamers and lined up sugar bowls, each imprinted with the gilt-edged crest of the Royal Victoria Hotel. He brushed crumbs from the tabletop into the path of Miss Marianne's broom.

"Don't fling the crumbs about, young man," said Miss Marianne. "We've had a few furry visitors this fall as the weather gets colder, and I do not want them to feel welcome!"

"So sorry, Miss Eversham. Don't mention it to anyone, but it's the same up in the hotel, mice nestling in for the winter. They're too clever to nibble any poison we leave out and go straight for the sugar sacks!"

"I've tried everything," said Miss Marianne. "I've got boxes of VerminRid in the pantry, but the little rascals just keep coming back. I don't like the idea of traps."

"Quicker though," said Roddy. "One sharp snap and

kkggh!" A sound meant to be the dying breath of a mouse. "Like a guillotine."

"Ugh!" said Rose. "Perhaps you simply need to use more poison?"

Roddy Fusswell would return in the morning, with his assistants, to cart away the dishes and the tea urn. Leonard would fetch the splendid bouquets, and Mr. Teasdale's volunteers would lug their bounty to the basement of All Saints Church. All foreign newcomers now resident in Torquay were invited to come on Sunday after the morning service to make selections according to their needs.

Miss Marianne was just finishing her sweep of the smooth wooden floor when the bespectacled stranger approached. In a low husky voice, he introduced himself as Mr. Augustus Fibbley, a reporter for the *Torquay Voice*. A reporter! I sidled closer, scooping up garments that had escaped from the donation boxes. Mr. Fibbley was gathering facts for a notice in tomorrow morning's edition of the newspaper, he explained. Might he please take a program with him, in order that her name be printed correctly? Oh glory! An actual reporter had heard the world premiere of my poem!

"Miss Aggie?" Charlotte held my coat so that I could slip my arms easily into the sleeves.

I buttoned it slowly. The Mermaid Room was once again its dear, drab self after a brief transformation into a shimmering theater. How odd to think that I'd been struck catastrophically mute while my poetry had filled the room to grand acclaim. I had both failed and triumphed in the same moment!

"Miss!" said Charlotte.

Only one thing was missing from this being the perfect evening. Papa. He would have loved to be here. I pictured him with a beaming smile, head tilted, listening to every syllable. Perhaps he'd heard it all from Heaven.

"Miss!" called Charlotte again. I hurried to catch up. Leonard was here to fetch us in the pony cart. Belle neighed softly as we climbed aboard. Pulling on my gloves, I realized that I'd left my notebook behind. Not a big worry, I'd be back for my lesson in the morning.

Whoever could imagine that a corpse would be waiting upon the same floorboards where my poem had just been read aloud?

(cut from the *Torquay Voice*)

TOWN TALK

A collection was made last evening, of clothing and household items, to benefit needy immigrants and refugees who now are living as our neighbors in Torquay. Miss Marianne Eversham, proprietress and instructress of the Mermaid Dance Room, hosted an evening of entertainment and generosity. Students performed a dance arrangement and recited poetry created for the occasion. The pleasant gathering was supplied with fresh flowers and tasty refreshments from local benefactors.

A.F.

CHAPTER 4

A GHASTLY DISCOVERY

THE NEXT MORNING, a little after eleven o'clock, I was at the head of the line, waiting for my dance lesson to begin. Classmates shuffled and giggled behind me in the stair-well. The familiar notice, stitched in curlicued needlepoint letters, hung aslant on the door: PLEASE WAIT. But we'd *been* waiting simply *ages* and Miss Marianne was emphatic about punctuality. We were all agog to discuss last evening's concert. I confess to hoping for a little more praise of my poetic contribution, despite my lapse in the performing of it. Miss Marianne might marvel at my cleverness loudly enough to quash any remarks made by Florence Fusswell.

Being in front, I wished to show a flash of leadership without needing to speak. I put down my dance bag on the top step and nudged the door with my elbow so it might drift ajar in an accidental manner.

"Miss Aggie!" Charlotte was ever alert to misdemeanors. I ignored her as the door creaked slowly open, and I slid inside . . .

The chairs used by last evening's audience were tidily lined up in front of the mirrors along one side. The donation boxes, brimming with garments and bric-a-brac, had already been removed to the church by Mr. Teasdale's team of husky volunteers. The piano stool was overturned and the fringed cloth dragged to the floor. A sugar bowl and milk jug sat atop the piano, next to my notebook. Pieces of a shattered teacup lay strewn on the floor in a puddle of milky tea.

And between the elegant legs of the grand piano lay a body.

Not, thank goodness, Miss Marianne. This woman was much rounder. Her head seemed crooked, mouth agape. Her legs—sticking out in a most unladylike way from beneath her skirts—were short and thick-ankled, encased in knitted stockings. Her feet lay at odd angles, as if they'd been kicking in protest. Nothing was kicking now. The contorted body was eerily still. I stepped closer and regarded the face, swollen and bluish-gray in color. One glazed eye stared sideways and a lace of foam ringed the open lips.

I felt the room sway. The woman was most certainly dead. And despite her disarray, I knew who it was. Who she had been.

Had she suffered a heart attack? Some sort of conniption? Was dull indigo the usual color of a dead person's skin? Weren't bodies meant to be ghostly white? Or was that only if the blood had been drained by leeches—or by the stab wound made by a knife? Might this be a *murder*? I could see no blood, but an unpleasant smell hovered in the air. Where was Miss Marianne? Was our dear teacher also dead? I scrutinized the mirror-lined studio.

What if . . . a ferocious tramp had crept in, or . . . a runaway madman from the Broadmoor Criminal Lunatic Asylum . . . or—more sordid and compelling—a cast-off sweetheart of Miss Marianne? *Intent on revenge he'd gained entry by crawling through the window in the small pantry but found two women instead of only the one he was seeking . . . The stiletto knife was so swift and accurate that it pierced the heart, permitting no drop of blood to fall. The scoundrel gagged and bound his long-ago love, before stuffing her into a cupboard to writhe amongst the tambourines and dance tunics. The other woman lay beneath the grand piano, too portly to be shifted.*

"Come away, miss!" Charlotte was suddenly beside me, pulling urgently on my arm. Common sense made a brief appearance. We must prevent the other girls from seeing.

"Don't come in!" I pushed past Charlotte to halt the others. "Do *not* enter." I caught hold of the ballet barre for a moment's support. I had just met a corpse. I willed the quaver from my voice. "There's a dead body on the floor! Possibly murdered!"

Why did my mind fly to murder? Last night, Rose had wished her mother dead. Roddy Fusswell and Miss Marianne had suggested that Torquay would be a better place without Irma Eversham. And here she was, as dead as the elephant whose tusks had provided the piano keys above her head . . .

"Aggie Morton, you are the biggest fibber," said Florence Fusswell. "You can't get through one single day without making up a story."

She stepped around me. My thumping heart skipped two beats when she began to shriek. Her nursemaid, Miss Boyle, tried to budge her from the doorway. Other curious girls attempted to peer beyond Florence, but soon retreated to shudder and sob in the stairwell.

Charlotte clamped a firm hand on my arm. "Come, Miss Aggie. Easy now."

Easy? No. But I would rather lie down next to the body under the piano than to start mewling like Florence Fusswell. Talking to strangers might be a challenge, but I would *not* lose my nerve before a corpse! Charlotte guided me toward the door. Her arm across my shoulders was something of a comfort, I confess.

"Move aside, girls, for Mercy's sake!" Miss Marianne was at the bottom of the stairs, her voice several notes higher than usual.

And then a man. "I am a doctor. Let me pass." He removed his top hat, scowling, and unbuckled the clasp on his black leather case. "All of you, clear off! This is a medical emergency." He closed the door almost upon our noses. He had spoken a flagrant untruth. An emergency? A doctor could do nothing but look at the corpse and agree that she was dead.

Most of the girls had seen scarcely more than a stockinged foot, but a collective howling commenced as they obediently shuffled their way into the street.

I sagged against the stair railing.

I had not been permitted into the room last year after Papa died. Mummy said she was protecting me from a memory too heavy to bear. It was intended as an act of kindness, however vexing at the time. This meant that the corpse I'd just met was my first, thrilling and grim. It was thoughtful of Mummy to prevent me from seeing Papa in a similar state.

"I know who it is," I whispered to Charlotte. "Who *she* is."

Charlotte squeezed my hand and said yes, she'd seen too.

"Rose's mother," I said.

"Yes," said Charlotte.

"So mean-tempered last night, leaving before we'd even begun."

"She was never friendly," said Charlotte.

I closed my eyes. "Rose is an orphan."

Being unpleasant was not really a good enough reason to take one's final breath under the legs of a grand piano. Poor, poor Rose! It was all so horrible. If Mummy ever died . . . I felt weak just thinking about it. Only last evening I'd been agonizing about reading my poem when something so very much worse was waiting to happen.

My *poem*! My eyes flew open. My writing book still sat atop the piano where Rose had laid it down last evening after the recitation.

Right over the corpse!

"Miss Aggie, no!" said Charlotte, but I had opened the door and slipped inside.

The doctor knelt on the floor, his hand encircling the dead woman's wrist. He shook his head slowly, the back and forth motion making his extra chin waggle. The message was clear and no surprise to me.

Miss Marianne slumped awkwardly on the piano stool, twisting her hands together. Her face showed horror at my entrance.

"You may not be here, Aggie. Take her away, Miss Graves."

"I'm so sorry, Miss Marianne," I whispered. "I just . . . I left my . . ." I was reluctant to admit that I was intruding on a death scene for the sake of a notebook. But would it not be worse to have come in for no reason at all? I raced to the piano, snatched up my book, and retreated backward, dropping my eyes for only a moment to those ghastly, sticking-out legs.

"No!" Miss Marianne half-stood and waved her hands. "You mustn't take . . . You cannot touch—"

"We're so sorry to have disturbed you," said Charlotte.

"Since you're here," said the doctor, "could you be of some assistance? We have need of a policeman."

"We'll go at once." Charlotte snatched my hand and tried to yank me down the staircase, putting our balance in peril. I wrenched free, took up my dance bag and stuffed my notebook inside. My throat was thick with some feeling I could not name, my breaths rough and loud as I clattered down the steps.

Charlotte's rebuke was swift and unpleasant. "That was shocking behavior! As if a notebook matters at such a time! Your mother will be woefully upset." The skin around her nostrils had gone white and her freckles positively gleamed. "I cannot allow any further association with this grim affair. You will remain in the safety of Mr. Dillon's shop until I return with a constable."

"But I'm the one who—"

Charlotte raised her palm. "Not another word." She maneuvered me through the sweet-shop door, and briefly told Mr. Dillon of the occurrence upstairs.

"Well now," he said. "That's not something that happens every day."

No, indeed, it wasn't, Charlotte agreed, and asked if, please, could Miss Aggie wait under his care until the police were fetched?

"Do not let her out of your sight, Mr. Dillon," she added. "Though what greater woe she might encounter than a dead body, I cannot conceive!"

Tra-ling went the bell, and *bang* went the door.

Mr. Dillon sat me down and offered me a sugar lolly, as if I were an infant five years old. It was, admittedly, delicious and soon soothed my shivers. I'd been a loyal customer since I was younger than five. Mr. Dillon knew which sweets I liked best, and I knew him well enough to chatter as freely as with our own cook.

He turned to his telephone, asking to be put through to the Torquay Police Department.

"A constable is required at the Mermaid Dance Room on Union Street. At once!" Mr. Dillon hollered into the mouthpiece. "Above Dillon's Sweets and Sundries. We've got what you'd call a candidate for the graveyard."

He put the telephone speaker back into its cradle, and then tapped his lip with a plump finger. "Dead for certain, were she?"

I nodded, my mouth full of the sharp, sweet taste of lemon.

"Not long dead, though," he said. "That I know. I only just saw her."

I straightened up. "You *saw* her?"

The bell on the door jangled sharply, and in came the black-haired boy from last week.

"Well, well," said Mr. Dillon. "My rescuer."

"Hector!" I hopped off the stool.

"Hello, miss." He pronounced it *meese*. "I bid you good day."

"Wait till you hear!"

Agitation tangled my words and the story was not well told, but I believe he caught the gist. *No teacher. Body! Piano. Spilled tea. Blue face! Pudgy legs. Screaming. Doctor. Notebook. Victim. Possible murder! Police!*

"And Mr. Dillon has just informed me that he saw the dead woman enter the premises! Before she was dead. He was nearly the last person to see her alive!"

Mr. Dillon turned a bit pink at this notoriety, but objected at once. "I were far from the last, I assure you. The workers on those stairs were as busy as ants on a jar of honey this morning. Miss Marianne Eversham were up there overseeing all manner of backing and forthing."

"So, if it was murder . . ." I said. "Oh, Mr. Dillon. If you saw the victim, think how likely it was that you also saw the murderer!"

"Let's not go about making up stories, Miss Aggie," said

the confectioner. His fat cheeks trembled as he wheezed out a chuckle. "There's nobody saying that it were murder."

Hector's eyebrows shot up and down while he listened.

"What is the manner of her death?" he said. "Is she afflicted with—" He broke off to pat his chest right over his heart.

"Word has it," said Mr. Dillon, "that she'd got no heart at all. You could have knocked me over with a rope of licorice, seeing Irma Eversham puffing up the street and going through that door." He tipped his head toward the entrance of the Mermaid Dance Room. "I never saw her visit here, not once."

"She was here last night," I said. "For about six minutes. She was meant to watch our concert, but she went home early in a huff."

With everyone hating her and wishing her gone.

"On the premises two days in a row?" said Mr. Dillon. "That's rare, that is. They say those Eversham women are like a pair of pitchforks, jabbing at each other morning till night. The old Captain kept them civil, but since his passing . . . May he rest in peace."

"At what time does she arrive?" asked Hector.

"When did she get here?" I said, at the very same moment.

Mr. Dillon rubbed his chin. "I noticed her pacing out front. She were waiting for the stairway to be empty. Blokes from the church were doing some heavy lifting with those crates. The gent from the hotel, he were up and down a number of times with his urns and his platters. She followed him up, finally. The flower chap came and went, maybe some others before that. Saturday's a busy day in a sweet shop. I don't see everything."

"What is next to happen?" said Hector.

"A few minutes of blessed quiet and then Miss Marianne Eversham goes scurrying out. Soon after, you girls start coming."

"I was first," I said. "At the front of the line. That's why I found the body. Miss Marianne wasn't there to let us in."

"I didn't know there were trouble," said Mr. Dillon, "until Miss Eversham come back with the doctor. She might've used my telephone, but perhaps she doesn't know I've got one. I'm one of the first hereabouts. She fetched that Dr. Chase, who never smiles and never ate a sweetie in his life."

"He was a bit curt," I said. "I expect it was due to not finding a pulse. He might have felt badly, not saving her."

"How far away is the home of Dr. Chase?" said Hector.

But I was thinking about Miss Marianne's clothes.

"She was wearing her dance skirt," I said. "I mean, *only* her dance skirt, and a blouse. No coat or hat. Not even a shawl over her shoulders."

"This is very important," said Hector. "When a lady is improper in her clothing for a chilly English October, it is logical to deduce great distress. How is she forgetting to bring with her a shawl?"

"She just didn't think," I said. "She was in a terrible hurry."

"She'd have been mighty unnerved," said Mr. Dillon, "with her sister-in-law dropping dead at her feet."

"But you don't rush to fetch a doctor for a corpse," I said.

"She is believing that the fallen may be revived," said Hector. "She runs into the street while Mrs. Irma Eversham still breathes."

Unless . . . A dire thought crept into my head.

"Unless . . ." said Hector.

"Unless . . ." I said. "Miss Marianne was only pretending to get help, when really she is a murderess."

CHAPTER 5

A HULLABALOO

THE MOMENT I SAID out loud that Miss Marianne could be a murderess I knew it to be a ludicrous notion. Yes, she had an ongoing dispute with her sister-in-law, but that had been true for nearly a lifetime and she had never killed her before! So why today? It seemed highly unlikely. I had witnessed her anguish as she sat beside the corpse.

A commotion outside brought us all to the door. Thudding hooves, clattering wheels, shrill whistles and bells. The police had arrived.

"What an almighty din," said Mr. Dillon. "No respect for the dead."

Five men jumped from the police wagon, carrying a canvas stretcher and other implements of rescue. A burly man wearing a tweedy Ulster overcoat shouted directions, a thick mustache jumping on his lip.

"The senior detective," said Hector. "No uniform, but much noise."

"Look there." I recognized the young officer holding open the door. "It's Charlotte's constable! The one who came too late to pick you up off the floor, Mr. Dillon."

Charlotte burst into the shop, gasping, as if she'd run beside the police wagon all the way from the station. The men thumped and bumped their way up the narrow staircase that shared a wall with the sweet shop. Then, silence.

"Well, now," said Mr. Dillon. "Some of those young men may find themselves a bit sick seeing what they're about to see."

Hector and I looked at each other. Our entire acquaintance amounted to little more than a half hour, but I knew in an instant that we both wished with all our hearts to be upstairs watching the constabulary perform their duties. A tickling thrill of conspiracy raced up my spine.

"Time to go, Miss Aggie!" said Charlotte. "We've been dawdling far too long."

"It can't be called dawdling at a death scene," I said. "We're making crucial observations."

"*My* crucial observation is that your grandmother will have sharp words if we're late for tea," said Charlotte.

"Thank Mr. Dillon for the unnecessary sweets and we'll be on our way."

"Come with us!" I spoke to Hector, not looking to Charlotte for permission. Why did an afternoon so perfect as this need to end? "There's always plenty. It would be ever so nice to have you." I was depending on Charlotte being too polite to interfere with an invitation just given. "Mummy will love to meet a new friend, won't she, Charlotte? Please, Hector. We've so much to discuss!"

It used to be that Mummy would be sitting with Papa in the library after lunch, sewing perhaps, and quietly chatting. When Papa was still alive. Naturally she wouldn't be sitting so pleasantly with a ghost, would she? Though perhaps his ghost had remained a faithful companion these many months, giving Mummy some small comfort. I considered the idea that memories and ghosts are knitted together as closely as stitches of yarn on a needle, part of the same warming shawl that each of us wears. Occasionally my mind strayed to consider what my father might look like now, not his ghost, but inside his coffin. Or, what if he hadn't been buried, but picked clean by helpful carrion, leaving him a skeleton, shining white and elegant?

Mummy was most impatient with what she called my Morbid Preoccupation. Papa being dead was the very last thing she wanted to think about, though she clung to his memory with her own melancholy resolve. Quite recently I had discovered a memento tucked under her pillow—the stub of a pencil in an envelope labeled *Last Pencil Ever Used by Fletcher*. Its end was dented with the marks of Papa's teeth, as he would gnaw in concentration while he tabulated numbers.

It was my fervent intention to tell Mummy the afternoon's news in a calm and factual manner. Despite my plan, I dashed across the drawing room and draped myself around her.

"Oh, Mummy!"

The clicking of Grannie Jane's knitting needles paused, as if waiting to hear what came next. Tony hopped off his mat by the fire and pushed his head against my leg, accepting my ear pulls as merely his due.

"Whatever has happened?" Mummy's voice was muffled by me squashing her. "Gracious, Agatha!"

She caught sight of Hector hovering in the doorway. "And who is this?" She tried to rise, but my hug impeded her. "Are there now boys in the Mermaid Room?"

Grannie put her knitting back into its basket. This was a novelty not to be missed.

"This is Hector, Mummy. Hector Perot." I tried to remember the sequence one should follow when making introductions. "Hector, this is my mother, Mrs. Morton. And this is my darling Tony Dog." Tony sniffed Hector's shoes and seemed to approve. But, oh dear, perhaps Grannie Jane should have been first because she was so old and also a person?

"This is my grandmother, also Mrs. Morton."

Hector performed perfectly. He gave a small bow to each woman in turn and even clicked his heels together.

"Oh," said Mummy, a bit surprised.

"Mummy, I told you how we met Hector last week in Mr. Dillon's shop. Today I have invited him for tea."

"Lovely to have you here, Hector. And how was the dancing lesson? Were you all resting on your laurels after last evening's triumph?"

"The lesson didn't happen at all! You'd best stay sitting, Mummy, because when I tell you . . ."

I took a breath.

"There was a dead body, under the piano. Not crushed by the piano, just lying there, under it. With one side mashed up against the pedals. I was the one who saw her first, wasn't I, Charlotte?"

"Yes, miss."

"Goodness!" cried Mummy. "Not dear Miss Marianne?"

"No, no!" I said. "Miss Marianne is perfectly well, but she'd rushed off to find a doctor. So there I was, with—"

Mummy was on her feet, hands pressed to her face. "Agatha! This is frightful!" She turned on Charlotte, hovering in the doorway. "How could you let her see such a thing? You're meant to be protecting her!"

"Certainly, Mrs. Morton, I attend Miss Aggie at every moment." Her tone made clear that the task was not a restful one.

"It's not Charlotte's fault, Mummy! I just happened to be the first through the door."

"You haven't said who died!" said Grannie Jane. "I'm trying to be patient, but, really, this is the most slipshod report."

"It was the Captain's wife," said Charlotte.

"The Captain's widow," I corrected. "Rose's mother, Mrs. Eversham, from next door."

"Irma!" Mummy's hands reached backward for the arms of her chair.

"Cora!" Grannie stepped toward Mummy, but Hector was closer.

"Please to sit, madame," he said softly. He held her elbow and guided her into the chair. Tony's nose gently nudged Mummy's hand until she stroked his neck. He was very good at knowing where he was needed. He'd been sleeping on her bed since Papa died, and they were now the best of friends.

Grannie Jane opened a cabinet and withdrew a bottle with a gold label, embossed with a red seal. She poured amber liquid into a teacup and added a spoonful of sugar.

"Brandy for shock, my dear. Sugar, for sugar's sake."

Mummy drank it in two gulps, giving a little shudder in between. "I should like to go to my room," she said. "Charlotte? Will you bring a hot pan from the kitchen to warm the bed?"

Their footsteps had scarcely faded down the hallway when the front door knocker banged. We all jumped a little. Most visitors knew to come to the less formal side door—or even all the way around through the garden to the kitchen.

Grannie clasped her bosom in surprise. "Who is making that appalling uproar?"

"We haven't any servant to answer the front door," I whispered to Hector. "Robertson left months ago, when we turned out to be poor because of Papa's bad investments."

Another knock.

"I will go." I hurried into the hall, with Hector close behind.

I peered through the pane that overlooked the doorstep. "Oh!" I cried. "It's a policeman!"

Charlotte's policeman! Tall and ruddy-cheeked, his knuckles raised and ready to knock again. Next to him, stamping enormous boots, was his bushy-lipped superior. I opened the door.

"I am Detective Inspector Locke," the man announced. "And this is Police Constable Beck."

I bobbed my head and stared at his boots, willing the words to come out. In rather a mumble, I managed that Mummy was indisposed but Grannie was in the library.

"Then take me to the library," said the inspector.

I imagined that I was handsomely attired in the sharp tailcoat and striped cummerbund of an excellent butler as I stepped to the library door.

"Detective Inspector Locke and Police Constable Beck," I told Grannie in my best posh voice. "Ma'am."

"Oh, for Heaven's sake," said Grannie Jane.

The inspector paused on the threshold, eyes scanning the book-lined walls, the floral arrangements from last evening's concert, the deep velvet chairs, a cozy fire in the grate. His survey refreshed my own appreciation of the best room in all the world. Grannie's keen eyes awaited the inspector's attention until he finally approached. The constable and Hector slipped in behind him.

"You may go, Agatha," said Grannie. "Please ask Mrs. Corner to make a tea tray for the inspector."

"No, thank you, ma'am. No tea on duty. And the young lady is to stay. She's the one we're here for."

"We'll also need to interview the girl's . . . uh . . .

51

nursemaid," said Constable Beck. "The other witness at the scene."

"Charlotte," said Grannie Jane, "is with my daughter-in-law, who is unwell."

"She's not a nursemaid," I muttered. "I'm not a baby." I sounded most uncivil, but at least my voice was emerging.

"Who's this?" Inspector Locke peered down at Hector as if he were a fly on a cream biscuit.

"Hector Perot, at your service, monsieur." Hector made it sound as noble a position as the Prince of Wales.

"Were you also at the crime scene?"

"Non, monsieur."

"Crime scene?" said Grannie Jane.

Crime scene? Just as we'd guessed! Hector lifted one eyebrow and I did my best to lift one in return. It was official. I had seen a murdered person!

How grim for poor Rose to hear that her mother was a victim of murder! But thinking back upon what Rose had said—aloud—before the concert, would she consider it such grim news after all?

"Your attendance is not required here," the inspector said to Hector. "Go away. See if you can find this Miss . . . Miss . . ." He flipped open his notebook to retrieve the name.

"Miss Graves," said Constable Beck, from his position near the door.

"Graves," said the inspector.

Hector bowed neatly.

"Remember every word!" he whispered to me as he passed. I slid onto the ottoman at my grandmother's side.

"You may speak with Agatha only if I am present," said Grannie Jane to the inspector. She gestured toward what I called the Sofa of Rigor Mortis, the very hard one that leaves a person rather stiff. The inspector's eyes widened slightly as his bottom met the surprising plank of tufted satin.

"Now then," he began.

"The child has had a most distressing afternoon," said Grannie Jane.

"Indeed. We will keep this brief, but she was the first to arrive on the scene. Her impressions may be important."

I kept the smile from my face but I preened a bit inside. As a poet, I had *practiced* having first impressions. This would be a good test of my observational skills. If only I could write them down instead of talking. My fingers began to itch.

Grannie leaned forward, pinning the police inspector with her fierce gaze. "I believe, Inspector Locke, that you said *crime* scene?"

"That is correct, ma'am. The news will be all about town by morning, so there is no point in trying to keep it quiet. The woman was poisoned. Clear and simple."

CHAPTER 6

A Probing Interview

"What kind of poison?" I asked.

"That, miss, is confidential information." The inspector shifted his bottom and the sofa legs creaked. "I'll thank you to be discreet about anything we ask here today. There is a villain at large and we mean to arrest him as soon as possible."

"Or her," I said.

Inspector Locke's furry eyebrows lifted. "Why do you say that, miss?"

"Poison is so conveniently domestic," said Grannie Jane. "Suitable for use by ladies."

"Our delicate constitutions," I said, "are not so fond of blood."

I would far prefer to administer poison than to shoot a gun. One needn't even be present at the time of death!

"Who better to administer the poison than she who prepares the food?" said Grannie.

Inspector Locke tapped a heavy finger on his notebook. "Ladies, this is a very serious crime. You"—he pointed a finger at me—"are a witness. Do not obstruct the investigation with fancy."

I stifled the temptation to salute and sat up straighter. "Yes, sir."

"I'd like to ask you, Miss Morton, to close your eyes for a moment. Tell me what exactly you saw when you entered the dance studio."

Closing my eyes was a clever suggestion. The library vanished and the inspector's hairy face with it.

"The stool was on its side with its cloth pulled off. The cloth is yellow with a tatted edging, embroidered with peonies. Miss Marianne would never let it lie upon the floor. The room looked wrong before I even noticed the body."

"Can you describe the position of the body?"

"Really, inspector, she's a child!"

"I'll show you." I dropped to the floor and contorted myself into the same shape in which I'd found Mrs. Eversham. I turned my head and opened my mouth into a silent scream, but closed it at once because the carpet smelled so dusty.

"My word," said Grannie Jane.

"Indeed," said Inspector Locke. "Children often make the best witnesses. They report what they see instead of making assumptions about what we want them to have seen."

"An interesting point," said Grannie. "However—" She broke off to glare at me. "That's enough, Agatha. Up you get."

"*However.*" The inspector said it just the way Grannie had. "You are finding it difficult to remain silent. I need the girl's impressions with no interference. You can stay with your lip buttoned or depart for a room where your chatter is welcome."

No one had ever, not *ever* spoken to my grandmother with such cheek! I held my breath—but it took only three seconds for Grannie to respond.

"I'm quite comfortable here, inspector, thank you." She made a great show of settling into the cushions, displaying not even a hint of the affront. She was disguising herself as we watched, becoming a fluffy old woman. I could hear in my head what she would say later. *Uppish man. Needs to trim his mustache.*

A knock at the door caused Constable Beck to spin briskly around. I rolled onto my tummy and pushed myself up to standing. I heard Charlotte from the hallway, asking was she needed?

"Shall I take Miss Graves elsewhere, inspector?" said Constable Beck. "We'd have independent witness statements that way, without . . . er . . . each other's influence."

I imagined Charlotte's blush beginning at her throat and rushing to her temple. He wanted to be alone with her! Inspector Locke dismissed them with a wave of the hand. I watched the door close. If only I could see what happened next!

The manly policeman, his brow a bit damp from nerves, turned to the young woman with the dimpled chin.

"Oh, Miss Graves," he sighed, his large bony hands cupping her freckly face. "I have longed for this moment, praying that you would share the secrets within your—"

I blinked. I had nearly used the word *bosom*!

"Miss Morton?" said Inspector Locke. "Can we proceed?"

"*May* we?" murmured Grannie Jane, so quietly that only I could hear. A good thing, as I did not think the inspector would appreciate a grammar lesson.

"Think very carefully, miss. Was the victim holding anything in her hand?"

I shook my head no.

"Take your time. Something white, perhaps?"

"No." I closed my eyes again, to improve my recall and my ability to report. "Her hands were . . . puffy, and a bit gray, really, more than blue. The closer one, the right one, was . . . open. Palm up, and certainly empty." Rather like a gardening glove left on the path.

"And the other?"

"The left hand was curled over. I suppose it might have held something, but it would have been very small. I couldn't see properly, either time."

"*Either* time? You had more than one encounter with the deceased?"

"I . . . I . . . left when the doctor came in," I said. "But then . . ."

"Spit it out, Miss Morton. We are not chatting for pleasure."

"I'd forgotten my notebook," I whispered, examining my hands. "On the piano. I popped back in to fetch it."

The inspector cleared his throat. "And when you re-entered the room, can you tell me, did your dancing teacher have anything in *her* hand?"

"No." I remembered clearly. "She was sitting on the piano stool, so she must have set that to right . . ."

"Moved the piano stool . . ." The inspector scribbled in his book.

"Well, yes, but I expect she needed to sit down, didn't she?" The words came more easily now. This was quite diverting. "She . . . she *sagged* a little, shoulders hunched, not anything like her usual dancer's posture. And she was wringing her hands." I turned my own hands over each other to show what Miss Marianne had been doing. "They were certainly empty."

"Nervous, was she?" He made another note.

"Upset, I'd say. *Grievously* upset! Who wouldn't be? Her sister-in-law was dead at her feet!"

"Indeed she was," said Inspector Locke. "Quite dead. To someone's great satisfaction."

His words sent a chill up my back. Did he already have a suspect?

Grannie Jane leaned forward and spoke confidentially. "Surely no one we know, Inspector?"

"In cases of murder, ma'am, the killer is nearly always closely related to the victim."

Life would certainly be smoother, Miss Marianne had said, *if she were not in Torquay.*

And Rose's words. *At least once a day, I find myself wishing that she were dead.*

"You *can't* be thinking—" I broke off. I'd had the same ghoulish ideas but they sounded worse coming from him.

"What I can or cannot think is up to me, young lady. Your task is merely to give me a picture of the room. Tell me about the tea things. Was she so careless as to move those too?"

I closed eyes that were suddenly blurred with tears. Could I tell him anything to prove the innocence of the Eversham ladies? *Were* they innocent?

The puddle on the floor was milky tea, not clear, so it must have come from the cup, not the teapot. The pot . . . where was the pot? Had Miss Marianne poured the tea in the pantry and carried it out to her visitor? That would suggest she'd prepared the tea in private. But perhaps I should not tell him that.

"There isn't a tea trolley in the dance studio," I said. "It would take up too much room. I don't remember seeing the teapot, but a smashed cup on the floor had tea spilled around it. The floor is wood, of course, for dancing on, so there is no carpet for the tea to soak into. It just sat there in a puddle."

I squeezed my eyes tight. "Miss Marianne's little blue milk jug was sitting on top of the piano." My notebook had lain nearby. "And next to it was a sugar bowl." As I noted that, my skin prickled in recognition that something was wrong.

Grannie was paying close attention. "Was the sugar bowl blue as well, dearie?" she said. "Was it part of a set, with the milk jug?"

I stared at her in admiration. "No," I said.

I looked directly at Inspector Locke to deliver what suddenly felt like very important information. "The sugar bowl was imprinted with the crest of the Royal Victoria Hotel."

"I believe my destiny is decided!" Hector's green eyes shone, and there was a shell-pink hue to his pale cheeks. His grin stretched in true delight. "I like very much this occupation of knowing other people's business! The job of a policeman is for me an excellent match."

"Not if it means you have to grow a nasty great bramble bush on your face." I was thinking of the inspector's shaggy upper lip and jaws. "Only slightly better than a furry, crawling caterpillar like Mr. Roddy Fusswell's!"

"Mais, non! My mustache will be elegant. Sleek. With ends to here, fine and pointed . . ." Hector rubbed his fingertips together close to his earlobes, as if his mustache would be as grand as that of a circus ringmaster.

"Ugh." I was quite firm.

"The asking of questions that no polite person may ask!" said Hector. "Unwrapping the thoughts of the suspect, seeking always the solution to a puzzle! Is this not a wonderful endeavor?"

"I want to hear about Charlotte and the policeman!" I said. "What happened?" I had already described my forty-two minutes with Inspector Locke. Now it was his turn.

Hector had been miserable—"desolate!"—when told to leave the library. "Excluded from the heat of the fire," he said. "But the policeman's infatuation with Miss Graves, this is lucky for me, non?"

"Go on, tell!"

Hector had been sitting on the hallway settee, nursing his wounded spirit and wondering how he should go about informing Miss Graves that she was desired for questioning. He hoped that a servant would pass through the hallway, for where in a big, strange house should he begin to look? Happily, Charlotte herself appeared from upstairs and tapped on the library door. Constable Beck, face aflame, informed her that he had official questions to ask, and would she please step into the dining room. Hector used the moment while the young officer gained approval from the inspector to slip in ahead of them and hide under the dining table.

"Just as I would have done!" I told him. "That's one of the best hiding spots! When Papa was alive, my parents had fancy dinners with lots of people wearing evening clothes. The champagne made them terribly chatty. It was an excellent game. Now it's only ever family, and I already know their secrets."

Tony's paw nails clicked on the wooden floor as he padded over from his spot in a shaft of sunlight. He made a small, polite yip.

"We need to take Tony outside," I said. "Better that you make your report out there." I dropped my voice to a whisper. "Grannie Jane says that servants listen to everything."

I ushered Hector along the hallway to the kitchen, with Tony skittering at our heels.

"Hello, Mrs. Corner!" I patted Cook on the arm as we crossed to the garden door. "This is my friend, Hector. He's the extra for tea."

"I hope you like fruit pie, laddie," said Mrs. Corner. "As much as Miss Aggie does."

"Mais oui, madame!" Hector performed a quick bow, managing not to trip over Tony.

"I'm going to show you a favorite place." I dragged him past the grove of pear trees to a spot at the edge of the little wood that separated our property from the Eversham villa next door.

"See?"

Groveland was so far above the town that when winter came and the trees were bare, we could see the sea. Today, though, the warm yellow of a few remaining October leaves still blocked the view, casting dappled shadows on a wooden bench and the row of painted gravestones at our feet.

"What is this?" said Hector, peering.

"Mummy would say it's a symptom of my Morbid Preoccupation. But really, it's perfectly genteel. This one is for Marigold, my canary. She was my first pet when I was six. Then Kiki, here, and Tom-Tom. They were mynah birds, that's why I put the colored stripes across the headstones."

"Most thoughtful," said Hector, admirably unperturbed. "And this?"

"That's just a squirrel," I said. "He wasn't a pet, but I named him Squiffy to make the tombstone more personal. And the big one, here, was the kitchen cat, named Ivy. That's why I've painted leaves, you see? When Ivy died, I played the mandolin at her funeral. It was ever so doleful and reverent. Cook cried and cried. We never got another cat, so we've got mice instead, like everywhere else in Torquay."

"You make a pleasant rest for the animals," said Hector. "And a good place to discuss death."

"Let's sit," I said. "While you tell me everything."

Hector brushed the bench with his hand and checked his palm to see that nothing had stuck. He sat carefully, knees and ankles touching. I supposed it was best not to tease him for something so inconsequential as being a fussbudget. Not while there was a murderer on the loose.

"Well?" I said. Tony was snuffling in a patch of tall grass overlooked by Leonard's mowing.

Hector picked up the story. "I am under the table, twisted into a knot like a serpent in a basket," he said.

"And what did you hear?"

"The policeman, he asks many questions. Who is standing where, how does the body lie, can she name anything out of position? Miss Graves, she answers most efficiently. She tells the same details that you tell to me already."

Tony yipped twice, excited by something he'd found near the tree.

"Ssh, Tony," I said. "Go on, Hector."

"However," said Hector. "There is one curious item. Constable Beck is particularly interested in the piece of paper."

"What piece of paper?"

"You do not mention such a thing in your description of the murder scene, so I try very much to hear, but my limbs are becoming most cramped. A missing paper is indicated because of the scrap."

"What scrap? Did you find out why it matters?"

"A tiny scrap of paper is squeezed between the thumb and the forefinger of the deceased, discovered by Doctor Chase during his examination." Hector's eyes narrowed. "You do not know of this?"

That's what Inspector Locke had been prodding me to remember! *Think very carefully,* he'd said. *Was the victim holding anything in her hand? Something white, perhaps?*

How irritating not to have seen it! "Nothing visible was clutched in the corpse's hand. It must have been very small." The only paper in the room that I knew about were the pages of my poetry notebook, sitting on top of the piano.

"Your nursemaid also reports no evidence of a paper or a scrap," said Hector. "After this, the interview between Constable Beck and Miss Graves becomes what I believe you English call *gooey*. The words of inquiry turn to mur-murings of . . . romance. This is when I put fingers into my ears and cease to listen."

"*Romance*? Really?" Plain and earnest Charlotte? I could not think of a less *gooey* person!

"They do nothing improper, I assure you," said Hector. "Simply the whispering of lovebirds." He twirled his imaginary mustache.

"They only met a week ago!" I said. "It's rather saucy of Charlotte to be whispering like a lovebird, don't you think?"

Tony yapped and began to paw furiously at something amongst the weeds.

"What have you got there, Tony?" I got up to look. "Something nasty, I expect, since you're so excited."

A rabbit lay dead, its stiff fur ruffled and its little head torn open, a trickle of blood seeping from a gray puddle of muck.

CHAPTER 7

A SLEIGHT OF HAND

"I'VE ALWAYS THOUGHT my brain was pink." I leaned over to get a better look at the earthly remains. "Are rabbits different from people?"

"No, no," said Hector. "I am a devoted student on the topic of the human brain. For something so intriguing, it is notably a dull gray in color. As you can see."

"*Ugh*, Tony, no!" I caught the dog's collar and tugged him away from his prize. "Let the poor bunny rest in peace." I pulled up fistfuls of grass and sprinkled them over the mutilated carcass. Mrs. Eversham's feet appeared in my mind.

"Losing one's brains is undignified enough," I said. "Let alone being mauled by a frenzied terrier. Not that a rabbit has much to lose, with a brain the size of a plum."

"Au contraire," said Hector. "A rabbit is a creature of much character, most playful and clever."

"Clever?" It took a bit of strength to wrestle Tony along the path, away from the corpse.

"Inside the brain . . . ," Hector tapped his forehead, "are billions of nerves dancing together, telling to each other many messages. This *friction* is the essence of how we think."

"And a rabbit has an abundance of *friction* amongst its brain cells?" I said.

"Not so much as a human," said Hector. "But for its size, yes. Alas, the size makes him prey to nearly every other animal, including us. He is born expecting to die."

"Aren't we all?"

Tony raced ahead, circled back, and bounded onward again.

"Look, there's Leonard." I waved at the garden boy. He looked up from his digging and pushed back his cap, freeing a curl over his eyebrows.

"Miss Aggie," he said, and glanced sideways at Hector.

"This is my friend, Hector Perot," I said. "He's staying for tea. Hector, this is Leonard. He works here in the garden."

Leonard nodded at Hector and Hector nodded back.

"We found a dead rabbit." I pointed. "Tony did, actually. Its brain is . . ."—I wiggled my fingers beside my head—"leaking out."

"Maybe a fox got him," said Leonard.

"As we didn't know him, we needn't hold a funeral," I said. "But could you . . . Would you mind digging a hole? Near the others?" I looked toward the leafy awning of the beech tree protecting the creatures buried below.

"Yes, miss," he said. "I'll do that before dark."

"Thank you, Leonard. I'll think of a name, and make him a stone later."

"Yes, miss." He shifted the shovel to his other hand. "I was wondering, is there trouble? I saw the police wagon."

"There's been a *murder*!" It was thrilling, being the one to tell such news before anyone else. "In the Mermaid Room where you brought the flowers last night. I was meant to be having my Saturday lesson, you see? And I found the body!"

Leonard stared. Perhaps I shouldn't sound so eager. I took a breath.

"That's why the police came, to interview me and Charlotte. I was practically a witness to a monstrous crime!"

I could feel Hector fidgeting next to me. "This is perhaps not an item to be trumpeted," he said. "If indeed it is murder, there is still a murderer to be found."

"Of course it's murder! Do you think she poisoned herself? I'm only telling Leonard," I said. "Not advertising in the *TorquayVoice*! Goodness! That means I've found *two* dead bodies in one day! First Mrs. Eversham and now the poor rabbit."

Leonard gazed at me with those enormous brown eyes. "Mrs. Eversham, miss? She's *dead*?"

"As dead as dead," I said. *As dead as the rabbit in the grass. As dead as a coffin nail. As dead as Papa.*

Leonard looked faintly perturbed, so I allowed the corpse to rest and turned instead to the police.

"They asked a lot of questions," I told him. "I had to demonstrate the position of the body. And I'm sure to think of more clues later. The police seem a bit plodding, to be honest. But goodness! You were there this morning as well, Leonard! Did you see anything suspicious when you collected the bouquets? Thank you, by the way, for hauling them back to Groveland. It's like having spring in the drawing room. Nice for us that Miss Marianne didn't want to keep them."

Leonard was fiddling with the brim of his cap. "I nipped in and out quick as I could," he said. "The stairwell was plugged up like an old pipe, with the vicar's men shifting those whopping crates. That bossy chap from the hotel packed up his tea things as if they were as precious as the King's china. And there I was, doing my best with the vases."

"Did you see Mrs. Eversham?"

"In a proper snit with your teacher, she was." He looked at the ground, kicking a clot of dirt off the path.

70

"Have you thought of something?" I said.

"It's nothing." Leonard pulled his cap off and put it back on at a new angle over his brow.

"Nothing can be considered nothing," I said. "She's *dead*."

"I'll tell you who I don't think much of," said Leonard. "That Mr. Fusswell. He nearly stepped on me more than once, but never actually went anywhere. Just took his time, stacking teacups one by one." He looked from my face to Hector's and back again. "You want to steer right clear of it," he said, quite urgently. "No reason to get mixed up in anything so—"

"So shockingly macabre?" I said. "So horrifically gruesome? So morbid and grisly?"

Leonard didn't smile as I'd hoped he would. Perhaps he'd cheer up if I asked for his specialty.

"Will you do a trick for us, Leonard? Hector will be ever so baffled. Please?"

"Aw, miss."

"He does conjuring," I told Hector. "Watch."

Leonard shuffled his boots. "I haven't got a sixpence."

I hadn't got one either, my pocket money being minded in Charlotte's pocket.

"But how about I have a look around, eh?" Leonard laid down the shovel and pulled his trouser pocket inside out to show how empty it was.

This was part of the trick!

"Oh dear," I said. "Nothing there."

Leonard examined the ground for a moment, as if he might spot a coin in the grass. He took off his cap and peered at its lining.

Then, "Aha!" His fingers nimbly plucked a sixpence from behind Hector's left ear. He held it up with a victorious grin.

I laughed and clapped my hands.

"This is much skill," said Hector.

"Do another!" I cried.

"I believe," said Hector, "that your policemen are departing."

Indeed, the horses were tossing their heads and clopping away from the house.

"Good-bye, Leonard!" I set off across the spiky yellowing grass at nearly a gallop, with Hector stumbling along behind.

"Can we not travel along the path?" he called. "The dirt on my shoes is . . ."

I kept running.

". . . Dirty," he finished.

"I've thought of something," I said over my shoulder. "I must tell the inspector."

But the police horses had picked up speed. They were around the curve and gone before we'd reached the drive.

My stockings drooped after running. I pulled them straight.

"Why are you panting like an old dog?" I asked Hector.

"I have no practice in scampering through the nature." He plucked stray blades of grass from his trousers. "I wonder if your thought is similar to my thought?"

"Here it is," I said. "I do not believe Miss Marianne to be a murderess. I love her. I will vouch for her goodness, though I suppose that even heinous villains have friends who would swear to their innocence. But, also, she lives in the same house with the victim. If she were going to kill her sister-in-law, would it not be simpler to do so at home?"

"Most certainly," said Hector.

"She could have mixed poison with cocoa and brought it to her in bed . . . Or she might have left a bucket on the cellar steps and let her tumble to the bottom to break her neck. Or stabbed her with a paring knife and said it was a cooking accident. Or tampered with her medicine, if she takes . . . if she took . . ." I trailed off. Hector's eyebrows had lifted up to his hairline.

"So many resourceful suggestions. I shall hope not to displease you." He grinned. "But is it Miss Marianne who brews the tea?"

"I expect so. It *is* her pantry." Not an answer in her favor. "Was the poison in the teapot or in the sugar bowl, do you suppose?"

"A question we must strive to answer," said Hector. "Either way, at first glance, Miss Marianne is the most suspicious character."

"Then we've got to look deeper!" I said. "We must activate the friction in our brains to a frenzy. The inspector does not know Miss Marianne as I do and will not try so hard."

"For a moment, let us say that she is not the killer we are seeking," said Hector. "She does not make a perfect accident happen in her home. She does not imagine that vanquishing her nasty relative will make life better."

"Well, she did do that," I said. "But everyone else did too. Especially Rose. And even . . ." A smirking face came to mind. "Even Mr. Roddy Fusswell."

"If it is not Miss Marianne who performs the murder," said Hector, "it means that *someone else* arranges for Mrs. Irma Eversham to drink the poison, yes?"

"The poison must have been in the sugar bowl," I said. "That's why the inspector was so interested when I told him about the crest! The sugar bowl was only in the Mermaid Room because of Mr. Roddy Fusswell! That makes him awfully suspicious, don't you think? More suspicious even than Miss Marianne?"

"However the poison is administered," said Hector gravely, "there is the important matter of why does it happen in the Mermaid Room? Why *not* at home with the cocoa? Does somebody know that Mrs. Eversham will be present to drink the tea on this particular Saturday?"

My heart turned upside down inside my chest. "Mrs. Eversham had never visited before. Mr. Dillon said so, remember? No one could have known ahead of time. That means that either the killer saw her arrive, or . . ."

Tony whined at my feet. A gust of wind brought a spatter of rain. Hector and I had come up with the same idea. This was precisely what I had wished to suggest to Inspector Locke.

"Miss Marianne was the one who was always there. Alone, except during lessons," I said. "Was it *Miss Marianne* who was meant to drink the poison?"

CHAPTER 8

AN AWKWARD MOMENT

CHURCH ON SUNDAY MORNINGS was often a pleasant diversion, but on this day, Mr. Teasdale did not deliver one of his better sermons. He usually thumped and rumbled, which was much more elevating. He'd had to write this one quickly, I realized. If a person were murdered on a Saturday, the vicar was obliged to soothe his flock the very next morning, which must put dreadful pressure on his pious creativity.

Some poor soul had taken a wrong turn, he said. Veered off the road to Heaven and tumbled into a pit of vipers. It fell upon the rest of us to show compassion to the lost, to those in darkness, to our brethren in need. The notion of *our brethren in need* allowed the vicar to move smoothly to his urgent invitation. Would we please adjourn to the church basement after the service to aid his effort for indigent strangers from foreign parts? He skipped right over the likelihood that the murderous lost soul in question was very possibly among these very parishioners. I cast an eye along the pews staring at each upturned face. Which of them might have wished Miss Marianne dead? Many in town thought she was a bit of a nut. She wanted corsets banned. She thought women ought to be allowed to vote. She thought *all* adults, whether they owned property or not, ought to be allowed to vote. She had never been married, which caused great suspicion among the other ladies, I'd noticed. Suspicion or pity. But how might any of that be reason to kill? Which member of our parish could be so disturbed by a spinster's oddities? Everyone stood for a final hymn—"Behold! A Stranger's at the Door!"

My question had borne only further questions. Who? Why? How?

The basement of All Saints Church had been transformed into a street market, tables dragged into long rows. Ever-growing piles of useful offerings came not only from the Mermaid Room concert but from all over the parish, carried to All Saints in crates and baskets, boxes and bags, which now covered the floor. Women sorted and folded and stacked. Children scurried back and forth, carrying books or trinkets or teapots from one spot to another, helping to organize the offerings.

"Thank you, Mr. Teasdale, for a heartening sermon," said Charlotte. "And how gratifying to have received so many donations! You must be proud!"

"Not *proud*, my dear, but *humble* in the face of such generosity." Mr. Teasdale beamed, and then, remembering, looked grim instead. "And sorely tested by the evil we have so recently met," he said. "I pray that no unknown foreigner has performed this despicable act."

Charlotte dodged that idea by proffering our services. "Let us help as we may today," she said.

I had already found a task, unpacking books and setting them up in rows. Mr. Teasdale's prayer felt like a wasted one, in my opinion.

"How and why would an unknown foreigner sneak into the Mermaid Room carrying poison?" I whispered to Charlotte, once the vicar had moved on.

"Shush!" said Charlotte. "Do not think upon such things!"

"All these boring books!" I said a moment later. "Why would a foreigner want to read one?"

"To learn the English language, naturally," said Charlotte.

"But . . ." I held up a book to show gold lettering on the cover: *The World as Will and Idea* by Arthur Schopenhauer.

"Surely a child's primer would be more useful than this? Something with pictures, perhaps?"

"Just dust them," said Charlotte. "We are not here to question."

"But—"

"Oh, good morning, Mrs. Teasdale," said Charlotte.

The vicar's wife hovered like a seagull, waiting to pounce on any scrap she might spear with her beak.

"Good morning, Miss Graves." Her smile was always hard to discern because her lips were so very thin. "Good morning, Agatha."

"Mrs. Teasdale." I bobbed my head.

"You've had a shocking time," she said to me.

I bobbed my head again, it being easier to agree than to explain that finding a corpse was a stimulating sort of shock, rather than one of the unpleasant variety.

"I was with Rose Eversham, you know," said Mrs. Teasdale. "When she got word of her mother's death. She was here helping to set up the tables and such."

Rose Eversham was in the church basement while her mother was being murdered?

"That was good of her," said Charlotte.

That was *lucky*, I thought. She could not have done the dreadful deed. Not alone, anyway.

"She did not help us with goodness in her heart," said Mrs. Teasdale, "but as penance for using the Lord's name in vain during choir practice. My husband is cunning when it comes to gathering volunteers for church functions."

I noticed then that the vicar's wife seemed to be holding someone's arm. A smallish someone out of sight behind her.

"I'm sure Rose Eversham was grateful to be in a place of refuge when the news came," said Charlotte.

"I had my smelling salts ready," said Mrs. Teasdale. "But they were not needed. The girl barely flinched. Her spirit is a briar patch, that one. If I were not a Christian, I would say she'd smiled when my husband spoke with her."

"A man of great insight," said Charlotte. "No doubt he coaxed a smile of bravery with words of comfort."

"Have you met our visitor?" Mrs. Teasdale pulled on the arm, trying to bring its owner into view. "He has come to stay with us at the vicarage for a few months, so that we may set an example of charity to our parishioners. Our own little immigrant."

Hector!

"Aren't you, dear?" Her voice got louder when she spoke to him. I saw that Hector wished the stones of the floor would split open and swallow him into the earth below.

"We're waiting to hear whether the rest of his family will be joining him." Mrs. Teasdale spoke extra slowly. "Belgium is quite civilized on the surface of things, but their wretched king has behaved so badly. I'm not surprised that Hector's father has sent his son away for a time."

"Mrs. Teasdale," I began. "I know Hec—"

"Madame," said Hector. "I have already the pleasure of—"

"The schools in England are better, of course," said Mrs. Teasdale. "Think what they might be teaching in a country where everyone speaks French!"

"French or Flemish, madame," said Hector.

"Goodness, what have you got there?" She poked at the collection of things that Hector held in his arms. "Are those for your father, dear?" Her voice was loud to the point of being shrill. She tried to tug free a shiny black shoe from Hector's collection. "These are quite impractical," she said. "Shall I help you find something else?"

"Non, madame. These are for me."

I'd seen those shoes dropped into one of the bins at the Mermaid Dance Room, the night before the murder. Hector might be the only person in Torquay who would consider them a treasure worth fighting for. They had found a good home! He also held a woolly green hat and a book.

"*A Study in Scarlet!*" I said. "Sherlock Holmes is my favorite!"

Hector smiled. "I am now to read in English," he said.

Mrs. Teasdale sighed and relinquished her grip on the patent leather shoe. She asked Charlotte to assist in moving a stack of table linens. I stayed by the books, immobilized by revelation.

Hector's jacket was neat and fit him well, with no visible patches. An English boy might be seen wearing the very same item. His hair was clean, his teeth bright and his manners good enough to have impressed Grannie Jane. His accent was odd but he did not smell of any exotic spice. Admittedly, my experience of boys was limited to those I saw in the street, or roller-skating on the Princess Pier. Hector was not especially different from any of those, aside from being clever and unusually polite.

He liked sweets.

He liked mysteries and read Sherlock Holmes.

And yet, he was also a charity boy.

His eyes held an urgent question. I guessed that he was wondering what I would wonder if we were to change places. *Will you still be my friend?*

I nodded yes. Yes, yes, yes.

His smile was wide, but lasted only a moment.

He held up a folded piece of paper, pale blue and wrinkled. He beckoned me to watch closely as he carefully revealed its inner folds. It was dusted with white powder like a fine fruit sugar, gathered more heavily in the creases. Hector displayed it open on his palm like a jewel of great value.

"I find this inside my new left shoe," he whispered.

"What is it?" I licked my finger to dab a sample.

"Do not taste it!"

My finger froze.

"It is possible that I am mistaken," said Hector. "But to me it looks very much like poison."

Charlotte, so good at appearing where unwanted, snorted out a small laugh. She plucked the paper from Hector's hand.

"You children are getting entirely too fanciful. Poison, indeed! Your mother is already concerned about your Morbid Preoccupation, Miss Aggie, without a new chum to encourage it further. This will be the end of it."

She crumpled Hector's discovery and dropped it into a box of rubbish under a nearby table. "No more foolish chatter about murder. Do you hear me? I believe your friendship will benefit from a hiatus. Master Perot, we shall now take our leave. Good afternoon."

Hector had listened with his eyes cast down, his pallor a shade whiter. I yearned to exchange a grimace, but alas, Charlotte's hand on my elbow led me firmly away. I looked back once, to see Hector swiftly extracting his precious clue from where it had been tossed—and flashing me a grin of fervent conspiracy.

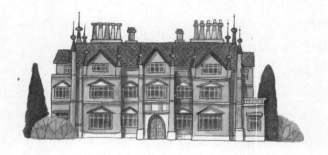

CHAPTER 9

A BRIEF INSTRUCTION

HOME FROM CHURCH and following a lunch of turbot in cream sauce, I now prepared for the afternoon's excursion, admiring my reflection in the hallway mirror. The black felt mourning hat was quite becoming atop my ringlets. One of the small consolations when Papa died last year had been a new wardrobe of vividly doleful clothes. This adorable little hat was one of my favorites. I would not say that I was *happy* for an excuse to wear it again, but I was not precisely *unhappy* either.

"Bereavement," said Grannie Jane. "As you well know . . . 'To have lost a close relation or friend because of death.'" She tugged on her second purple glove, finger by finger. Only the color purple, with black or gray, was considered acceptable when visiting the bereaved.

I suspected that Grannie was as attached to her purple gloves as I was to my hat. My pleasure was diminished at having to wear a dove-gray Sunday coat handed down from my sister, despite its wide shoulders.

"I suppose it is good fortune that our own loss allows us to be correctly costumed to express bereavement . . ." My grandmother paused in the glove-tugging battle. "Thanks to your own dear Papa."

Grannie Jane's own dear son, I thought.

"Naturally, a year ago, you were in no state of mind to consider the etiquette that surrounds the departure of every soul to Heaven."

The funeral for Irma Eversham had not yet occurred, and would wait until the police permitted. The family, however—Miss Rose and her aunt, Miss Marianne— would be "at home" this afternoon to receive condolences.

"Where do you suppose her soul might be?" I wondered. "Since her body is detained at the Torquay Hospital morgue?"

"Most distressing," said Grannie Jane, "to have one's earthly remains loitering about. The soul no doubt must linger with it. All the more important that we appear for the visitation today."

But how exactly did one express polite sorrow when a person had been murdered? A person for whom there was no great affection? Especially when one had so many questions! How, for instance, had the large and unwieldy corpse been moved down that steep and narrow stairway into the bustle of Union Street before riding to the morgue? She looked heavy. And awkward! Did they carry her at a vertical angle, with that oddly arched spine and those crookedly flung limbs?

I shook my head vigorously, banishing the vision. Did Grannie and Mummy ever have these dreadful sorts of thoughts about Papa? Mummy would not be joining this afternoon's excursion because her own bereavement for Papa had been refreshed by Irma Eversham's demise. She had not risen from her bed since the inspector's visit yesterday.

I forced my thoughts along a more poetic path. Bereavement made me feel . . . like a jar full of freshly collected garden worms. My innards were wriggling in the most unsettled way. But I had no interest in lying about beneath the bedcovers in a darkened room. I was ferociously curious to know who in Torquay was a wicked assassin.

"Grannie Jane?" Just to be clear. "Is bereavement necessarily only for a loved one? The whole town knows that Rose's mother was a crosspatch. She and Miss Marianne fought like cats over a fish's head."

Squabbled like seagulls over a sandwich crust.
Battled like God and the devil over a dying soul.

Grannie Jane made a harrumphing noise. "You've been listening to gossip, have you?"

"No, Grannie, I've been gathering evidence."

She was taking a turn in front of the mirror to adjust her hat. She laughed her rare, dear, horsey laugh. One of my greatest pleasures was to inspire that laugh.

"I am gratified that you understand the tremendous value of listening to the conversation of your elders," said Grannie Jane. "Please remember, however, that gossip is like river silt. One must sift it carefully to discover gold amongst the pebbles. Do you understand?"

"Mmm," I said. Not really.

"Only what you see with your own eyes can truly be trusted," she said. "Or that which you hear with your own ears."

"No one can see God," I said. "Are we not meant to trust Him?"

Grannie Jane sighed. "We shall address the matter of God on another day. Young Leonard is waiting to drive us to EverMore."

The Eversham villa was mostly hidden by trees. I could have got there in a wink—past the animal cemetery, over the stile with my skirts hiked up, and across the creek on stepping-stones. But for someone so rickety as Grannie Jane (*May I never be sixty-six*, I frequently prayed), taking the cart was a necessity. The poor old woman did not like to walk even so far as the end of the drive, let alone out onto Bertram Road and all the way up the winding path to EverMore.

Although today's venture must not be called *exhilarating*, visiting the home of a murder victim was not a usual outing. I vowed to remain alert to suspicious behavior on the part of our fellow guests.

"Never shirk your duty, my dear," said Grannie, as we jounced along, "when it comes to visitations and funerals. Mourn unto others as you would have them mourn unto you."

"Oh, Grannie, please don't speak of dying." I slid my white-gloved hand into her purple one.

"You are not to worry about me, my dear. I am not yet ready for the glue-pot."

"You're not a horse, Grannie Jane." I smiled up at her. "You won't be turned into glue."

"A worm's breakfast, then," said Grannie. "But let us assume that is some time in the distant future. Today we are to comfort Miss Eversham and Rose, who have had such a grievous loss."

Belle, pulling the trap, began the turn into the EverMore drive. Coming straight toward us was a police wagon drawn by huge black mares. Leonard got down and led Belle backward, making room for the shouting fellow on the other vehicle.

"What a palaver," said Grannie Jane, *tsk*ing her disapproval of the police. Our trap creaked back into motion. Grannie craned her neck, watching the police wagon clatter its way down the road.

"An inspector gobbling his mustache," she said, "is the last thing a bereaved family needs while they prepare for a visitation."

I was in a bereaved family too, I thought. Nothing had been right since Papa died and that was nearly a year ago. How long did it take for grief to fade?

"Grannie?" I whispered, after a moment. "Sometimes I think about Papa in the most unexpected moments . . . as if a garden snake has slithered through the grass and arrived unbidden on my shoe. It sends a jolt right up my legs."

The trap stopped. Grannie put her arm about my shoulders and gave me a hug. "Well put, my dear. You will be a poet yet."

Leonard helped us down and offered my grandmother the use of his arm for the journey to the front step.

"Thank you, young man. You may wait in the carriage yard until we are done."

Leonard touched his cap and led Belle away.

Grannie paused to look up. "Such a lovely house," she said.

"Not to be gloomy," I said, "but does it now belong to Rose?"

"No, no, my dear," she said. "This is gossip of the most pertinent variety. With a stroke of unexpected wisdom, the Captain willed the house to his sister and the money to his wife. This is why the two were forced into such uneasy proximity. Irma displayed enough good sense not to drag Rose from her childhood home, though I imagine she was waiting with bated breath for her daughter to be married so they could all go their separate ways."

"And now they needn't," I said. "Go separate ways, I mean. Rose and her aunt can just go on living here together. They love each other dearly."

"Indeed," said Grannie Jane. "Let us hope that continues to be true. If one of them has poisoned Irma's tea, it might be quite an imposition on the other's loyalty, might it not?" She patted her lip with a handkerchief and snapped shut her black tasseled handbag. "Unless they planned it together, I suppose. Shall we go in?"

The entrance of EverMore was dramatically draped with black crepe ribbon. Grannie Jane's remark was most unsettling, coming as it did one minute before I was meant to be expressing sorrow to the bereaved. With one idle comment from my grandmother, I must reconsider the list of suspects. My instincts were hollering NO! *Not* Miss Marianne! *Not* Rose!!! But my common sense, so often in hiding, was calling out just as loudly. The two people apt to benefit most from the death of Irma

Eversham waited beyond this door, receiving sympathy from friends and neighbors. Aunt and niece were the best of friends. Had my admiration assumed their innocence without sufficient examination? Were they, in fact, united in the gravest of deeds?

This was not the moment to explore such a possibility, for now here we were in the formal parlor, the shades drawn and elaborate wreaths resting on every chair, obliging mourners to stand. I struggled to bring out my memorized words, *Please accept my deepest condolences for your terrible loss.* Not a sound could I utter. Instead, I made a slight curtsy, which I thought Miss Marianne would appreciate, knowing how devotedly I had practiced.

When I raised my head, her eyes gazed most intently into mine. Eyes rimmed with red and shadowed with exhaustion.

Was this a woman meant to die by another's hand? Or could this be the face of a poisoner?

CHAPTER 10

A GLUM VISITATION

"DEAR AGGIE," said Miss Marianne. "I deeply regret that you were exposed to the vision of poor Irma's death." She squeezed my hand, which was damp inside its clean white glove. To Grannie she said, "Mrs. Morton, I apologize from the bottom of my heart . . . a shocking thing for a child . . ."

"We are here to give you comfort, my dear," said Grannie Jane. "Not the other way around. Agatha is quite a practical girl, and not unduly fussed."

Miss Marianne endeavored to smile, but weakly. "The police have been here again." She touched her hair, and let her eyes drop shut for two long seconds. "What more can they expect me to say? She died a hideous death. I'm the one who brewed the tea. But how can they imagine that—?"

She'd brewed the tea! That answered Hector's question. And she'd said so plainly, with no hint of hidden guilt. This renewed my confidence momentarily.

"We saw the police driving away," I said. "They came yesterday to Groveland and asked me questions too."

"What could they want from you? What did you tell them?" My idle wondering that she might have offered poison in a sugar bowl became preposterous under her imploring gaze. And yet, as Grannie had suggested, who other than she and Rose would achieve wealth and peace with one simple stir of a spoon? It seemed that every minute following such a crime held a new suspicion, a new question, a new puzzle.

Grannie Jane put a hand on Miss Marianne's arm, smoothing the black silk with gentle strokes. "They were merely doing their duty, interviewing a witness. Do not fret, my dear." She glanced at the door where more visitors were coming in. "You'll want to speak with others now. But keep us in mind. We live right next door, should you need us."

For someone who had suggested only moments earlier that this woman had conspired to murder, Grannie was being exceedingly tender! These were the manners, I supposed, that she expected me to learn: How to Be Gracious at All Times, Even with Villains. Miss Marianne, shivering in agitation, leaned close and whispered, "Have you written a poem about this? Do you have your little book with you?"

I shook my head. "No, miss. The circumstances are too sad to be inspiring."

"I should like to read your other poetry." Miss Marianne clasped my hand more tightly than I could slip from. "Would you bring your little book to me? Tomorrow perhaps?"

A Very Odd Request. I could not think what to say. She was giving an impression of being slightly unhinged. Perhaps it made more sense that she had killed Irma Eversham in a fit of madness, rather than part of a carefully devised plot. Seeing her so upset was most disconcerting. At last, she let me follow Grannie Jane to where we now must speak with Rose.

On Friday evening, when Rose had rescued me— partway, at least—from eternal embarrassment . . . Had she then been dreaming of killing her mother? Was she so full of hurt and anger that she somehow conspired to end her mother's life as a way to rescue herself? Or had some- one done this *to* her, by removing her dearest, if prickliest, person?

My eyes were spilling tears before I even spoke. I wished to express gratitude and condolence in one heart- felt sentence. Instead, I was struck mute. I wrapped my arms around her middle and let myself weep, for all the lost parents and left-behind children. I had seen some- thing that even Rose had not—her dead mother. It was as though I'd spied her in the bath, or heard her snoring, some intimate act that only family should ever know about. "Ssh." Rose patted me gently on the back.

I gulped in the next swoop of tears and stood straight again. Grannie Jane murmured her own words of sympathy and pulled me aside to dry my eyes with her handkerchief as others approached Rose. The room had become over-warm and stuffy, thanks to a crackling fire and the growing number of black-clad mourners.

"I am tempted to say . . ." Grannie used the low voice she reserved for improper observations. "Irma Eversham was never so popular alive as she has apparently become when dead as cinders."

I covered my laughter with a cough, and knew her to be correct. Years of eavesdropping had informed me that many of these townsfolk would have crossed the road rather than speak to Mrs. Eversham, or find themselves the target of her spite. But was any one of them—aside from Rose—genuinely distressed by her demise?

"Nothing like a murder," said Grannie Jane, "to gather a flock. Irma Eversham will be honored by more people as she enters her eternal slumber than she spoke to civilly in all of 1902."

We edged our way to the dining room, where somber men and women gathered near a splendid array of refreshments. Two plates of sandwiches, fish paste or sardine.

Tiered trays of champagne wafers, macaroons and lady-fingers. An enormous platter of sliced lemon cake. Eyeing the riches with anticipation, I was overtaken by a memory from after Papa died. Along with new clothes, another small comfort of being in mourning was the quantity of cake delivered to our house from many kitchens about town. I particularly recalled buttered slices of a caraway seed loaf, delivered by a distant neighbor. Only two days after losing Papa, I spent whole minutes devouring cake instead of pondering my bereavement.

A lady wearing a hat with four black-dyed ostrich feathers had snagged Grannie Jane in conversation. I sidled over to the refreshment table for a better look. I peeled off my gloves and stuffed them into the pocket of my coat before choosing a miniature cream puff sprinkled with powdered sugar. The plates and serviettes were at the end of the table, too far away to bother with. I popped the whole confection into my mouth and took another.

"I'm not one to speak ill of the dead," said a hushed voice behind me. "But it comes as no surprise that some-one should want to remove Irma Eversham. On her *best* days she was merely cranky."

"And that's being kind," whispered another voice.

Goodness! Who was saying such things? I dared not turn around to find out. The recently deceased seemed to have no friends at all.

I stopped my tongue from licking the cream puff. The sugar dusted on top was very like the powder discovered by Hector on the paper in his new shoe. I tucked the pastry into a serviette and chose instead a pale yellow meringue.

"What a trial it must have been to *live* with her! Like a cat among the pigeons, she was. I could scarcely abide her bossiness for the length of a Ladies Committee meeting, let alone share a lavatory!"

There were several gasps of swallowed laughter.

"Hush, Myrtle! You naughty woman!" said a third voice. "Though I do wonder how her daughter came to be so nice."

"Rose Eversham is not so nice as she pretends," said the first voice. "Very saucy when she's with the boys, I've heard. Not at all pliant to her mother's will."

"Only a spitfire could stand up to Irma," someone commented. "She'll have her own way now, without having to fight for it, won't she?"

"Do you recall," said the one called Myrtle, "early in Irma's marriage to the Captain? He did something she nearly didn't forgive him for. Wouldn't speak to him for weeks, as I remember."

A murmur: "And she never did say what he'd done."

A clucking of quiet guesses came in response to that.

Another lady? He must have been unfaithful. No, no, he just got drunk and told her she was a homely sow. Not true, he was never a drinking man. He caught her stealing guineas from his handkerchief drawer. Oh nonsense, he simply would not agree to having a cat.

I ate the meringue and considered another. This chatter was as good as a play and I had a front-row seat, though I had yet to identify the players. Staying as still as a cream puff, I studied the lace of the tablecloth, my fingertip tracing the intricate curlicues of thread.

"And now she's dead," said Myrtle. "Taking her secrets with her."

"Her secrets—or somebody else's," said one of the others.

"Agatha?" Grannie Jane beckoned from near the shaded window. It was terribly dim in here! Why did the rules say that we must mourn in darkness? Shaded rooms, shuttered windows, drab clothing, black-and-purple dahlias in the wreaths. I remembered Papa best in the sunny garden, sitting in his chair with an iced lemon water at his elbow, devising sums and puzzles for me to solve.

Next to Grannie was a man whose very stiff collar appeared to push his chin uncomfortably upward. His nose was beaky, but his eyes crinkled when he smiled, as if truly happy to make my acquaintance.

"This is Fletcher's daughter," said Grannie Jane. "Agatha Morton."

I furtively wiped the sugar from my fingers as I dipped into a curtsy. Standing straight again, my eyes flew across the room instead of politely meeting those of Grannie's gentleman. I wished to see whether I might spot Myrtle and her gossiping friends. A row of plump, motherly women stood nibbling pastries and looking entirely innocent.

"Agatha, this is Mr. Hugo Standfast. He is a solicitor and now lives in London. He and your father were chums back in their boyhoods."

"Ancient history, it will seem to you, Agatha," said Mr. Standfast. "Your father was a couple of years older than I, and knew all the ropes. Very able, he was, getting us into—and out of—all sorts of scrapes. Dared me to go off the gentlemen's diving platform my very first time. Must have been about nine years old. Had this ever since." He pointed to a tiny scar above his left eyebrow, pale as a dove's feather.

How odd to think that strangers had recollections of Papa entirely different from my own. This Mr. Standfast held memories of someone that I had never met! He knew the boy who'd plunged into the sea and spilled lemonade on his trousers at the town fete. The Papa of his memory was untarnished by weeks of illness, or the wheeze of troubled laughter.

"Your father was my hero," said Mr. Standfast. "I was most distressed to hear of his passing."

I did not know what to say. His distress was mere hiccups compared with Mummy's, or with Marjorie's and mine, and yet his sorrow should not be disregarded. Grannie's lesson on bereavement had not addressed this courtesy, but she would expect me to respond with more than a mute nod.

"Are you friends of the Evershams also?" I managed.

"Again I have Fletcher to thank," said Mr. Standfast. "He introduced me to the Evershams long ago. I was the Captain's solicitor and also prepared his wife's will." He paused to glance over his shoulder. The smile he offered Grannie was one that seemed tinged with apology.

"The will," he whispered, "is now of great interest to the police, in their pursuit of a motive. But I stand by my oath of privacy, that it must first be read to the family, which will happen in a few days."

"Surely the family is curious as well?" said Grannie Jane. And I knew she meant that she was.

"Is there any family?" I said. "Apart from Rose?" Miss Marianne was not related by blood. Would Rose not inherit everything? But how much was everything? Enough to kill for?

"Do you know what a will is?" the lawyer said to me.

"Yes." I knew exactly what a will was, how it could alter lives. The document that Papa had written and left behind had initiated our financial woes, being nearly fully fiction. Papa had not, after all, been astute in his accounts, despite his role as my maths tutor. His imaginary wealth was far greater than what he'd actually possessed, not enough to pay his debts, let alone keep his family secure. Luckily it was Mummy who owned Groveland or we should have lost our home. Luckily too, Marjorie had married rich, lovely James, who would help take care of us all. Grannie Jane had a bit of money of her own and wouldn't be a pauper. Really, only Mummy and I were the ones to feel the pinch, and the servants we had to let go, poor things. We never ate steak as we used to, and that was my favorite. Now I wore dresses for two years instead of getting new ones each season. All sorts of corners to be cut.

What if Captain Eversham and his wife had been similarly negligent? What if an impoverished fate awaited Rose? Perhaps she should not have been so generous in her donation to the refugee boxes! But if Rose had suddenly become a wealthy woman—and had known beforehand that this would be so . . . Mr. Standfast may be in possession of information that could prove—or disprove—a reason for Rose to initiate a conspiracy.

"What does the will say?" I was too eager to be shy. "Do you know what lies ahead for Rose Eversham?"

"Agatha." Grannie Jane was sharp and firm. "One *never* inquires about money."

Mr. Standfast took a large bite of cake, leaving a smear of icing on his upper lip. "My profession," he said, "is rather like being a detective or a spy. I, too, am concerned with other people's secrets, but the difference is that I do not pry. A lawyer waits for clients to come to him, and then listens to their confidential tales. But I certainly do not tell those tales myself."

"Hearing stories all day long sounds like an ideal occupation," I said. "Perhaps I shall become a solicitor."

Mr. Standfast chuckled. "A woman cannot be a solicitor," he said. "I cannot think of a law school that would care to accept a female applicant. The bar exams are far too difficult."

My eyes shifted to the doorway, where I could see Miss Marianne, her hands being held by another well-meaning matron. She must never have heard Mr. Standfast's opinion of women, or he would not be welcome in her home!

"Even if one or two members of the gentler sex were determined enough to succeed, what client would trust a woman with his secret? Not even a criminal would be so foolish. Females are known for being chatterboxes, which rather blights the oath-of-secrecy bit, you see?"

I did not feel quite so warmly toward Mr. Hugo Standfast as I had previously. I could keep an important secret, just see if I couldn't! And uncover plenty more. I took some comfort in how silly he looked with icing on his lip.

"Mr. Standfast." Grannie Jane handed him a serviette. "You must come up to Groveland for tea before you leave town, if you can bear to enter a household run by the gentler sex? Are you available on Tuesday? I know Fletcher's wife would be so pleased. Cora misses him dreadfully, and you will have reflections to share."

He agreed at once. I wondered how pleased Mummy would truly be about having a stranger thrust upon her. It would require serving a proper tea instead of having a bowl of soup on a tray. But perhaps I would be allowed to invite Hector? Unless Charlotte managed to convince Mummy that his friendship was in some way harmful. Why did some people, like nursemaids and vicars' wives, imagine they knew what other people should be thinking about?

This room was now as crowded as the parlor. Grannie Jane and Mr. Standfast lowered their voices rather than raising them against the chatter. The bespectacled man who had been at Friday's concert stood by the refreshments table, devouring a tart with precise little bites, shedding flakes of buttery crust all down his chest. Why had a journalist come to a visitation? Was he paying his respects? Or pursuing the story of a murder? Mr. Fibbley deserved closer scrutiny. I would say so to Hector, when I had the chance.

Miss Marianne and Rose had come in to join their guests. Rose sat on the bench of the pianoforte, looking bleary-eyed and weary.

Mr. Roddy Fusswell stood close by, one hand resting on her shoulder. She did not look at him, nor he at her, though he kept patting her shoulder for all to see. If Rose's mother's ghost had recovered from the surprise of having such a populated visitation, she would strenuously object to a man who publicly caressed her daughter. I squinted up to the shadowed corners of the ceiling, imagining a phantom's thin howl, *staaay awaaay from Rrrooosssse!*

"Roddy is devoted to her," someone murmured. "Very attached."

Attached like a burr to a silk stocking, I thought. *Like dog hair to a velvet cushion, like candle wax on a lace cuff.*

Rose closed her eyes and swayed slightly, leaning against Roddy Fusswell. Wearing a silly grin, he stroked her hair, which made her sit up straight again and bat away his hand. He promptly dismissed the woman talking to Rose and snapped his fingers at Norah, the maid. I knew Norah. She came often to visit our maid, Sally, in the Groveland kitchen. She'd told lots of naughty stories about Irma Eversham and had wished her evaporated many times over. How must she be feeling now?

Norah brought a small tray with a cup of tea already poured. She added milk, telling Mr. Fusswell that's how Miss Rose preferred it, with just a splash.

"She's still in shock," he said. "She'll have sugar too." He dumped in two teaspoonfuls, stirring briskly before handing the cup to Rose.

My skin prickled, as if suddenly there were ants

crawling inside my camisole. Had I just witnessed a demonstration of how the murder had been performed?

(cut from the *Torquay Voice*)

POISON!!!
VICIOUS MURDER IN THE MERMAID DANCE ROOM!
WOMAN'S BODY DISCOVERED BY CHILDREN!
IS THERE A KILLER ON THE LOOSE?
TORQUAY SWAYS WITH FEAR . . .
FULL DETAILS IN THE EVENING EDITION!
Augustus C. Fibbley

CHAPTER 11

A FEW QUESTIONS

ON THE AFTERNOON following the visitation, I waited in the garden with Tony lying across my feet like a furry, snuffling log. My Monday reading lesson with Mummy had been postponed in favor of an excursion with Grannie Jane to the Torquay Museum. I knew—from overhearing—that the outing was Charlotte's suggestion, to divert me from the frightful occurrence that was riveting my attention.

Murder.

Try as I might to dispel it, the vision of Mrs. Eversham's bloated face had not yet faded from my mind. This was not, in fact, alarming, but rather a logistical puzzle that I yearned to solve. I ought to be writing down my thoughts about the murder case before they got more muddled. Having a pencil in my hand was part of the machine that kept thoughts flowing from my brain to the page. The *scritch, scritch, scritch* of lead upon paper and the occasional pause to sharpen the point, allowed me to sharpen the next sentence at the same time. Whether writing poetry or a catalogue of crucial facts, a pencil and paper were essential.

My writing book, however, was upstairs somewhere, and my feet were immobilized under a dog. I would do my best to arrange the points inside my head, making an effort to follow Hector's example by proceeding logically instead of allowing a flight of fancy to take hold.

One. Miss Marianne rushed into the street in her dance dress with no shawl, meaning that she believed that speed might save a life, that Irma Eversham was still breathing, and a doctor must be summoned at once. This would indicate concern, an attempt to assist rather than kill her sister-in-law. *Unless* (though I truly did not think this was so) she was diabolically clever and had abandoned the corpse of her victim in order to cover her own deed. Point not settled.

Two. Rose Eversham would gain more than anyone from her mother's death. She was probably an heiress and would no longer be abused by Irma Eversham's tongue. But after a lifetime of tolerance, what had compelled a desperate act on Saturday morning? One which Rose cannot have performed herself, as she was a church volunteer all day . . . meaning that Rose Eversham was only guilty if she had a partner in crime. Point to be pursued.

Three. Mr. Roddy Fusswell had imported the sugar bowls from the Royal Victoria Hotel. Had he imported the deadly contents as well? Was he Rose Eversham's conspirator? Or had she been in league with her aunt? One crucial fact demanded attention: Miss Marianne did not own a sugar bowl. She made no secret of this, eager to lecture anyone who would listen on the ill effects of eating sweets. She urged her students to avoid Mr. Dillon's sweet shop for the sake of our health. Roddy Fusswell knew well enough that Miss Marianne loathed sugar and that Irma Eversham loved it. If *he* were the one who stirred poison into the sugar bowl, Miss Marianne was not the woman intended to die. But the question remained: *Was* he the killer? Point not settled.

Four. Somewhere there was a paper with its corner torn off, a paper that mattered very much to someone. Enough to kill for. What was it? And where?

Again, point not settled.

How exasperating! All my ideas led only to further questions. Far from scrubbing clean a glass through which to examine the picture, I was smudging the surface with grimy fingers! And none of the points even pointed anywhere.

I was inclined to think that Hector's find yesterday, of the powdered paper, advanced the progress of our detection well ahead of the police. That was one small triumph, no matter what Charlotte had to say about the matter. I had urged her, during the long walk home, to agree that we should inform Inspector Locke about the new clue.

"Clue to what?" said Charlotte. "Clue to the feverish delusions of two silly children?"

"But don't you think Constable Beck would—"

"Constable Beck?" Charlotte flushed scarlet. "He is *never* to hear of this, do you understand? You may play silly sleuthing games if it pleases you, Miss Aggie, but you are *not* to approach the police! Your pretend clue went into the rubbish bin where it belongs."

Into the bin and out again. I smiled to myself. That paper was safely in Hector's pocket, and the police had Charlotte to blame for another lapse in their investigation. I could keep a secret, just watch.

At that moment, Tony hopped up from a dead sleep to being on full alert, barking furiously. Was there a shrew in the meadow grass? Another bunny dead amongst the roses?

"Ssh!" I scolded. "Only me, Tony dearest. Sorry if I woke you!"

But Tony kept on, aiming his fury at the holly bushes that framed the garden gate.

"Stop!" I cried. "You'll upset Mummy's rest! Please stop!" I put a hand on his head to knead his ear but he *grrr*ed and then yipped a few more times, glaring at the shaking holly leaves.

"I'm afraid it's me he's riled about," said a voice from behind the bush.

My breath caught. *The solitary girl sat like prey in the garden chair, unaware of the grisly doom lurking nearby. A fiend had tromped the lanes awaiting just such a chance to garrote and flay an innocent as she reflected upon his previous brutish crime.*

"If you hold the dog, I'll come out."

Was it the killer? Honestly, it did not sound like a killer. I did not think that killers worried about barking dogs.

"Who's there?" I summoned a pretend self, a bolder self. "Appear at once or my dog will eat you."

A slim young man stepped into sight and leaned against the gate. *Aha!* Mr. Augustus C. Fibbley, reporter from the *Torquay Voice*, wore a brown checked cap and an ill-fitting jacket. He was not hollow-eyed and grizzled, as I imagined a killer should be. His cheeks were smooth— no mustache or silly whiskers. His spectacles were two circles of glass, framed with thin gold wire.

I opened my mouth and closed it again. My brief spell of bravery had vanished.

"Hello," said the man. His voice was a croaky whisper, as if perhaps he had a sore throat and needed a hot honey toddy. "Do I have the honor of addressing Miss Agatha Morton?"

My tongue was twisted in a knot but I offered a nod. Tony yelped.

"I thought so," he said. "You have the look of someone who can gaze coolly into the face of death and come up smiling."

I liked that phrase, *gaze coolly into the face of death*. That is what I had done, though not smiling, to be truthful. The young man found the gate latch and stepped into the garden, bringing his own ease with him.

"Tony!" I said sharply. "Do stop barking!"

"Quite the guardian you've got there. I startled him, a stranger appearing out of nowhere."

"U-usually, he only barks at girls," I said, wishing fervently to quell my nerves. This was someone who wrote words for his livelihood! It mustn't appear that I could not use them myself. "The girls who aren't me."

"I apologize," he said. "But I do so want to speak with you." He glanced down at the notebook in his hand and gave it a little wave.

This morning's headline flashed in my mind. *Woman's Body Discovered by Children!* He must have learned that I was first at the scene of the crime! He wanted *my* answers to his questions! First mentioned as a poet in the press and now an interview subject! If I could summon words and spit them out.

"I should have introduced myself first thing," said the

young man. "My name is Augustus Fibbley. I prefer Gus. I am a reporter for the *Torquay Voice*."

I nodded. I knew that.

"I understand you were the first person to see the poor lady in her deceased state," said Mr. Fibbley. "Did you swoon?"

I shook my head.

"Of course not!" said Mr. Fibbley. "Now that we've met, I can see that you're not the fainthearted type at all."

Our brief acquaintance had not yet shown me in a valiant light, but I was not so fainthearted as Florence Fusswell, to be sure.

"You were in Rose's parlor yesterday afternoon," I said, in a whisper.

"I was indeed." He came a step closer.

"And at the concert too. Befriend the Foreigners. I saw you in the back."

"I deduce, from having heard your poem, that you are an accomplished observer," said Mr. Fibbley. "I'll wager you soaked it up in a flash, am I right? The mayhem in the Mermaid Room?"

Tony had finally stopped yapping, but stood rigid by my knee, panting like a steam engine.

"And being a good witness, you told the policeman everything you'd seen, yes?"

"I think so." I needn't mention that Miss Marianne

had likely poured the poison brew herself. "The body, the blue face . . . the spilled tea, the sugar bowl."

"The sugar bowl?" said Mr. Fibbley.

"The crest," I said. "From the Royal Victoria Hotel. Where the poison was."

"Ah! You've proved me right already. Sharp as a needle in a dish of ice cream, that's you." Mr. Fibbley scribbled a note in his book. "It was Mr. Roddy Fusswell who donated the refreshments, was it not?"

Steps on the path made me turn. Leonard carried a bucket that slopped water across the flagstones.

"Leonard!" I said. "You gave me a fright!"

Leonard stepped out of reach of the growing puddle.

"Come meet Mr. Fibbley," I said. "He's a reporter."

"Does your Miss Graves know you're with a stranger?"

I squinted toward the house and shrugged with great nonchalance. "He's not really a stranger anymore. We've been talking for ages." Five minutes at least. He did not feel like an ordinary stranger. My speechless embarrassment had not lingered.

"Miss Agatha." Leonard's voice came from behind closed teeth. "Take the dog inside." He nudged Tony's flank with his toe and advanced.

"You think it's clever, creeping about in back gardens?" he said to Mr. Fibbley. "Is that how news is made these days? Drumming up gossip from a child?"

The young man shrank back and collided with the holly bush, causing it to tremble. "No harm intended, my friend. The girl is an eyewitness—"

"I am not your friend," said Leonard. "Try asking your nosy questions at the big flashy hotel. Don't let us see you again."

"Leonard!"

Mr. Fibbley flushed, pushed his glasses up his nose and strode briskly around the corner of the house. Tony renewed his insistent noise.

Leonard picked up his bucket and glared. "Reporters are goutweed," he said. "I'll have the cart 'round at the front in five minutes," he said. "For your excursion to the museum."

"I'm not a child," I said. "If you would care to remember." Tony finally stopped his yipping.

"Miss Agatha?" Sally called from the kitchen door. "Your grandmother is asking for you!"

I waved to Sally, but did not move at once. Leonard was being awfully churlish. Would he tattle to Mummy? Perhaps I should thank him for rescuing me from the clutches of a stranger! If it were possible to discover a body under a piano, could there not be a killer right here in our garden?

CHAPTER 12

A SENTIMENTAL OUTING

WHEN PAPA WAS ALIVE, we went together often to the Torquay Museum of Natural History, but I had not visited since his death. A fine, sharp needle twisted itself into my heart as Grannie Jane and I stepped through the arched doorway and into the dimly lit foyer.

"I know you have your special pets, Agatha, so off you go," said Grannie Jane. "There is a great deal to discover by following one's own nose. When you've had enough, I shall be in the Reading Room with the botanical drawings."

I went up the double staircase to the second-floor exhibition hall, to where a person could look at bones and taxidermied animals.

Papa had been the sort of museum visitor who paused before each glass case, perusing the contents, reading the cards of explanation and examining the display again. But I was a roamer, ambling back and forth until something called out and demanded my notice.

I began with one of my favorites, the diorama of a lynx attacking a fawn. The lynx had long been extinct in England, but here it lived on in front of a stone castle with a drawbridge painted on a backdrop to indicate the era during which the beast had wandered the countryside. The lynx, with a spotted golden coat and elegant ear tufts, had been modeled in a ferocious pounce, springing from behind wild privet made of plaster. The cat's claws tore into the hindquarters of a baby deer, leaving long bloody scratches in the fur. Looking closely, one could see that it was red paint dotting the stripes of the wound, but the effect from afar was deliciously gruesome.

I imagined myself perched on a stool in a workshop, surrounded by pots of paint and glue, heaps of wood scraps and a jar of brushes . . . *The devoted artist wore a sturdy canvas apron with a special pocket for her hammer. The spectacles upon her nose glinted as she hummed. Repairing the torn ear of a badger with careful stitches, she imagined it had occurred during a duel with a raccoon. Each tug of the needle, each tap of the awl, became part of the story she constructed.*

Papa's favorite was a snake, jaws agape, caught in the act of stealing an egg from the nest of a flustered mother mallard. Papa laughed at the drake cowering amongst the reeds while the female's beak and wings were wide open in maternal fury.

I wandered past scenes featuring the gray wolf, the Canadian beaver and the leatherback turtle, more disconsolate with every step. It wasn't as much fun, being here without Papa. All the moments of my life, my poems and my adventures from now until I was a wrinkly old woman taking final breaths through yellowed teeth . . . it would all unfold without Papa. How could I bear it? Hot tears pricked my eyes. I must bear it, that's all. There was no choice. So think about something else.

Next time, I thought, Hector should come here with me. Which animal would be *his* favorite? I was certain he'd be pleased by the displays of bones as well. If only Charlotte weren't such a thorn to our friendship. We had so many other topics to discuss! A real newspaper reporter had sought my observations! If Leonard hadn't interrupted, I might have asked Mr. Fibbley a few questions of my own. Like, how did a person go about writing a story when presented with so many threads to follow? And if the story involved a dead body, how did one decide which details were irrelevant and which might be crucial to a solution?

I wiped my face with my sleeve. Was it possible that instead of needing distraction *from* the murder, I needed the distraction *of* the murder, to help dispel the gloominess of a world without Papa?

Grannie Jane was in the Reading Room as promised, peering at a framed drawing on the wall. A burly man with untidy side-whiskers stood nearby, murmuring instruction.

"*Lavandula*," he said. "Commonly called lavender, as you likely know. A member of the mint family, so the aromatic quality is of no surprise. The species shown here has pinnately toothed leaves, but this is not consistent across the genus."

"Oh, hello, dear." Grannie touched my arm. "You remember Mr. Tunweed, the museum botanist?"

"Sir." I bobbed slightly.

"I am delighted to have you visit us again, Miss Morton. I believe your grandmother is finding me quite tiresome as a docent this afternoon."

My grandmother's eyes confessed to tedium. I guided her to sit in a chair. Purpose overcame my usual wish to avoid a conversation. Here was an expert, presented on a platter! "Grannie Jane already knows everything about buds and blossoms," I said. "And about knitting. But, I have a question."

The man brightened. "Of course, Miss Morton. How may I help?"

I scanned the small gallery of drawings mounted on the one library wall not lined with bookshelves. Surely he would know about poisonous plants?

How to ask without alarming my grandmother? "Have you any drawings kept away out of sight?" A tall wooden cabinet stood across the room with more than a dozen wide, shallow drawers. "I am most particularly curious . . ." I kept my voice only just above a whisper, "about poisonous mushrooms."

Among other poisons, I might have added but did not.

"That's an eccentric interest for a young lady," said Mr. Tunweed. He cast a worried look in Grannie Jane's direction.

"For the safety of my dog," I said. "Tony is quite adventurous in his appetite, and likes to eat all sorts of horrible things. Only yesterday we found a rabbit with its spongy little brain seeping out."

Mr. Tunweed looked decidedly concerned.

"Tony didn't kill it! But he was keen to get close, you see? So perhaps I should know more about potential dangers in the garden."

"Er . . ." said Mr. Tunweed.

"Cyanide," I said. "Doesn't that come from a plant?"

The botanist coughed. "Cyanide is present," he said, "in many fruit stones and pits. Cherries, for instance, or apple seeds, though in very small quantities. I think your little doggie will be quite safe if you prevent his eating of fruit."

"Have you drawings of anything else I should watch out for?" I asked. "What does deadly nightshade look like? Or opium?" It was a welcome insight that once I'd launched a conversation, I could keep it going simply by asking questions.

The botanist rolled open a drawer and showed me a detailed picture of a pale purple bloom. "I've never met a dog who liked to eat flowers," he said. "So I may assure you that Tony will not become a drug addict. This is known as *Papaver somniferum*, or the sleep-bringing poppy, used in the Far East to produce opium and morphine."

"What about strychnine?" I said. "In the Sherlock Holmes books, strychnine is very popular."

Mr. Tunweed coughed again, a small bark, and peered across the room at Grannie.

"I've heard that strychnine is often an ingredient in mouse poison," I said, coming finally to my intended destination. Could it be a coincidence that Roddy Fusswell and Miss Marianne had both complained of rodents on the night before the murder? That poison was on both their minds? "Mice or rats. *That* would be perilous for a small terrier, would it not?"

"Undoubtedly perilous," said Mr. Tunweed. "But the use of such a compound would normally be restricted to a cellar or a kitchen. Not a concern with your dog in an outdoor garden."

"What might be the symptoms," I pressed, "if such a substance were consumed? I'm wondering about something that might cause a person to become blue in the face when dead?"

"A *person*?" Alarm rang loud and clear in Mr. Tunweed's voice.

"Agatha, dear," said Grannie Jane.

Oh, dash it! How long had she been listening?

"I believe Mr. Tunweed is quite worn out from our visit this afternoon. And I am feeling anxious for my tea."

I was gracious with my thanks and my farewell. We got all the way to where Leonard was patiently waiting with the cart before the scolding came.

"I can see this outing was quite useless as a diversion from the fate of poor Irma Eversham." Grannie Jane had to raise her voice because of the clopping hooves and the squeaking wheel. "I don't suppose you learned anything of value?"

"Not really," I said. "But you should be applauding my efforts, dear Grannie. My brain cell friction is at a high velocity this afternoon."

We arrived at the Royal Victoria Hotel with hearty appetites. The Royal Victoria Hotel high tea was a treat saved for rare and special occasions. I supposed that distracting a person from a murder investigation could be considered rare.

"How does a young lady feel about hot chocolate?" said Grannie.

"A young lady," I said, "feels particularly warmly about hot chocolate when it is garnished with a dollop of double cream."

My favorite sandwiches were the cucumber with chopped chives, and the ones with ham sliced as thin as onionskin. After sandwiches came cakes and tarts. Plus an extra plate of scones and clotted cream, with a pot of strawberry jam.

"I don't suppose the vicarage serves tea like this," I said. "I wish Hector might have come."

"I expect that Hector attends school on a Monday afternoon," said my grandmother. "I understand he's at the Grammar, on a scholarship."

"He's very clever," I said. "And quite a suitable friend, don't you think?"

"Miss Graves appears to disagree on that point, Agatha, though I found him an appealing boy. Your mother will have the deciding vote, I daresay."

I buttered a scone with a layer thick enough to look like cheese. "Well, I think it's nice to have a friend. And to be puzzling about chemistry instead of moping around," I said. "I wish we knew for certain which poison was used. What do you think, Grannie?"

"It may surprise you to know that I am not well-schooled in poisons, Agatha. But I do recall a compelling case when I was younger, perhaps thirty years ago? A woman named Mary Ann Cotton was arrested for poisoning her stepson. A stepson from her fourth marriage. It came out during her trial—thanks to the dedication of newspaper reporters—that she had left a string of corpses in her wake."

"How many?" I said. "How did she do it?"

"If I remember correctly, she killed three of her four husbands and eleven of her children. All with arsenic. The victims suffered what were called 'stomach fevers.' It took years for Mrs. Cotton to be suspected. Her lawyer tried to suggest that the stepson died from inhaling the dye used to make the green wallpaper in their home."

I licked a dollop of butter from my thumb. "A stomach fever sounds slow," I said.

"I believe arsenic takes several days and is often mistaken for cholera or some such."

"Well, it wasn't arsenic for Mrs. Eversham, then. She went ever so quickly. Does anyone blend poisons? For speed and strength combined?"

"Your mother is quite correct that you are perhaps too entranced by morbid thoughts," said Grannie. "Though it is a mysterious affair."

I was quiet for a moment. "I do not choose my thoughts," I explained, after a while. "They seem to choose me, like the lines in a poem."

"There *was* a poem!" said Grannie Jane. "About Mrs. Cotton. Let me think . . . Most of it is gone." She tapped her forehead. "But the last lines are memorable. You'll like this, Agatha . . . *Mary Ann Cotton, dead and forgotten. Lying in bed with her bones all rotten!*" She laughed, pleased with herself. I agreed that it was an excellent rhyme.

"What was Mary Ann's motive?" I said. "Was she simply seething with hatred?"

"Hatred? No. It was more a matter of greed. You likely are not familiar with the particulars of life insurance, my dear. Back then it was quite a new idea. One could insure someone else's life like making a bet at the races, for just a few pounds. If the insured person died unexpectedly, the person making the bet would receive a sizable dividend. Mary Ann Cotton earned a substantial income by sacrificing her family members."

"She killed her own children and it was all for money?" I said. Such wickedness seemed inconceivable. "Sherlock Holmes was right, I suppose. The motive is nearly always money in his cases. Murder and greed must be the best of friends, do you think?"

"Money, or terrible hurt," said Grannie. She spread clotted cream on a corner of her scone. "Or both together. Intimate companions, as you say."

"Do you suppose someone insured Mrs. Eversham's life?" I asked.

"Despite our being inquisitive, certain details of a person's life are not any of her neighbors' business," said Grannie Jane. "If *pressed*, however, I would guess that, no, the Evershams are not the sort of people who stoop to vulgar equations such as putting a money value on human life." She rustled in her chair just enough to have the waiter spring to attention. She bade him bring the account. I turned away from the view of rollicking waves on the sea to look at who else was lucky enough to take tea at the Royal Victoria on a Monday afternoon.

"Oh!" I clamped a serviette over my mouth. "That's him!"

"Surely you meant to say, *that is he*?"

"It's the reporter," I whispered. "Mr. Augustus Fibbley, right there at the corner table."

Grannie Jane, naturally, could not writhe about in her chair to stare. "And how did you become familiar with the appearance of a newspaper reporter?" she said.

Lying came more easily than I expected. "He attended our Befriend the Foreigners concert." True but false at the same time. "He mentioned my poem in his little notice." Not my name though.

"And then today, not to be boastful . . . I was in the headline." I quoted, "*POISON!!! Vicious Murder in the Mermaid Dance Room! Woman's Body Discovered by Children! Remember? Torquay Sways in Fear?*"

"Scandal-snake," said Grannie Jane.

"He's talking to Roddy Fusswell," I said, watching. "Or, rather, Roddy Fusswell is talking to him. The reporter is scribbling things down as speedily as anything."

"A pity our table is so inconveniently distant," said Grannie Jane. She lifted her handbag from its hook under the table. "Come along, Agatha. I should like to meet the young man who has been assigned to the Mermaid Room murder."

Her face showed a grim resolve, except for the spark of mischief in her eyes. My sudden rise set the cake crumbs atremble. Grannie stood more gracefully, causing the waiter to fly to her side, but she waved him away.

The two men looked up as we approached. Roddy Fusswell's fuzzy lip made him appear older than clean-shaven Mr. Fibbley, but I guessed they were about the same age as Rose Eversham and my sister Marjorie. The reporter's schoolboy eyeglasses reflected darts of light from sunlight streaming through the windows. Roddy Fusswell rose nimbly to show respect for Grannie Jane. I supposed he was polite every day to old ladies visiting the hotel. Mr. Fibbley's chair made a dreadful scraping sound as he got awkwardly to his feet.

I stammered out the introductions, and didn't mix anyone up.

"I do like to partake of the news," said Grannie, "and even enjoy an occasional taste of gossip. But I must say that making one's living by nosing about in other people's business is rather *seamy*."

Pink flared in Mr. Fibbley's cheeks. Mr. Fusswell's went straight to red. "It's for a good cause, Mrs. Morton," he said. "I'm only talking to the chap because of Rose, just trying to set him straight about what a good egg she is."

"Does Mr. Fibbley have reason to believe that Rose Eversham is *not* a good egg?" Grannie Jane turned her gaze to the reporter, using what I long ago dubbed The Withering Look.

Mr. Fibbley pushed his spectacles up to the bridge of his nose and blinked. "I am delighted to count you among my readers, Mrs. Morton," he said. "Most stories go deeper than just the facts, as you'll have noticed. In this case, I'm looking for motives not necessarily visible on the surface of things."

"If Rose killed her mother, I could only wonder what took her so long," said Roddy. "That old woman was asking for something like this to happen, the way she bullied and bruised everyone who crossed her path. Myself included." He smirked briefly. "But Rose most of all."

Mr. Fibbley's eyes shifted to the notebook open on the table. I sensed his fingers itching to write down what Roddy Fusswell had just said. Was this an admission that Roddy had aided Rose in a homicide that he thought was justified because the victim was a nasty woman? Did Roddy know something that no one else could know? Or was he slyly stirring up interest in someone other than himself?

Grannie Jane raised an eyebrow. "A word of advice, Agatha dear, as you go forward into the world. Remember at all times with whom you are speaking and how your words may be interpreted by those hearing them."

"That's good advice, Mrs. Morton," said Mr. Fibbley. "Though I rather depend on people forgetting themselves in my company." And then he winked. At *me!*

"Now, just a minute." Roddy Fusswell finally understood that they referred to his own brash comments. "If you think—"

"Time to go," murmured Grannie Jane. "Our curiosity is becoming unbecoming. You have a lovely tearoom, Mr. Fusswell. We have enjoyed ourselves. Good day."

"If you think what I just said about the old biddy means I offed her, you'd be dead wrong," said Roddy Fusswell. "If I were going to kill someone . . ."—he glared straight into my eyes—"I'd do it with my bare hands."

CHAPTER 13

A LETTER AND ANOTHER

"It seems to me," said Grannie Jane afterward, "that Mr. Roddy Fusswell is similar in temperament to little Bertie Cummings who lived down my road when I was a girl. Bertie waited for the braver boys to climb the vicarage wall and sneak out with their pockets full of plums. When he managed to cadge one, he'd make a great show of munching it in front of the rest of us, as proof of great naughtiness on his part."

I thought it a peculiar notion that someone might pretend to be naughty, as I spent a great deal of effort pretending to be a Good Girl. Was Grannie suggesting that Roddy Fusswell had not, but wished he had, killed Mrs. Eversham? He was still very high on *my* list of suspects.

As soon as we were home, Grannie went to have an over-due afternoon lie-down. I hastily bundled my coat into the hall closet and hurried toward the staircase, eager to record the clues I'd been gathering inside my head.

"Miss?" Sally called from the back hallway. "There's a letter come for you." She waved the envelope. "The post-man's given up knocking on the front door and only ever comes to the kitchen."

Marjorie! Back from her honeymoon! I knew that script as well as I knew my own, though mine was never so tidy.

"Thank you, Sally! Did Mummy get one too?"

"Yes, miss."

I did not bother looking for the letter knife. Climbing the stairs to my room, I peeled off the seal with my fingernail.

Friday

Dearest Aggie,

Thank you for the letter and the darling drawing of Tony with his enormous lamb bone. It was waiting when we arrived home from our

*wedding travels, which were perfectly splendid.
(Your spelling is still atrocious! One of the
drawbacks of Mummy thinking you shouldn't
go to school!)*

*I am sitting in my Morning Room, sending you
the warmest of best wishes for the Mermaid
Room concert this evening. By the time you
receive this note, you will be looking back at
your poetry recitation with relief and triumph.
Congratulations, Missy.*

I paused. My last letter to Marjorie had been written
before I'd found Mrs. Eversham! How speedily one's view
of the world can change—especially when one has gazed
coolly into the face of death . . .

*James's niece, Lucy, is still chattering about
meeting you at the wedding. She says it was the
most wonderful day of her life so far. (It was
certainly one of my favorite days as well but, of
course, I was the bride!). I'm so pleased that you
and Lucy got on well.*

*James and I hope that you and Mummy and
Grannie Jane will all come to spend Christmas*

with us at Owl Park. Lucy will be here, and the rest of James's family, as well as various other friends and odd acquaintances who have nowhere else to go. Do say you're as excited for this as I am.

Many hugs, dear Agatha-Pagatha,

Your loving sister, Marjorie

I held the letter for a moment, closing my eyes against the sting of tears. I missed my sister dreadfully. But I missed Papa even more, and Marjorie had just reminded me of that. It was Papa who had used my name to make up a silly variation of the nursery rhyme.

Agatha-Pagatha, my black hen,
She lays eggs for gentlemen.
She laid six and she laid seven,
And one day she laid eleven!

I screwed up my face as hard as ever I could, teeth biting into my lip. Go *AWAY*, tears! Think of something else!

As I tucked the letter back into its envelope, I saw that Marjorie had scrawled a postscript on the reverse side of the page.

My goodness, Aggie!

I've just had a note from Grannie Jane telling me about Rose Eversham's mother. This is the most dreadful news. I shall write to Rose at once, but am horror-stricken that you made such a grim discovery. You are a brave girl. Best love, M.

My fame as a body-finder was spreading without me doing a thing. The harder task was finding the murderer. Being a clever sleuth was far more deserving of fame than simply walking into a room where a corpse was waiting to be found under the legs of a piano.

And being a clever sleuth involved taking notes. I'd come up here to collect my writing book, so where was it? Not in the drawer of the table at my bedside where I usually kept it. Not amongst the cushions on the window seat where I liked to write poetry. Not on the bed. Not under the bed.

Come on, think! Where had I last seen it?

My mind flew to the dreadful scene in the Mermaid Room. Doctor Chase on his knees next to the corpse of Rose's mother. Miss Marianne, ashen-faced, wringing her hands. Charlotte hissing at me to hurry back out. Me paying no heed, but scurrying over—almost close enough to step on poor Mrs. Eversham—to retrieve my notebook from where Rose had laid it on top of the piano the evening before.

Then what?

Charlotte had dragged me away, down the stairs and into Mr. Dillon's shop to await the police. Eureka! I had slipped the book into my dance bag, and not given it another thought.

How much brain cell friction had assisted in remembering one small detail? I pulled my dance bag from the bottom of my wardrobe and fumbled to open the clasp.

Hooray! My dear, tattered writing book quietly waiting to be of service. I riffled through, looking for my most recent entry. A loose page fell out and fluttered to the floor. Not my writing. Not writing at all, but words assembled from the cut-out bits of printed text.

PLEASE be InFORMED thAT ☞you ARE NOt the First CHILD of YOUR PARENTS' UNIon.

They hID A baBy BEFOre YOU WERE boRN. IS this A SECrET YOU CAN LIve WiTH? MEET AT ToPRE ABBEY 5 O'CLOCK sUNDAY SHOULD We nOT INHERIT TOGETHER?

froM FAIR PLAY

I turned the page over. Nothing was written or pasted on the reverse. I read it a second time, and then again, my face hotter and hands more trembly every moment. Who had written this?

Clearly it was not meant for me. My parents had Marjorie first and then me, no confusion about that. There could never be another because poor Papa was dead. So, who *was* it meant for? And how did it come to be inside my writing book? Despite being signed Fair Play, it whiffed of menace more than good intentions.

As well as a very big secret.

Each letter had been cut from other texts and then made into new words. Most of them were quite small and must have come from newspapers. Upper- and lowercase letters were mixed up so the sentences dipped and rose in crooked lines. I examined it so closely I could smell the paste and ink. The author had gone to great lengths to hide his—or her—identity.

I gave myself a shake. I was holding a real clue to a real murder. It simply must be connected. There could not be *two* ominous mysteries happening at the same time.

Begin at the beginning, I told myself. Proceed logically, as Hector would.

When I'd passed the notebook to Rose at the concert there had been no letter inside. Between then and the moment when I reached over the corpse to retrieve it, this letter had been slipped between its pages. Who by?

Was the writer also the hider? Or was the recipient the one who wished it to stay a secret? Were there two identities to discover . . . or three? Was my notebook meant to be a postbox of sorts? Or was the insertion an accidental one? Neither of these ideas made sense. My name was boldly written across the front, so no error could be made.

Rose was likely the last person to touch the notebook, since I'd picked it up from where she'd put it down. If Rose had slipped a paper into the book while reading my poem, the audience would have seen her. And later, when we'd all gone home? By then, there'd be no reason for secrecy. She could have simply put it into her handbag.

My head swam. How would I ever sort it out?

Just then came two taps on the door, and then another. Charlotte's usual knock. I crammed the letter back into my notebook and slammed it shut.

"Miss Aggie?" Charlotte poked her head around the door. My heart pounded as if I'd raced a pony rather than hidden a piece of paper.

"Hullo," I squeaked.

"We're all at table," said Charlotte. "And you are not."

I flattened a palm on the cover of my precious book. "Coming. Ten seconds."

As soon as she had gone, I flew to the window seat and tucked the book under a cushion. One thing was certain. I would *not* show the letter to Charlotte. She had been so rude about Hector's powdery paper. Offering a second clue would be begging for ridicule. She'd never be an ally in a murder hunt, I knew. I rushed along the hallway and down the stairs without pausing to smooth my hair or catch my breath. Deceit was an energetic pastime! How did criminals manage to live their lives?

Grannie Jane shot me a stern look when I scurried into the dining room, hot-faced and mumbling an apology. Charlotte passed a plate of cold tongue with sliced bread and butter. I *loathed* tongue. It looked so much like tongue!

"If I had known that an outing would result in the discourtesy of being late . . ." said Grannie Jane.

"Yes, ma'am. Sorry, ma'am." Well, *humph*! Grannie Jane could be so unreliable! One minute she was a person's best friend, and with the next breath she turned brusque and unhelpful. Best not to risk showing her the letter either. Grannie Jane in the wrong mood might toss it into the fire or, worse, send it straight to Inspector Locke. What an insult that would be to my sleuthing abilities.

"Are you quite well, darling one?" Mummy reached over to feel my forehead. "You look flushed."

"I'm fine." I nibbled on bread spread thickly with butter.

"You haven't touched your tongue," said Mummy. "A growing girl needs excellent meat, along with improving grains and lots of fresh air. Charlotte, come with me now to speak with Cook. We'll devise a restorative diet. I'm terribly concerned since Agatha's upsetting day on Saturday."

I did not protest as they made their way out. It made Mummy feel better to feed me bran and cod liver oil. But I wouldn't share the letter with her either. It was too easy to worry Mummy, and a worried Mummy was a terrible thing to behold. I had never done it on purpose, of course, but I squirmed to remember the time or two when I had caused distress by accident. Like when fat little Tony had fallen into the creek last summer and couldn't get himself out. I had waded to the rescue and come home caked in creek-slime. Mummy had swooned, actually swooned. If she saw the menacing letter, she would agree with Charlotte and forbid the very thing that I wanted most— to solve the puzzle of Mrs. Eversham's murder.

"Has hot cocoa in a hotel spoiled you for proper food?" said Grannie. "I recall a fervent promise that food at home would be eaten without complaint."

"I didn't know it would be tongue," I muttered.

Grannie unfolded the *Torquay Voice*. "How disappointing," she murmured. "Mr. Fibbley has not filed a story this evening, despite his promise in the morning edition. Too busy taking tea with one of the prime suspects, I presume."

"Is there *nothing* about the death of Mrs. Eversham?"

"Only a statement from Inspector Locke. 'The investigation continues, et cetera . . . Anyone with pertinent information should notify the constabulary at once, et cetera . . .'"

I stared at the nasty little bumps on the slab of tongue before me. If only Tony were allowed into the dining room, I could slip him a treat. Unbeknownst to the police—or to cocky Mr. Fibbley—Hector and I were holding *two* pieces of pertinent information: a paper dusted with possibly lethal powder, and a threatening, anonymous letter. But Charlotte had roundly scolded us for thinking we had something to offer the police. She'd forbidden me from further involvement. It seemed prudent to follow her instructions and refrain from passing along clues just yet. Who said a girl could not keep a secret?

"May I please, *please* be excused from table?" I said.

"You may," said Grannie Jane. "But do not imagine that putting a serviette over your plate disguises the uneaten tongue."

Finally released and back in my room, I kicked off my shoes. I pulled my notebook from under the cushion of the window seat and sat with my feet tucked up, peering through the window into the black beyond. Nightfall happened so quickly in the autumn. Above the branches of the little woods, a single light burned in Rose Eversham's bedroom.

The girl's fingers danced in agitation on the soft, peach-colored coverlet. She watched the candle splutter, imagining that she would never sleep again, so heavy with sorrow was her heart.

Or, perhaps . . .

The girl's dark eyes flashed in the candlelight, bright with barely contained exultation. Until Saturday, she had been flung like a feather on the wind by the whims of an angry woman.

But no longer! She was now queen of her own domain, rich and pretty, happily sharing the castle with her dear Auntie M.

Auntie M.

I arrived with a *thunk* at a nagging recollection, one I had been trying to ignore.

My notebook was usually of little interest to adults. Mummy said fondly that I was a poet, and Grannie Jane occasionally suggested that I record the correct spelling of a newly learned word. But no one had ever asked to read what I had composed.

Until yesterday.

CHAPTER 14

A SCHEME IS DEVISED

I RECALLED THE PLEADING look in Miss Marianne's eyes during the visitation when she'd asked—even begged—that I should bring her my notebook, expressing a sudden curiosity about my poems. And before that, when Mrs. Eversham was lying dead at her feet, Miss Marianne had objected to me taking my own same notebook from where it lay on top of the piano. At the time, I had assumed it was about disarranging the elements of a crime scene. But her request now made perfect, horrible sense. She had hidden the letter and urgently wanted it back.

Had she been intending to send it? To whom?

Or had she received it? From whom?

I needed help to untangle this knot. I would find Hector tomorrow and together we would decipher its meaning. I withdrew the letter and smoothed the page flat on my bed.

My neck prickled with cold, as if I'd forgotten my muffler on a winter day. One small corner at the bottom of the page had been torn away. The missing piece looked to be the size that might be trapped between a thumb and forefinger if wrenched from the grasp of somebody holding it.

Somebody dead.

I was looking at the very clue that Inspector Locke had been so keen to recover. I paced the room while daubing my teeth with tooth powder and a rough flannel. Back and forth, around and round, my slippered feet trying to catch up to my spinning thoughts. This matter could not wait until tomorrow after all. Something must be done at once. But what? *What* could I do?

I rinsed my mouth and swished and spat. I brushed my hair and braided it as best I could, though most bedtimes it was Charlotte's task to ready my hair for sleeping. My curls were so long they got in the most dreadful tangle if I left them loose at night. I'd got my dress unhooked and off and put away on a hanger when I saw the solution. An utterly simple solution.

A light still burned in Leonard's shed, a yellowy glow in the darkness of the chilly garden. Despite his bad humor earlier, I expected he'd be a brick and help in this small mission.

The lacy blossoms on Rose's curtains were still illuminated, as much a part of my evening sky as the moon rising over the sea. Bringing peace to the inhabitants of EverMore was the reason behind my plan, which I now put into action. I carefully tore a page from the back of my writing book and found a nearly sharp pencil in the drawer of my little table.

Vital new clue.
When can we meet?

I folded the paper twice and wrote HECTOR PEROT, CONFIDENTIAL on the outside. I tipped the candle and let drops of wax fall on the fold. I pressed my thumb into the blob, making a whorly seal.

The door opened. I jumped nearly out of my skin.

"Ready for me to do your hair?" said Charlotte.

I got clumsily to my feet, banging my knee while trying to block the tabletop from view.

Charlotte's gaze, naturally, went straight to the paper that I was hoping to conceal. "What are you up to?"

I felt a blush rising, warm and stupid. I shrugged, a gesture not permitted in the Morton house. Charlotte's eyes narrowed.

"You've done your hair all by yourself," she said.

"I'm twelve," I said. "I can braid my own hair. And I shan't need tucking in either."

"Well, then," said Charlotte. "Good night, Miss Aggie." She'd nearly closed the door when she turned back. "Does this have anything to do with your odd little chum?"

Which was worse, to be a liar or a soppy goose?

I sighed as aggravated a sigh as I could muster and thumped myself down on the bed. Finally the door clicked shut. I raced to the window. A candle still burned in Leonard's shed. Beyond the fruit trees, the Eversham villa was now in darkness.

I counted slowly up to one hundred and then backward all the way down. I wasn't the least bit tired. I pulled on the old knitted spencer jacket that I'd adopted from Mummy and often wore to keep warm in the evenings. The spencer made my pantaloons feel positively indecent. I fastened my petticoat back on to cover my legs. I counted again to one hundred and back to zero.

No sound from outside my door.

Shed still alight.

Time to go.

The hallway was empty and as black as a cellar. Were the gaslights always extinguished when I went to bed? How did Charlotte find her way when I occasionally pulled the cord in the night? How lucky that I'd outgrown sharing the nursery with Charlotte! How lucky that Tony now slept in Mummy's room and was not here to raise a fuss.

How *un*lucky that I didn't have one of those new electric Flash Lights, advertised in the *Torquay Voice*. I'd ask Father Christmas to bring me one. For now, I kept a hand on the wall and inched my way to the stairs. At the first creak, I gasped. At the second creak, I held my breath and waited, expecting Charlotte's door to fly open and a candle flame to shock the darkness. I was sneaking out! At the third creak, I began to giggle silently, part in terror and part with glee. Two full flights! And then along the back hall to the kitchen, small hiccups of laughter bubbling up. At the garden door I scooped Cook's egg-collecting jacket from its hook and pulled it on over the spencer, making my arms a bit stiff, but a tad more presentable for visiting a young man in a shed in the dead of night. I tucked the letter for Hector deep into one of the pockets.

The frosty night air whistled straight through my cotton undergarments, chilling my legs, making Cook's jacket all the more welcome. How could I have waited twelve whole years to be out of doors alone at night? Stars shone in glorious constellations, and a glowing moon peeked between nearly bare branches as it rose. Far off was the gentle roar of the sea, a constant lullaby.

Except, of course, that there'd been a murder, and I, Agatha Caroline Morton, was in possession of a crucial piece of evidence. Make haste!

The grass glistened with droplets from a sprinkle of rain. My crocheted slippers were sopping within moments. The garden shed cast a moon-shadow across my path and I bumped into the wheelbarrow. Reaching out to steady myself, I jostled Leonard's bicycle, leaning against the wall with its tire jutting out.

I was making enough noise, as Grannie Jane would say, to wake the dead. It was no surprise that the shed door creaked open before I had summoned my nerve to knock.

Leonard wore a woolly hat and a ragged grass-colored muffler wrapped twice around his neck and pulled up over his chin.

"Oh," I said. "You're going out. I'm ever so pleased I've found you first."

"Miss Aggie!" Leonard's eyes were as round and dark as chestnuts. "I'm not going nowhere, just keeping warm." He peered over my shoulder, concern on his face. "Is there trouble, miss? Is your mother taken ill?"

"Nothing like that, Leonard. I need you to help me. It's a bit urgent, if you don't mind."

"What is it?"

"Well, I've found something crucial. Related to the murder. I mustn't tell you, because it's not my secret to tell." I thought briefly of Mr. Standfast, the lawyer, insisting on discretion. "But . . . Rose, you see, had my notebook

147

at the concert . . ." I found myself stuttering a little. After being so very careful and quiet all evening, the words were pouring out in a jumble.

"I couldn't speak in front of all those people at the concert on Friday. I freeze up sometimes. So Rose read my poem aloud. She was the last person to hold my book. When I opened it tonight, there was a . . . paper inside, and it's a clue."

Leonard stared at me. Why, when I was usually struck dumb, did I sometimes—with handsome, friendly Leonard, for instance—turn into a foolish chatterbox?

I took a deep breath. "This is rather a confidential matter. Do you suppose I could come inside? It's awfully cold out here."

"No!" said Leonard. "It wouldn't be right, miss. Your mum would have chickens just knowing you're out of your bed at this time of night. It's too small in here for a visitor, a young lady besides." He moved slightly, allowing me to catch a glimpse.

I saw a cot with its wool blanket mussed, as if it had been worn as a cloak. I saw the candle wedged into a jelly jar and a tidy stack of newspapers rolled into pretend fire logs. I knew that's what they were because two of those logs were smoldering in a large tin bucket, edged with gleaming orange, smoking rather than burning and surely not providing much warmth.

"You don't have a fire."

As if he didn't know. I was mortified that I hadn't considered this before. Why would the garden shed have a stove or a chimney? And here it was, late October! Even Hector—a foreigner—surely had a fire in his room!

"I'll tell Mummy in the morning," I said. "We'll find a place indoors, I promise. But . . . but tonight . . ."

It seemed harder now to ask him what I had come to ask. But how else would I get my note to Hector by morning?

"Tonight I wonder if you could deliver a letter for me? Not so very far, just down a ways on Bertram Road. You can ride on your bicycle. Please, Leonard?"

Leonard was shaking his head.

My fingertip found the wax seal on the folded paper in the pocket of Cook's jacket.

Leonard squinted in the dark. "A letter for who, miss? The police?"

"I'm not telling the police," I said. "Not yet anyway. They'd try to stop me finding out more and I—"

"Miss Aggie," Leonard interrupted, "it's too late at night to play fanciful games. Burn the letter before your mother has more to worry about. You be a good little girl and get yourself tucked into bed."

Ouch.

He put out a hand, as if beckoning to the note in my pocket. A hand wrapped in an old sock, with the toe cut off for his fingers to peek out and the heel bulging at his wrist. I stepped out of reach.

"Never mind," I said. "I shouldn't have bothered you." I gave him what I hoped was an innocent-looking smile. He summoned one in return.

"To bed, miss." He gave my shoulder a little push, compelling me to turn around. "Go on," he said.

He closed the door with a firm click.

Grrr. My hands balled into fists, itching to hammer on the door of the shed. But then the ragged socks-for-gloves came to mind. The narrow cot and thin blanket.

What an awful place to live! All those spades and rakes hanging on hooks over one's bed, ready to smash a person's skull. All those pots and jars and earthy things, probably hosting spiders and caterpillars. Poor Leonard. I couldn't fault him for being in a foul mood on a cold night. Perhaps we could let him stay in the wine cellar, now that Papa wasn't here to care about wine. At least for the winter. I would ask Mummy at breakfast.

But that was tomorrow. Tonight, I had a decision to make. I touched the envelope in my pocket. If I sent it with the first post in the morning, Hector would not know about the new clue until tomorrow at teatime. We could not meet before Wednesday! It mustn't wait so long. We were confounded by two simple pieces of paper—the letter with a corner missing and the blue square with powdered creases found inside a shoe . . .

I blinked, struck by what Hector might call logic. His new shoe, the one that held the powdered paper, had been in one of the Mermaid Room boxes. But those boxes had been hauled away *before* the murder happened. If the killer had poisoned the sugar early enough to dispose of the evidence in a charity box as Hector had guessed . . . how could he—or she—know that Mrs. Eversham would be requiring sugar sometime later in the morning? Mrs. Eversham had not yet arrived in the Mermaid Room! It seemed too unlikely. I did not think that anything inside those boxes could be connected to the murder at all.

I began to hum, to drown out the scolding voice inside my head. I had no choice now about what I must do. The stranger's letter falling out of my notebook had set a sequence in motion, one thing leading to the next. And next was telling Hector that his paper clue was no clue at all—but that I had another one, even more valuable.

As if part of a plan all along, I pulled Leonard's bicycle upright and got myself balanced on the seat. The sodden toes of my slippers, just reaching the pedals, started to pump. The fender was out of alignment and clicked against the wheel, the tires were not perhaps as fully inflated as they should be, but I bounced along the drive under a starlit sky, with an unfamiliar boldness in my heart.

CHAPTER 15

A WEARY MESSENGER

I KNEW WITHIN THREE turns of the wheels that my petticoat was an impediment to pedaling. Little wonder that lady cyclists were now wearing bloomers on the fashion pages in Mummy's *Tatler* magazine. With an awkward jerk of the handlebars, I steered the bicycle into a privet hedge to guarantee it stopping. I unhooked my skirt, rolled it tightly and pushed it in amongst the brambles near the bottom. Chilly air bit through my pantaloons, almost as if they weren't there. I was about to ride to the vicarage and back wearing one flimsy layer of cotton on my legs! What if Mrs. Teasdale should be having a late-night stroll about her garden? *With her hair in pins under a kerchief! Yes! Smoking a cigar! A thick, leaf-wrapped cigar, imported from Morocco! Saying curse words between puffs . . .*

Well, if Mrs. Teasdale was tapping ash into the laurel bush, she deserved to see me in my pantaloons! I looked about in the dim, blurred night. Not so much as a fox or an owl was stirring. No one to see me. So, get a move on! It wasn't as far as all that . . .

The bicycle wobbled along, meeting each pebble as if it were a boulder. I concentrated on balance, and also on steering. The pale, holy glow of the moon transformed familiar hedges into monstrous tree sprites.

"Thank you, Papa," I said out loud, my voice a funny quack next to the clickety-clank of the bicycle and the silence beyond. Papa had spent many hours holding the seat of my child-sized bicycle while I learned to pedal up and down the drive. He'd tricked me in the end, trotting alongside in a pretense of holding me up, but having let go many minutes before.

Up and down the drive, however, was sorry preparation for the up and down of a hilly road. Part of what made Groveland my favorite place was how far it was from other houses—which tonight meant how far a person had to pedal on a rickety bicycle to get to where she wanted to be. The other homes along Bertram Road and then St. Vincent's Close stood shadowed and forbidding.

My foot slipped, making my shin bang hard against the pedal. *Ouch!* Pay attention! I bumped over a ridge of mud at the side of the road and nearly toppled. It wasn't safe to drive a vehicle and be lost in thought at the same time. Despite the cold and chafing web of my slippers, I pedaled harder. I coasted down one more hill, braking on and off, the rush of air chilling my legs. What a sight I must be, with the lace edging of my pantaloons poking out beneath Mrs. Corner's jacket, bare ankles winking above muddy slippers.

I had arrived at the vicarage without being noticed by anyone! The gate was hemmed in by shrubbery, the house itself out of sight. I rested the bicycle against the fence and reached over to unhook the latch. I was now on somewhat holy ground—if a vicarage counted as holy— so I said a silent prayer. *Forgive us our trespasses . . .*

Was this trespassing? Somewhere, a dog howled. Did the vicar have a dog? Three worried breaths. All quiet. The path to the verandah lay in deep shadow. I could barely feel my feet but trusted that my toes were still there inside the spongy slippers. I extracted the letter, crumpled and a bit damp, from the pocket of Mrs. Corner's jacket. The wax seal still sat firmly, and Hector's name was clear enough on the outside.

Was the Reverend Mr. Teasdale an early riser, or did he take his tea in bed? If I were lucky, Hector would be the first to leave in the morning, on his way to school. I tucked half the note under the bristled mat in front of the door. I crept away and steered the bicycle onto the road, my feet feeling as if I were ankle-deep in cold spring mud, squelching with every step. My heart sank a little as I realized that the homeward journey was uphill all the way.

Then *GONNnG!* I jumped nearly out of my skin! *GONNnG! GONNnG!* The bells of All Saints clanged twelve clamorous times. Goodness, had I ever before been up so late as midnight?

With my ears still ringing, I heard something else, a whoosh and a creak. Before I could dart into hiding, another bicycle hurtled toward me with a torch beam jiggling from its handlebars and a police officer upon the seat.

"Steady on there!" Constable Beck. His long legs dragged his bicycle to a stop as he shone the light straight into my face, rendering me quite blind.

"Miss Morton, is it?" Surprise painted his words. He redirected the torch to the middle of my chest and then to my saddle and wheels. "What the devil brings you out in the middle of the night?"

I stared at the faint gleam of buttons on his chest, any answer I might muster stopped in my throat. I was standing in front of a grown man whose duty it was to apprehend anyone misbehaving. I was outdoors on a dark road wearing Cook's battered jacket and only my underthings beneath! If greater mortification were possible, I prayed never to know.

"Are you . . . Are you . . . *awake*, Miss Morton?" Alarm shot through his voice.

Would it make things better if I pretended to be sleep-walking? The frozen lumps that had formerly been my feet chose that moment to fail me. I sagged at the knees, let go of the bicycle and collapsed to the ground. A spinning wheel scraped rudely against my calf, which was horribly, nakedly illuminated under the glowing moon.

The policeman gave a small cry of consternation. He swung off his own machine and scooped me up in strong, Papa-like arms, the damp wool of his uniform smelling slightly of camphor. Setting me back on my feet, my rescuer looked very stern.

"What sort of lark is this?"

"Please don't tell Charlotte!" I was flustered by the brief embrace, flummoxed by my likely doom if he were to tattle. "Miss Graves, I mean."

I had a fleeting picture of the policeman murmuring in Charlotte's ear, his stubbly chin against her neck. I pushed that thought aside.

"It will ruin the surprise, you see? I delivered a letter to a friend . . ." I vaguely waved a hand so that he wouldn't guess about the vicarage. "It would be dismal if all my planning was for naught."

The policeman sighed. "Hop on," he said.

In a rather impressive display of strength, Constable Beck pushed his own bicycle with his right hand while propelling mine with the left. He managed to keep both steady, with me upright on my seat, my poor feet resting on the gently turning pedals.

"Am I the only person," he said, "who knows you're running about at midnight?"

I wondered for one distressing moment, might *he* be the killer? *The wicked man had only pretended to court the plain and earnest nursemaid. His murkier intent was to watch the inquisitive nuisance of a girl. And here she was, alone and unchaperoned in the dark of night, easy prey for a murder near the vicarage! A brisk blow to the head with his truncheon would quiet her infernal curiosity for once and for all!*

Constable Beck was breathing noisily, pushing two bicycles and a tall-for-twelve-year-old girl up Bertram Road. If he were going to bonk me on the head, would he not have done it before climbing the hill?

"Second time today," said Constable Beck, "that I've been waylaid by a pesky child sleuth."

"Whatever do you mean?" I said.

"Your little friend, the funny French chappie—"

He broke off to lean his bicycle against his hip while he fished a handkerchief out of his pocket and mopped his forehead—all while keeping me upright on my own vehicle. I counted to ten.

"Hector?" I finally asked, as he replaced the square of linen into his jacket pocket.

"Ha, yes, well, he come into the station today with a look about him so serious that we thought he was there to confess stealing the head off Queen Victoria's statue."

Oh, dash it all! The powdered paper! He must have taken it—

"He walks right up to the desk sergeant and says, ever so gravely, he says, 'I am wishing to speak with the inspector, if you please.'" Constable Beck began to chuckle, as if it were a great joke. " '*If you please!*' "

It was not amusing to hear Hector's accent being mocked. I rather doubted that the policeman could speak French so well as Hector spoke English.

"The *inspector*!" Laughter lingered in Constable Beck's voice. "If you please! We told him the inspector was not available—which was true, as it was the middle of the afternoon and everyone but us was gone for their tea breaks."

Hector must have walked to the station directly from school, I thought. He'd probably stewed all day and then summoned his courage and—

"Constable Rushton was on desk duty," said Constable Beck. "A great pal of mine. 'And how might we be of assistance, as Inspector Locke is not available?' Rushton asks the little Frenchie."

"Hector is Belgian," I whispered, "not French."

"And out of his pocket he pulls this bit of folded paper,

158

like he's going to show us the Duke of Buckingham's cuff links."

I squirmed on my seat, causing the bicycle to wobble, but Constable Beck straightened it out with a jerk of his wrist and carried right on with the story.

"Your friend tells us that he has discovered a piece of very important evidence in a charity box taken from the scene of the murder. Rushton calls me over and we lean in close to have a better look. Young Mr. Perot shows us white powder clinging to the creases of a piece of paper. 'I believe it to be poison,' he says."

Constable Beck whispered with exaggerated solemnity as he reported the next bit.

"'That is a very serious charge,' says Rushton. And then he lifts the paper up close to his face and takes a sniff. He's examining the evidence with the greatest attention, you see? Then he says to me, 'Tell my Julie I loves her truly . . .' Like he's heading into battle. He puts the paper up to his lips and . . . he licks it!"

CHAPTER 16

A PROFITABLE EXCHANGE

CONSTABLE RUSHTON'S TONGUE, broad and pink, met the white dust for a tentative appraisal. At first touch, the taste was slightly sweet, but as he greedily slobbered on the paper, his mouth began to burn. Too late, the policeman groped for water, his scorched tongue taking on a yellow hue, darkening to purple as foam bubbled up from the wretched man's throat . . .

"Did he die?"

Of course he had not. Constable Beck would not have been in such good humor if he'd been telling the tale of a colleague's demise.

"It was paper from a square of Turkish delight!" cried Constable Beck. "He'd brought us a sweetie wrapper! We had a good laugh about that, we did."

Oh, poor Hector! A warm flush swept up my neck on

his behalf. How foolish he must have felt! First, how determined and brave in approaching the police, and then how small and foolish. I hated Constable Beck just then, and I hated Constable Rushton even more.

I bristled on Hector's behalf. "I suppose your investigation is tearing along, and you have a suspect behind bars?"

"I think you know perfectly well that I am not at liberty to discuss the case," he said. That sounded to me like a phrase he'd practiced in front of the mirror, making himself feel important. "But it won't be long, Miss Morton. Not long now."

Not long now? Getting some answers would be the best revenge for Hector's humiliation. I mustn't back down. When might I have another chance to interrogate a police officer?

I waited until we reached a flat bit of road.

How to begin? I knew what Grannie Jane would say. No man has yet been born who does not like to be admired for what he knows.

"Miss Graves . . ." I managed.

"Oh, yes?" said Constable Beck.

"She speaks of you." She never did. Not out loud. But I fancied I knew what she was thinking. "A policeman's job is terribly difficult, she says. Catching robbers, being kind to old ladies, keeping clues straight in your head. You can do it all, Miss Graves says."

Constable Beck grunted. He was sweaty but not scowling.

"Miss Marianne was not the killer," I blurted.

"We know that, do we?" puffed the constable.

"I believe it to be certain," I said.

"And why is that?"

"If I lived with a person I wanted dead," I began, "I should contrive a convenient death at home. Preferably an accident." I refrained from sharing my full catalogue of creative murders. "Would you not do the same?"

Constable Beck grunted again, most unhelpfully.

I persisted. "Would it not be wiser to avoid the complications of using a public place?"

"If you drops your corpse in a public place," said the constable, "you've saved yourself the trouble of disposal."

Chopped up in a suitcase, shoveled into a well, hurled from a clifftop, locked in a cupboard . . .

"An excellent point, constable!" Why had that not occurred to me already? "If you do it at home, I suppose the suspect list is cut down to those who live there with you."

"That's why the Mermaid Room was a clever choice. Your dance teacher made it look like a spur of the moment murder, in a public place with plenty of suspects!"

I felt sick.

"She had enough poison on the premises to kill ten old ladies," added Constable Beck. "Or two hundred mice."

VerminRid! I'd had my suspicions . . . had even inquired of Mr. Tunweed at the museum, after hearing Miss Marianne and Mr. Roddy Fusswell chatting about rodents quite freely. And here was official testimony. No one had carried poison to the Mermaid Room. It had been already waiting there, to serve its demonic purpose! No wonder the police were so rude to Hector about his powdered paper if they already knew the source.

"Unless there is a mighty clever character laying down false evidence," said Constable Beck, "Miss Marianne Eversham is our murderess."

For someone not willing to discuss a murder, the constable had become usefully forthcoming.

"I don't believe it," I said. "It just can't be."

Or could it? Was I wrong about everything?

"The daughter, Rose, she'd be the second choice," said Constable Beck. "Except that—"

"She wasn't there," I said.

"That's right," he said. "And there's no trickery involved with the alibi. The vicar's wife is witness for every minute of Saturday up to the moment Rose learned of her mother's death. If Rose Eversham wanted her mother dead, she would have needed help."

What about Roddy Fusswell? I wanted to say, but refrained. I wished first to know that if he'd done it, Rose was not a partner in the scheme.

"It's usually someone in the family, going after money. I expect Marianne Eversham imagined she'd be getting some residual of her brother's estate, once his wife was out of the way, never mind Rose being the daughter. You'd be downright disheartened to know how often an inheritance enters the picture."

"What if Roddy Fusswell thinks he could marry Rose and get rich from her inheritance at the same time?"

"That's a bit far-fetched," said Constable Beck. "Would you marry someone once he'd murdered your mother? I think we can knock out Fusswell and his helpers, along with the unrelated casuals, like the flower delivery boy and the reporter coming back in the middle of the morning to find the case for his spectacles."

"Mr. Fibbley was there too?" He certainly had a knack for turning up wherever there was a hint of drama. A knack? Or a darker purpose? Was he also smitten with Rose?

The canny reporter had fallen in love with the beautiful heiress from afar. He asked her disagreeable mother for permission to propose, but she sneered at his audacity and sent him away, little knowing the dangerous strength of his resolve . . .

Actually, I had some questions I'd like Mr. Fibbley to answer. What had *he* noticed in the Mermaid Room on the morning of the murder? Who had used the pantry? Had anyone aroused his suspicions when he thought about it afterward? Which part of the story was I missing?

"There's only one thing stopping us from putting Miss Marianne Eversham in prison this very night," said Constable Beck.

"What's that?" I whispered. The bicycle seat seemed suddenly very hard.

"What if the nasty cuppa was meant for her? We've got to make certain that she wasn't the one that someone wanted dead."

"She wasn't." The words slipped out before I had considered whether or not the policeman should hear them. "Unless she was not well-known to the killer." Like Mr. Augustus Fibbley. Or even Mr. Roddy Fusswell. It is doubtful that either of those men was overly familiar with her personal habits.

"What makes you think that?" said Constable Beck.

"Miss Marianne is a dancer," I said. "She never eats sweets. Anyone who knows her knows that. She does not take sugar in her tea."

I thought again of Miss Marianne's little blue milk jug, and next to it the gilded sugar bowl with the crest emblazoned on its side. "Mr. Roddy Fusswell had to bring his own sugar from the Royal Victoria Hotel because there isn't any in the pantry of the Mermaid Room."

"I shall make a note of that irregularity," said Constable Beck. "You've been of considerable assistance, for a person of a youthful nature."

I let myself grin for half a moment in the dark. I had offered common knowledge—Miss Marianne's dislike of sweets—after learning a small important detail: Mr. Fibbley's timely presence in the dance studio just before it became the scene of a crime.

"I can walk from here," I said. "You've done the hard part." We had reached the top of Bertram Road and were minutes from home.

"Pardon me for mentioning," said the policeman, as I climbed down from the bicycle seat. "But you appear to be underclad for the weather."

He'd reminded me just in time. I found my bundle under the privet hedge. "Turn around," I told him.

I turned my back to his back and pulled on my petticoat, chilled and wrinkly, but giving me an extra layer, however thin.

"We'll have to wake someone up," said Constable Beck, "and get you safely inside."

"I'll just slip in the way I came out," I said. "Through the kitchen. If you ring the bell, you'll give Mummy nightmares and set Tony barking like a fiend!"

"Letting you go unreprimanded will not be adequate to the situation," he said. "You go in and send down Miss Graves."

"You want me to wake Miss Graves at half past midnight? To speak with you alone, wearing her nightclothes?"

166

I felt the sing of an arrow winning its mark.

"Well, perhaps not. But I'll be back in the morning. And for now," he said, "I want a promise from you that I will never find you prowling the road at night, not ever again."

"I promise." That was easy! If I were ever again prowling the road at night, I would certainly avoid being found by Constable Morris Beck.

"And," said the constable, "I want a promise that you will stop trying to do my job. You get into your bed and be a good girl after this. No more detecting, do you hear me?"

"Bed sounds delicious," I said truthfully.

"And?"

I crossed my fingers inside the pocket of Cook's jacket to counteract the lie. "And . . . no more detecting."

Until tomorrow.

"Off you go, then." Constable Beck tipped his chin toward the kitchen door and I squelched up the path, sighing a gust of relief when I rounded the holly bushes and was out of his sight. I leaned Leonard's bicycle carefully against the back of the shed, intent on silence. I was halfway up the path when I heard, "*Hey!*"

I went still.

Had Constable Beck changed his mind and followed me to insist on seeing Charlotte? Or was it Mr. Fibbley, again lurking in the garden?

But no, it was Leonard who stepped out of the shadows.

"You scared me witless," I said. He peered toward the road.

"Your copper gone then?"

"He's not my copper!" I said. "I nearly ran him down on Bertram Road and—"

"On my stolen bicycle," said Leonard. "After I told you no."

I bowed my head. "I'm sorry, Leonard. I will not take your bicycle again."

"No, Miss Aggie, you will not. I won't tell you again." He slunk away, back to his awful shed. I must speak to Mummy about that in the morning—if I weren't in terrible trouble for tonight's adventure.

My feet were so numb I wanted to weep. I hobbled to the kitchen door, imagining the moment of pulling on my bedsocks. Tucked under the door latch was an envelope. With my name on it. I held it in both hands, staring. I had not seen his script before, but I knew it was from Hector. The letters were precisely formed, with a flourish to the A that resembled the mustache he one day planned to wear.

Inside the door, I put Cook's jacket back on its hook. Hector had also been sneaking through the streets in the middle of the night! Delivering news to a trustworthy friend, just as I had been! My note would greet him upon his return to the vicarage. I stripped off my slippers and pushed them deep into the bin of kitchen refuse. I clutched Hector's letter and limped to my room. By the flickering light of the candle, I read his admission of failure:

POWDER NOT POISON.
HECTOR PEROT IS AN IDIOT.

CHAPTER 17

AN UNSETTLING NOTORIETY

TOO FEW HOURS AFTER I'd crawled into my bed, stiff and chilled to the very bone, Charlotte tried to waken me. I protested by telling her I'd do for myself, and then tucked my head under my pillow to sleep a few minutes longer. Eventually, with my hair brushed as well as I could manage, and wearing my thickest stockings over sore feet, I came down for breakfast.

"Good morning, Grannie Jane." I kissed her soft, rosy cheek.

"Hullo, Charlotte. I apologize for being a bear earlier." I kissed her too. If Constable Beck kept his vow to report on last night's encounter, this might be the last kiss of mine that Charlotte ever accepted.

Grannie Jane rose early, before the sun, and was always beautifully dressed for breakfast. Today she wore the pale violet, its bodice embroidered with tiny dark blooms.

"That's my favorite dress of yours, Grannie." I took a boiled egg from the warming basket and two pieces of toast from the rack.

"Mmm." Grannie Jane read the newspaper while she ate, just as if she were a man. She did not pay attention to what was said around her until she had absorbed the news of the day. Papa had been the same way—unapproachable until all world disasters had been digested along with his morning trout.

Charlotte was reading *Sense and Sensibility* by Jane Austen for the ninety-ninth time. Often I brought Sherlock Holmes to keep me company until Mummy showed up. But I'd forgotten my book this morning, what with trying to think up a story to explain where my slippers had gone, and anticipating a visit from Constable Beck. Being naughty and deceitful certainly put clever thoughts out of one's head.

"Wait! What does that say?" I'd caught sight of bold print on the front page of Grannie's *Torquay Voice*.

MERMAID ROOM MURDER!
IS DANCING SPINSTER A POISONER?

"Grannie? What has happened with Miss Marianne?" I leaned over and rattled the corner of the newspaper. "Grannie Jane? Please tell me!"

She pulled the *Voice* out of my reach. "Have we sunk so low that my grandchild is snatching things at table?"

"No. I'm sorry." I could not risk having her miffed on a day when there was likely to be plenty more reason than bad table manners. I waited three long seconds. "But I do so wish to know . . ."

"When I'm finished." Grannie Jane made a show of turning the page, lining up the edges, and folding the thin, rustling paper into a rectangle small enough to read.

I thought of Leonard's supply of rolled-paper kindling, yesterday's stories going up in smoke each evening while awaiting fresh fuel each morning after breakfast. Another thing to worry about! How best to approach the topic of the garden shed being unsuitable for habitation—without revealing that I'd seen its interior? Could I proffer an innocent question, perhaps? *Do you suppose it's getting chilly in Leonard's shed?*

Charlotte finished her bowl of porridge—topped with cream and brown sugar—and poured herself a cup of tea. She asked did I want some? But at the same moment, my grandmother refolded her newspaper so that the front page beamed its headline again.

"It is unsettling," she said, "but not surprising, to hear of the strange evil of humans in our midst." She held the newspaper out and shook it gently. "As much as I understand your curiosity, I wish you had not participated quite so much in the story's action."

Charlotte's head popped up from her book, alert to any wrongdoing that could be assigned to me.

"Me? But I—"

"What have you done now, Miss Aggie?" fussed Charlotte.

"Do not concern yourself, Charlotte." Grannie Jane handed me the *Voice*. "It is merely a lesson for Agatha."

The story filled several columns and was utterly absorbing. I ignored my boiled egg and let the toast go cold.

TORQUAY VOICE

MERMAID ROOM MURDER!
IS DANCING SPINSTER A POISONER?

by Augustus C. Fibbley

On Saturday last, Irma Eversham, 44, widow of the esteemed Captain Giles Eversham, was taken suddenly ill in the Mermaid Dance Room on Union Street, operated by Miss Marianne Eversham, sister to the victim's late husband.

According to the unmarried dance instructress, her sister–in–law arrived at the studio unannounced and in a state of high anxiety. "I made her a cup of tea," said Marianne Eversham. "But she soon worsened." At the first indication of distress—a struggle for breath—the 39–year–old dancer claims that she assumed the apoplexy was due to the victim's odious habit of tight–lacing her corset. Marianne Eversham is well–known in town as an advocate for certain female liberties such as forsaking binding undergarments—and having the right to vote in the nation's elections.

The corset was not, however, the cause of Irma Eversham's trouble. As the older woman fell to the floor, Marianne Eversham rushed to find medical assistance, leaving her relation insensible but not yet deceased.

"I knew it!" I cried. "Insensible, but not yet deceased!" Though even Mr. Fibbley had only Miss Marianne's word for that.

"Miss Aggie," said Charlotte sternly. "Did you not bring your book this morning?"

Sally pushed open the door from the kitchen.

"Excuse me, madam," she said to Grannie, "but Miss Graves is wanted."

Charlotte took a gulp of tea and followed Sally out.

I raced on.

Dr. Frank Chase, the physician called upon, stated that Marianne Eversham expressed great alarm and urgency in her request for his attention, claiming that an illness had befallen her sister. Dr. Chase accompanied the distraught dancer and examined the patient, whereupon he pronounced life extinct, and noticed details of the woman's aspect that indicated death by poison.

There was great distortion of the face and a disarrangement of her garments. No apparent loss of blood was indicated but there was evidence and a reek of vomit. This reporter can confirm that an open box of VerminRid, a common solution to domestic rodent infestation, was discovered in the Mermaid Room pantry. Mice have invaded many homes and establishments in Torquay as the seasonal temperatures drop.

The crime scene was interrupted by Marianne Eversham's eleven o'clock dance students, notably Miss Agatha Caroline Morton, a twelve–year–old neighbor—

"Oh!" I cried. "My name!"

My finger rested on the place. **Miss Agatha Caroline Morton** right there in black lettering, for all of Torquay to read this morning. Under this paragraph was an illustration, drawn tidily with pen and ink, of a sugar bowl bearing the crest of the Royal Victoria Hotel. I, Miss Agatha Caroline Morton, had made the observation of that particular murder weapon! Well . . . not precisely the murder weapon, but rather the vessel for the weapon. Like the holster for a gun, or the sheath to hold a knife.

I read on . . .

a twelve–year–old neighbor of the Eversham villa on Bertram Road, first on the scene. Miss Morton spoke candidly in an interview, saying that Mr. Roddy Fusswell of the Royal Victoria Hotel had supplied the sugar bowl full of poison and that the police would be wise to look beyond her dance teacher to find their killer. Mr. Fusswell was heard to say in Miss Morton's presence, "If I were going to kill someone, I'd do it with my bare hands."

"I never accused Roddy Fusswell!" I protested. Even if I'd wanted to.

"But I firmly believe that Miss Marianne is innocent." Florence Fusswell's face flashed through my mind, pasted with a ferocious scowl. I would never be able to meet her eyes again. "I . . . I mentioned the sugar bowl, but I did *not* accuse him." I intended to be in possession of a little more evidence before I did that.

"When exactly did this candid interview take place?" said Grannie Jane, head tilted to one side. I had evaded that question when she'd asked in the hotel tearoom. Now I had no choice but to tell the truth about Mr. Fibbley appearing at the garden gate. She listened with grave attention.

"I see now why he assumed such familiarity during our encounter," she said.

"He twisted my words!" I said. "It sounds as if I'm making a careless accusation! If Roddy Fusswell *is* the killer, I shall be the next victim!"

"And I should not fault him for it," said Grannie Jane. "Having one's reputation trampled by a twelve-year-old goes a long way in explaining his irritation yesterday, if the reporter provoked him with these suppositions."

My pleasure at being named in the newspaper turned quickly to mortification. Not so severe, however, to stop me from reading the remainder of the news story.

Schoolgirl guessing aside, the police are conducting their inquiries under the direction of Detective Inspector Henley Locke. On the afternoon of the murder, the body of the ill-fated woman was conveyed to the mortuary at Torquay Hospital. Due to the continuing investigation, the burial of Irma Eversham has been postponed until further notice.

Grannie poured a second cup of black coffee and took a sip.

"It is your good fortune that I am the only person in the house who will read the story," she said. "Being quoted by a journalist in reference to a murder is not an accomplishment to please your mother."

I looked at the page, and then back to my grandmother. "Can it be considered a quote if I did not say what he reports that I said?"

"I will repeat what I said to Mr. Fusswell yesterday," said Grannie Jane. "Be wary to whom you speak your mind."

Sally came in with the morning's post.

"There's one for you, Miss Agatha," she said.

"Marjorie!" I reached for the pile.

"I don't think so, miss."

Grannie passed the letter, in a creased envelope, addressed with the same precise lettering as the note I'd found at the kitchen door last night. Goodness! How had I forgotten? Reading Mr. Fibbley's story had pushed all other worries from my head. Grannie watched me over the rim of her teacup. Sally moved spoons on the sideboard, her eyes on me as well. I supposed they were waiting to see who, other than Marjorie, might be my correspondent and expected me to pick up the letter knife or warble with pleasure at receiving post.

I put the envelope in my lap. Sheltered by the tablecloth, I untucked the flap and pulled out a thin piece of paper with seven words.

Sally straightened the silverware at Mummy's place and removed Charlotte's bowl.

"Sally, where is Charlotte?"

"I come to fetch her a moment ago, miss. She's in the kitchen. Outside the kitchen, really, by the gate. With that police constable. Trouble brewing, I'd say."

CHAPTER 18

A CLANDESTINE ENDEAVOR

MY NECK PRICKLED WITH COLD. Catastrophe was moments away. Charlotte was hearing Constable Beck's account of last evening's misbehavior.

"Agatha?"

"Yes, Grannie Jane." With enormous effort, I spoke normally. "I was just thinking how much I'd like to go roller-skating this afternoon."

Grannie raised an eyebrow but was interrupted by Charlotte coming to the door of the breakfast room and crooking her finger at me. My heart turned over. I very slowly folded my serviette and rose to my feet, thinking of phrases to describe Charlotte's glare. *A face as dark as storm clouds. Scowling like a mad dog. Looking as if she might spit sparks.* I briefly considered options for escape:

a somersault through the terrace doors to the garden where a snorting steed awaited, a swift kick to Charlotte's bottom before fleeing through the front door, a scramble up the chimney to the roof and a heroic use of ivy to descend on the other side.

In the hallway, Charlotte's voice was fully vexed. "Can you guess who has just come to speak with me?"

I stared in fascination at my shoe buckles, as if not meeting Charlotte's glare would cancel my transgression.

The church bell tolled as a solemn procession led the girl past a horde of onlookers to the sturdy scaffold in the village square . . .

And yet, Charlotte's voice was unusually quiet. She was not trumpeting her indignation as she normally might, nor using Grannie Jane as an ally on the topic of disobedience. Indeed, it would appear . . . was this possible? *Charlotte was scolding me in secret.*

I moved my gaze from the worn carpet to Charlotte's flaming face and to her eyes, glossy with held-back tears. I nearly smiled. Charlotte, enraptured by Constable Beck, was practically confessing that she had more to hide than I did! Dare I hope that Mummy and Grannie need never know about last evening?

"I only wanted a very small adventure—" I broke into a stream of words that had been coursing along unheard for several minutes.

"I do not give a pin for your explanation, Miss Aggie,"

she whispered fiercely. "You have been the cause of great indignity! Your inconsiderate disregard of—"

"Good morning, young ladies."

Mummy appeared on the landing, hair not coiffed but tumbling across her shoulders like that of a schoolgirl, and still wearing her peach silk wrap. Since the murder, Mummy had been breakfasting from a tray in her bed, and we didn't see her until lunchtime. But here she was, having one of her bright days, drifting down the stairs with Tony dancing at her heels, as if content with her corner of the world.

"Sweet pea." Mummy kissed me. "Let Charlotte brush your hair today, will you?" She ran a hand over my wayward curls.

I nodded. "Mummy, please may I go skating on the pier this afternoon? It's ever so sunny. Charlotte's having a sulk and doesn't want to accompany me, but—"

"Nonsense, of course you'll go. You spend far too much time with your nose in a book. Fresh air will perk you up as well, Charlotte. I'm having Leonard drive me to the church directly after lunch, but he can take you in the pony cart later on. Will that suit?"

Leonard. I'd meant to plead his case this morning, but daren't do it now, with Charlotte ready to pounce on any misstep. Maybe at teatime.

"Yes, Mummy. Thank you, Mummy."

Charlotte's pique crackled the air, but she said nothing. Not a word. She bobbed her head and disappeared to the kitchen. I watched the door swing shut. Could my luck be so excellent? Might Charlotte be so smitten with her policeman that I would go unpunished? Mummy sailed calmly in to breakfast, unaware of the nest of spiders harbored within her own household.

I hurried upstairs to find woolly stockings for skating, and a jacket to shield me from the wind at the seaside roller rink. I collected my writing book with the letter inside and sharpened a pencil in case I needed to make detective notes. I tucked everything into the odd-shaped case that carried my roller skates and was back in the breakfast room in fewer than five minutes.

Mummy and Grannie were still at table.

"Oh, dear," said Mummy, looking up from her kipper. "Your wrists are two inches below your cuffs, Aggie! You are taller every day."

"Even without tongue," I muttered.

"Well, you've quite outgrown that jacket."

"But I like it." I tugged, as if to magically lengthen the sleeves.

"Your Grannie says we must ask poor Rose Eversham to come for tea," said Mummy. "Along with this Mr. Standfast. I should never have gone anywhere so soon after Fletcher died, but we must ask nonetheless."

She used the tongs to deliver a lump of sugar from the bowl to her cup. "Will we invite Miss Marianne as well?" Mummy stirred her tea and shook her head in answer to her own question. "I should think she'd be grateful for an hour to herself. But you'll be especially sweet with Rose, won't you, darling?"

"Yes, of course, Mummy."

She stirred and stirred. "And there is the small matter of etiquette," she said, "as to whether it is wise to have a possible murderess at one's table."

"Mummy! Miss Marianne didn't do it!"

"I hope you're right, dear heart. I couldn't sleep at night if we learned we'd lived next door to a poisoner."

The pony cart jounced so horribly that we could scarcely keep our bottoms on the seat. Leonard used a switch on Belle to make her go faster. Happily, a bone-shaking cart ride prevented Charlotte from scolding me in front of the garden boy. As Leonard had not forgiven me borrowing his bicycle, they both were grim and silent the whole way to town, as if I were to blame for all the woe in the world. Down the last hill, Belle stepped as carefully as a farmer's wife over a basket of eggs, and finally here we were! The sea glittered in unexpected sunlight, rolling gently under the fishing boats in the harbor.

Leonard brought Belle to a halt and we sat for a moment reveling in the pleasure of not being bounced like bags of potatoes.

Before us, the pier stretched into the sea, an avenue that offered an array of pleasures to be found nowhere else! It always made me think of the magical, wicked place in the book called *The Adventures of Pinocchio*. The marionette in the story was terribly naughty, telling lies and being disobedient, despite his dream of becoming a real boy. After many misdeeds, Pinocchio and his friend arrived at a land of toys, where children were allowed to play all day long, with hoops and wooden horses, putting on plays, eating sweets and never going to school . . . until being transformed into donkeys as punishment!

The Princess Pier had even more amusements—and with no fear of a nasty ending. Pennants snapped in the sea breeze; vendors called out from stalls selling toy watches and saltwater taffy, glass figurines and hot popped corn in paper bags. It cost a penny to look at the flea circus, and stilt-walkers loped up and down with stiff knees, breathing notes through mouth organs. Couples canoodled under striped parasols, nannies pushed pram-chairs, old gentlemen watched from wrought-iron benches. The roller-skating rink was my favorite of all, where I could pretend for a time to be chums with the other skaters, gliding and whooping with real people, not just with the friends I made up in my stories. Tinkling music from player pianos floated together with birdcalls. It was the best place to be on a sunny afternoon.

I scanned the crowd near the entrance to the Princess Pier. No sign of Hector. Two policemen were laughing under a lamppost. Charlotte's fingers fluttered to her lips. One of them was Constable Morris Beck!

"Everybody out!" said Leonard.

Charlotte climbed over the side of the pony cart, wearing a foolish grin. I was not eager to meet the man who had so recently seen me in my pantaloons. And— oh, goodness!—only a few feet beyond him, there stood Hector, waving like a demented pigeon. I clambered quickly out. Leonard jiggled the reins. The cart lurched forward and away.

Charlotte called, "Leonard! When will you—" But he was gone.

I used that moment to frantically signal Hector—to get out of sight, to stay close by, to wait two minutes . . . Who knows how he interpreted my finger talk, but per- haps being foreign he was skilled at such things.

"Well, well, well." Constable Beck had clapped his col- league on the back and ambled over. "Isn't this a special stroke of luck!" As if he'd been given extra pudding. "Fancy having the pleasure twice on one single Tuesday."

Charlotte's freckled cheeks were now a sincere shade of maroon. It occurred to me that their discussion of my midnight bicycle ride may have included *kissing* . . .

"It's a pleasure to see you also, Miss Morton. By the light of day, and warmly dressed."

Ooh, didn't he think he was clever? I wished I were four years old and could kick him on the shin.

"We are not yet able to laugh about that matter," said Charlotte. "Miss Aggie has not apologized for—"

"Ahoy there! Aggie Morton!" Someone called out my name, followed by a gust of giggles. I had never in my life been so pleased—or pleased even a bit, actually—to see Florence Fusswell and Lavinia Paine, each carrying a pair of roller skates.

CHAPTER 19

A NEW MOTIVE

"WELL, IF IT ISN'T THE world-famous eyewitness," said Florence. "Or shall we say, the meddling fabricator?"

Charlotte's gaze sharpened so swiftly I'd swear her eyelashes trembled. I did my best to smile, perilously situated between Florence Fusswell and Constable Beck, each heavily armed troublemakers. Charlotte had departed from the breakfast table before the discussion of Mr. Fibbley's interview, and did not usually read the daily newspaper. Already peeved over my midnight escapade, she'd be in a frightful twist to learn about a reporter in the garden!

Florence was a dubious good luck charm, but she was the only one present who might assist in escaping Charlotte's watchful eye. Do not hesitate, I told myself.

"Florence!" I cried. "Are you going skating? Or have you already been?"

"We are on our way now," said Florence. "But I should first like to speak with the policeman."

"There is a plague upon us!" Constable Beck put up his hands in mock horror. "Run for your lives! Torquay is being swarmed by infant detectives!"

"I would rather bathe in vinegar than become a detective," said Florence. "I merely want to make a statement."

Constable Beck made that familiar grunting sound.

"My brother was in the Mermaid Room on Saturday," Florence said. "He was one of the last to see Mrs. Eversham alive."

"I believe we are aware of that," said Constable Beck.

"However," Florence went on, "despite his failings as a brother, despite the fact that the Royal Victoria Hotel does indeed have a small rodent problem in the kitchens and a shelf full of VerminRid, despite what the newspaper has reported this very morning . . ." Here she paused to glare at me. "Here is my statement. Roddy Algernon Fusswell is not a murderer!"

Did she think such a statement would settle the matter?

"That reporter was desperate to speak with me," Florence went on. "But my father would not permit me being questioned. He said it would taint the hotel to have our name in a tawdry story about poison."

"Uh, thank you, Miss, uh . . ." Constable Beck was trying to stem the flow.

"Fusswell," said Florence.

I jumped in. "Charlotte? Will you be content if I skate with my friends and meet you afterward?"

Charlotte opened her mouth but the policeman spoke first.

"I will be most agreeable to keeping you company, Miss Graves," he said. "I am off-duty in ten minutes." He brandished his pocket watch like a vital piece of evidence.

"Where is Miss Boyle?" Charlotte looked about for the taciturn woman who usually accompanied Florence.

"She's fetching us cocoa." Florence pointed toward the tea hut. "Too bad you won't have one, Aggie."

I held my breath, watching Charlotte choose the smitten policeman over circuits on the roller rink.

"One hour, Miss Aggie. We shall meet back on this spot. Agreed?"

Florence clapped her gloved hands together. "Whee!"

Whee? Florence was so difficult to read! One moment scalding in her rudeness, the next minute crying *whee!* What was she hoping for in return for her false enthusiasm?

I was very soon informed.

"Now!" said Florence, once we'd moved out of Charlotte's hearing. "Before you tell me everything you know, allow me to confide how much you are despised by my father and my brother!"

"The police went to the hotel!" trilled Lavinia. "Her father is fuuuurious because of the picture in the newspaper."

My innards flipped over, giving me a very sick feeling.

"The hotel sugar bowl, for all the world to see!"

"Shut your blithering mouth, Lavinia Paine," said Florence. "This is *my* family and *my* hotel, not yours."

"Florence was *gasping* to be interviewed. But they only wanted to hear about—"

"Hush, Vinnie," said Florence.

"About Roddy and the missing money—" said Lavinia.

"Lavinia Ethelwin Paine," said Florence, curt and low, "I will slap you silly if you say another word."

"From the hotel safe!" Lavinia ducked away from her friend's swatting hand.

Florence looked as steamed as a runaway train, as spiky as a hothouse cactus, as fierce as a stampeding rhinoceros, ready to erupt like a volcano . . .

"That has all been straightened out," said Florence. "And is no one's business but my father's. Roddy will pay back what he borrowed, *and* he'll stop betting on dogs."

"On dogs who rip apart live rats for entertainment," said Lavinia.

"Lavinia," growled Florence.

"Fancy *borrowing* from your own family," said Lavinia. "And being so stupid as to get caught!"

"As this has nothing to do with Miss Marianne poisoning her sister-in-law," snapped Florence, "I suggest you stop talking this instant."

My heart, meanwhile, had sped up. Roddy was in debt from gambling! He'd taken money from the hotel safe! Exactly the sort of motive to inspire a murderous act. Did Rose know? I thought of Rose resting her head so trustingly against Roddy during the visitation. Was it trusting? Or just weary? Because how could someone like Rose care for someone like Roddy?

I needed to get away from these girls and find Hector. I would tell one more fib.

"Oh dear." I pretended to search. "Charlotte has my pocket money!" No Leonard here to produce a sixpence from behind my ear!

"Don't bother about that!" said Florence. "Lavinia will pay for you, won't you, Vinnie? You're paying for *me*, isn't that right? Since you can't keep your mouth shut when required?"

Lavinia nodded, but rolled her eyes.

"My mother does not like me to be beholden," I said. "I'll find Charlotte. I will meet you on the roller rink once you've had your cocoa."

"I hope you don't mind interrupting a slobbery kiss!"

said Florence. "Your Charlotte was bug-eyed for that constable."

More giggles from Lavinia. That was all I needed. Attention being paid to the new inconvenience of my nursemaid flirting with a policeman. If only just once I could toss out a clever retort to one of Florence Fusswell's pin-sharp barbs. Clever retorts, in my experience, usually showed up a week later—not, alas, when they were needed.

Back at the ramp to the Princess Pier, I turned frantically about.

"*Psst!*"

There! Sitting on one of the ornate iron benches, Hector's bright eyes matched the color of his green hat, the one he'd acquired in the All Saints bazaar.

"Enfin!" said Hector.

"Finally!" I said. "I've had to be awfully wily to get to this bench!" So much deception is required simply to meet a friend! "But our wiles have worked, and here we are!"

"Alas, you find me shamed," said Hector. "I am hanging the head."

Finding the paper dusted with sugar was now such a distant moment that I had forgotten to think that Hector might still be recovering.

"Don't be silly," I said. "It was an understandable caution, and you were brave to take your clue to the police."

His face showed a glimmer of gratitude, but then he shrugged. "In this matter, I fail."

"We simply didn't think things all the way through," I said. "Logically, I mean, the way you're usually so good at. Or we would have seen . . . Unless the killer cared not one bit who the victim was, and carried about a packet of poison to pour at any random moment into any available concoction—"

"This does not seem practical," said Hector. "This suggestion I disregard."

"I agree. So. Using the friction of my brain cells, I surmise that because the donation boxes were removed from the Mermaid Room before the murder happened, no evidence discovered inside them could have been put there *after* the murder."

Hector grinned at me. "You see the value of methodical deduction?"

"However," I said, "I have another clue."

I presented the folded letter. Hector was suitably respectful, holding it gingerly between trembling fingers. He raised his arched eyebrows even higher as he read, looking up with obvious excitement.

"Mon Dieu," he said. "This is a new ball on the playing field, n'est-ce pas?"

"Yes!" I breathed. "At last I have someone to talk to. I've been bottled up like a jar of fizzy lemonade!"

I told him everything from the discovery of the letter in my notebook right up to the midnight encounter with Constable Beck—omitting only how I had been clad at the time. I added my deduction that it was Miss Marianne who must have hidden the letter, Florence's reluctant admission of her brother's money woes, and Constable Beck's revelation that Mr. Fibbley had been in the Mermaid Room on Saturday morning.

"I think that's everything," I said. "Except that I cannot decide whether Rose likes Roddy Fusswell or is only putting up with him." I had been speaking so rapidly that the pause here felt considerable. We listened to the hungry cries of seagulls and the faint flurry of piano notes from the roller rink.

"None of this seems to touch upon the letter I am holding," Hector said.

"But, do you see?" I pointed to the torn corner.

"Oui, I see. This is evidently the source of the scrap for which the inspector is seeking, yes?"

"I expect so," I said.

"And so . . ." Hector tapped the paper several times with his fingertip. "These few words are so critical to Madame Irma Eversham that she holds on even while she is dying."

"And so important to Miss Marianne," I said, "that she tore the page from between the fingers of a dying woman. And then hid it." I sighed from the bottom of my lungs. "She must have been desperate, to imagine that my notebook would keep a secret safe, even for a few hours."

Hector put a comforting hand on my arm. "I believe this is not proof that she is a killer," he said. "The friction here . . ."—he touched his forehead—"tells me that it may be proof that she is not."

CHAPTER 20

A FURTIVE ENCOUNTER

"HOW CAN AN ANONYMOUS letter prove innocence or guilt?" I said.

"This letter upsets both women, yes? We do not yet know the reason, but it compels both to act as they do not normally act. Rose's mother comes—as never before—to visit Miss Marianne in the Mermaid Room, and—"

I saw at once. "And Miss Marianne conceals a clue that may be essential to finding a killer!"

"We too are hiding the same clue," Hector reminded me. "It is time, do you agree, to consult the police?"

"No!" I cried. "They think Miss Marianne is guilty of murder! This might be a clinching factor. We need to protect her at least until we know why she hid the letter."

"Is she in need of our protection?" said Hector. "It appears she is already protecting herself."

"Or someone else," I said.

"We must look carefully at the cast of characters in the Mermaid Room on Saturday morning."

"Not every one of them wished Mrs. Eversham dead."

"But one of them does," said Hector. "One most particularly wants her dead, and promptly." He withdrew from his pocket a small notebook, half the size of my own, and held a pencil ready. "Which one is it? Who benefits, now that Irma Eversham is dead?"

I wriggled on the bench. "Rose would be the first choice," I said. "She likely inherits buckets of money *and* gets rid of a nasty mother. But Rose never went to the Mermaid Room on Saturday. Her alibi is as firm as bricks."

"Unless she has a lethal accomplice willing to commit this most terrible act."

"I don't think she even likes Roddy Fusswell. Why would she trust him to murder her mother? Let's not be narrow-minded. It wasn't Rose or her aunt. We need to consider other suspects, whatever their likelihood at first glance."

"I am not ready to put aside Miss Rose," said Hector. "But I am willing to consider Mr. Fusswell with full attention. You think someone else beyond these two?"

"What if Rose's mother learned that Mr. Teasdale is not really a vicar at all, but a jewel thief in disguise who steals from old ladies in the All Saints congregation. He has amassed a fortune in pearls and rubies, but Mrs. Eversham discovered his cache in the alms box. He was forced to silence her in order to protect his reputation."

Hector's eyebrows lifted a little. "This is not a logical conclusion from the facts that we—"

"Or perhaps," I said, "Mrs. Eversham fell in love with Mr. Augustus Fibbley and would not leave him in peace. She followed him everywhere, pleading that he relent and take her for his bride. Finally, he cracked, luring her to her death under the piano so that he could print the sordid details in the *Torquay Voice*."

Hector sighed. "You are mocking me, I think. But we must be serious in the face of a letter such as this. The exposure of a secret is announced. A secret so great that no signature can be attached." He folded the paper and gave it back to me. I tucked it carefully into my left roller skate, somewhat chastened by his scolding.

After a moment of silent consideration, Hector said, "We must answer three questions."

"One," I said. "Who wrote the letter?"

"Two," said Hector. "To whom is it written?"

"And who is the mysterious baby?" I said. "Three questions of who."

A small boy went past, clutching his mother's skirt with one hand and holding a toy trumpet to his lips with the other. *Blatt! Blatt!*

"I would like to be a spider for an hour," I said. "It is the spider's good fortune to see the world from eight different directions. Would that not be useful while detecting? Every possibility could be considered."

Blatt!

"Equal consideration of eight views is wasting the time," said Hector. "Most points of view can be ignored. We need only logic to tell us where to look next. We must ask who is most easily tainting the sugar?"

"That's easy," I said. "Roddy Fusswell was king of the sugar bowls and no one looked twice. *And* he wants Rose to be rich. All her money would become his if they got married. He could pay his debts without stealing anything more from his family."

"We are in accord. I will commence the watching of Mr. Fusswell," he said. "What will you do?"

"Rose is meant to be coming to tea. Although the will has not yet been read, I will be watchful for any sign that . . ."

Grannie Jane's stern look darted through my mind.

"It wouldn't do to ask directly," I said, "but Mr. Standfast may slip up and give a hint of her expectations."

"This is good." Hector adjusted the collar of his sailor

jacket so that it lay smoothly over his shoulders. "I go now to the Royal Victoria Hotel."

"You know how to get there?" I pointed across the harbor to the stately building that perched atop the cliffs beyond. Sun sparkled on the water, reflecting flashes of light as if stars floated just beneath the waves.

"I see it," said Hector.

"From here you must go the whole way around the harbor," I said. "At the foot of the cliff there is a path that goes down to the Ladies Bathing Cove. That's where I go swimming all summer. But you will take the road *up* the hill, not the path *down* to the cove, and—"

"If I were a bird, I would be there in one minute," said Hector. "I am not discouraged by the distance."

"Today is Tuesday. Let us meet again on Thursday on this same bench. But be discreet if you see Charlotte or Constable Beck."

"I shall avoid Monsieur Beck wherever we may encounter. I am not at ease with those who consider me foolish," said Hector. "I go now."

"Excuse me?" Florence Fusswell's voice pierced the breezy air. "Is this boy bothering you? He looks rather foreign."

Florence, with Lavinia peering over her shoulder, spoke loudly and slowly, "Are. You. Foreign?"

"Oui, mademoiselle," said Hector, making a small bow. "I am quite foreign."

The intruders inhaled in unison, Lavinia's eyes so wide that she looked like a startled owl.

"May I introduce Hector Perot," I said. "Miss Lavinia Paine and Miss Florence Fusswell. Florence is the sister of *Mr. Roddy Fusswell*. Of the *Royal Victoria Hotel*."

"Ah!" said Hector.

"I do not think being Roddy's sister is much of a commendation," Florence said, "since he is an arrogant worm."

"Or should you say dog?" asked Lavinia.

"But you are worthy in your own name," said Hector, "for which I must give thanks. You are the girls who dance for friendship with the foreigners, yes? As you have so astutely noted, I am a foreigner, and now the owner of a fine pair of new shoes!" He lifted his right foot and pointed a shiny black toe.

Lavinia giggled, but Florence eyed him suspiciously.

"We danced," she said. "And we also provided the refreshments. Guineas worth of cakes and biscuits! It would not have been a successful evening without the Royal Victoria Hotel."

"Did you provide also the sugar in the sugar bowl, mademoiselle?"

Florence's mouth dropped open and then snapped

shut. "If you've nothing better to do than make slanderous remarks, you should probably go straight back to France," she said. "It is not permitted to bother girls on piers, not in England. I shall summon Miss Boyle to assist."

"It *is* permitted to speak with a friend," I said quickly, before Florence could disturb her nursemaid, who was poking the pointy nib of her parasol at a seagull on the boardwalk. "Which is what he is. A friend. Of mine."

"A friend who now is saying the farewell," said Hector. His eyebrows did a small caper, telling me *good-bye*, and *as-of-this-moment-I-am-a-dedicated-sleuth*, and also *Beware! Look-over-your-left-shoulder!* He bowed once more and slid away as I turned to find Charlotte trotting along the pier, lifting her skirt several inches above her ankles to permit better mobility.

"There you are, Charlotte," I said.

"Hello, girls," she said. "Good afternoon, Miss Boyle."

Miss Boyle nodded a brusque greeting while using her parasol to indicate a jumble of bags on a bench across the pier. "Your skating gear, ladies, is to be carried by you. Come along." She marched away, but Florence and Lavinia made no move to follow.

"I'm glad you're ready, Miss Aggie," said Charlotte, briskly. "Did you manage to remain upright on the rink?"

"Her hour was most upright," said Florence.

I wished to clamp my hand over her mouth. And hold it there.

"If," she said, "sitting rather too cozily on a bench with a foreign boy can be considered *upright*?"

Lavinia snorted a laugh, and Charlotte turned to stare at me. If Charlotte consulted with Miss Boyle, my absence on the rink would be discovered within seconds.

"Aren't we rather late for tea, Charlotte?" I said. "Thanks to your appointment with the constabulary?" I paused to let her cheeks go pink. "We have a long walk ahead, as Leonard is not here to fetch us. Good-bye, everyone!"

"Ladies?" Miss Boyle was calling.

I speared Florence with a furious glare, and set off toward The Strand, taking the longest steps I could manage.

Charlotte caught up, panting slightly. "Was Florence referring to Hector?" she said. "Or have you sprouted a wider acquaintance with foreign boys in the last few hours? You were most particularly instructed not to—"

"Would you have me rudely ignore a poor foreign person when he says good afternoon?" I said. "That would be most uncivil."

"Saying good afternoon does not require sitting on a bench!" said Charlotte. "What would your mother say?"

"What would my mother say if she knew where *you* spent *your* hour?" I asked her calmly.

Charlotte stopped walking right in the middle of the pavement. "Miss Aggie, that's blackmail."

So easy to slip into a life of crime, I thought.

"ARREST IN MERMAID ROOM MURDER!" hollered a newsboy. "PENNY FOR THE PAPER!"

"READ ALL ABOUT IT!" cried another boy from the opposite corner. "MERMAID KILLER CAUGHT!"

CHAPTER 21

A MATTER OF THE UTMOST IMPORTANCE

CHARLOTTE WOULD NOT let me purchase a newspaper, even with my very own pocket money. There'd be one waiting at home, she said, and we were late. True enough, Mummy and Grannie Jane were entertaining Mr. Standfast in the drawing room when we arrived, and the tea trolley had been rolled in, brimming with Mrs. Corner's best offerings. Tony slept as near to the fire as he could be without singeing. Charlotte did not join the family for meals if there was company, and so excused herself.

"Where is the newspaper?" I asked. "And where is Rose?"

"The evening edition has not yet come," said Grannie Jane.

"But the newsboys had it!" I said.

"Rose will be here," said Mummy. "Alas, a grieving person occasionally loses her sense of time."

"There has been an arrest," I said. "The newsboys were hollering like jackdaws. Where is the paper?"

"Agatha, dear," said Grannie. "Your fussing will not speed its arrival. Say hello to our guest."

Dutifully, I bade Mr. Standfast a good evening and accepted the cup of tea that Mummy poured for me.

I had just dropped in three lumps of sugar when there came a frantic hammering on the front door, followed by the scuffle of Sally's running steps. A ruckus in the foyer brought us all to our feet.

"Rose, at last," said Mummy. "Why such a clamor?"

Someone crying, more of Sally's hurried footsteps, and the door to the drawing room burst open.

"Oh, please, ma'am, come!" Sally's eyes were wild, as if she'd met a leopard in the vestibule. "It's Miss Rose," she said, "Rose Eversham. She's quite undone."

Mr. Standfast pushed past the maid and returned a half minute later, supporting a weeping Rose.

"Sorry," said Rose, gulping a bit. "It's just that I finally have someone to tell, and, and, I seem to be—"

"More tea," Mr. Standfast told Sally. "She needs sweet tea."

"Whatever has happened?" said Mummy.

Arrest in Mermaid Room Murder! I thought. But who?

"Brandy," said Grannie Jane, opening the cupboard that held rows of stemmed glasses and glimmering cordials in dark bottles.

Rose was whisked to a chair—Papa's favorite—and handed a snifter before she'd even settled into the cushion. Mr. Standfast urged Rose to drink, but one small sip of brandy made her cough. She couldn't talk for ages, and we had to wait politely to hear her news, though clearly the headlines shouted in town and Rose Eversham's miserable disarray must be parts of the same story.

Grannie Jane was the first to succumb to curiosity. "Well, dearie? What has happened?"

"They've taken away Aunt Marianne. In the police wagon." Rose paused to collect herself. "They say she murdered my mother!"

Nooooo! Miss Marianne? They'd got it wrong!

We pummeled Rose with questions, but the police had not been forthcoming. How vexing that the newsboys on The Strand—and probably Mr. Augustus Fibbley—knew more about Miss Marianne's situation than we did.

"If you'll excuse me, Mrs. Morton," said Mr. Standfast, bowing slightly to Mummy. "And Mrs. Morton." Another bow, to Grannie Jane. "I regret that I must leave your hospitable domain, but if Miss Eversham is being detained, I must be present. I will insist on speaking with the prisoner at once."

"The prisoner!" whispered Rose. Tony padded back and forth in front of her chair, as if in consternation.

"Do you suppose your man could drive me into town?" said Mr. Standfast.

Mummy and Grannie glanced at each other, both a bit pink.

"Our *man* is the garden boy, for the time being," said Grannie, capping the brandy bottle with a sharp click. "And the vehicle is a cart. But there is nothing young Mr. Cable likes better than driving like a chariot-racer."

"Mr. Cable?" said Mr. Standfast.

"His name is Leonard," I said. "Grannie calls him mister to make him sound more respectable."

"I'll come with you!" Rose tried to stand, but swayed and sat back down with a bump.

"You will not," said Mr. Standfast. "I'm quite certain that Mrs. Morton will serve you soup of some sort, and then you will rest for a while. I shall return to see you, Rose, when I have met with your aunt and know better of her situation."

"I'll tell Cook at once that we need broth." Mummy led Mr. Standfast away with the intention of finding Leonard.

I pushed the ottoman close to where Rose sat, but did not quite have the courage to take her hand. Grannie Jane asked more questions. Despite Rose's disquiet and her hiccupy way of answering, we eventually had a jumbled sense of the afternoon's story.

They'd had poached pears and cheese for lunch, Rose and her Auntie M., sitting in the kitchen near the fire. It was their habit to seek comfort below stairs rather than to use the grand dining room for just the two of them. Their maid, Norah, had been humming while she washed the crockery and waited for the kettle to boil.

(I wanted to tell her, Oh, do skip the humming maid and get to the point, but Rose was in shock and not to be hurried.)

Inspector Locke and two young constables had come banging on the kitchen door, Rose reported, and tromped across the stone floor with their muddy boots, making Norah awfully peevish. Auntie M. was to go with them to the police station, the inspector said. Her previous statement was lacking particular details, they said, including the *truth*. Auntie M. laughed at such nonsense. "She's done nothing wrong!" cried Rose, and the inspector said they'd see about that. One of the constables (with dreadful spots) said there was new evidence to implicate her. Auntie M. asked what could there possibly be? The inspector said would she come without a fight or had they got to restrain her? Auntie M. said that she'd best speak to her solicitor. The spotty constable sneered to the other, well, that's the sign of a guilty conscience. Auntie M. was

211

ever so plucky, according to Rose, though her eyes were too bright, and her hair became disheveled. They said to come along, it was only questions for now. Rose helped her on with her coat. She'd paused, brave and tender, to look at Rose, leaving firm but hurried instructions, Rose being blind with tears and deaf with worry. "It's all a mistake," Rose said. Is it now? said the inspector. They'd got an eyewitness confirming that Miss Marianne Eversham did not take sugar in her tea, proving that she was not the intended victim. First step toward a death sentence, in his opinion. After that they bullied her out the door like a common criminal.

Grannie Jane examined the row on her knitting needle. She had slipped a stitch. "Inspector Locke," she said, "reminds me of Mrs. Winkey, the greengrocer's wife. She'd insist on selling you cucumbers—because she'd got so many that week—even though you'd come into the shop for a cauliflower." She sighed and pulled the wool to release the errant stitch. "What happened next, Rose dear?"

Rose sank back into Papa's chair. "That's everything," she said. "Norah wept at the sink, while my blood turned as cold as January."

As cold as January. That exactly described the dread that overtook me now. But also the prickling heat of shame. This was a terrible lesson in the curse of vanity. I'd thought myself to be so clever, telling Constable Beck about dancers and their aversion to sweets. I'd been so entranced with my own cleverness that it seemed I'd knotted the noose for Miss Marianne!

"And then!" Rose sat up straight. "Not five minutes later—he must have been watching the house and waiting for his chance—there came another knock, a reporter from the *Torquay Voice*!"

Tony barked, startled by the sudden rise in volume.

"Mr. Fibbley?" Another chill followed the first. Was there something even colder than January? Mr. Fibbley had an unnerving ability to appear without any warning, precisely where he wasn't wanted.

"He said to call him Gus," said Rose. "As if I'd call him anything beyond an interfering scribbler!"

"What did he want?" said Grannie Jane.

"He got as far as mentioning the word *sugar*, when I slammed the door so hard I believe I cracked the glass."

"It is nearly six o'clock," said Grannie Jane. "What have you been doing all afternoon?"

Rose's eyes were rimmed with red and looked smudged beneath with ashes. "I am ashamed to tell you," she said. "I wept like a brokenhearted child. Mother is dead! The police believe that Auntie M. killed her! I'm not sure which is worse! I wandered through the house, asking my father's spirit to come and guide me. I really did that. Out loud."

Grannie Jane leaned over to pat Rose on the hand. "And what did he tell you, my dear?"

Rose exhaled, a small, sad sound pretending to be a laugh. "He did not answer, of course. He never was much good at having a conversation. I crashed about the house in a rage, pounding cushions and kicking chair legs. Behaving, my mother would say, like a savage."

"That is not so surprising, dearie." Grannie Jane kept patting Rose's hand. "Sorrow does not lie easily on anyone's shoulders, least of all the young, who have not yet learned how to carry such weight."

"Eventually," said Rose, "the fog in my head began to lift. I went over the scene in the kitchen and recalled Auntie M.'s last-minute directions, which I should have been acting upon far sooner."

Her eyes again filled with tears, but she brushed them fiercely away.

"She told me, in the most urgent voice. She said—" Rose broke off and looked directly at me, making my stomach whoosh with trepidation. Did she know that I was to blame for the afternoon's calamity?

"I had one task to fulfill!" Rose cried. "I've let my aunt rot all afternoon when she most particularly wanted me to—"

What did she want you to do? The question rang inside my head.

Before Rose could finish her sentence, Mummy came backward into the room, having pushed the door open with her bottom. She held a steaming mug in one hand and the evening edition of the *Torquay Voice* in the other.

"Lamb broth for you, Rose dear. Mrs. Corner's best." She nudged a doily into place on the occasional table by Rose's chair and put the mug down. She drew a rolled serviette from her cardigan pocket and laid it across Rose's lap. How nice to see Mummy as nurse instead of patient.

"Mr. Standfast has gone off with Leonard in the cart, though it threatens to rain at any moment and he hasn't had his supper."

Grannie held out a hand to receive the newspaper, but Mummy shook her head, no. Grannie Jane raised an eyebrow, and Mummy raised an eyebrow back. Did Rose notice? She sipped her lamb broth and said, "Mmmmm."

My eyes were now riveted on the newspaper tucked under Mummy's arm, evidently being kept from Rose. News of Miss Marianne's arrest was festering in those pages, and I ached to know details.

Rose put her mug carefully back on the lace doily.

"I'd like to freshen up, if I may? I must look frightful."

As if Rose Eversham could ever look frightful.

"I'll show you where." I hopped up, surprising Tony, who sneezed. "There's a mahogany seat on our loo!"

"Agatha, really!" Mummy scolded. "Not a subject to be mentioned in the drawing room."

I led Rose along the hall. "Just in here," I said.

But Rose did not go in. She looked both ways, took my hands in her own, and began to whisper. The weepy-eyed maiden of a few moments before had disappeared. A more familiar Rose, intrepid and determined, was suddenly talking to me as if it were a matter of life and death.

"I don't want anyone poking their noses in," said Rose. "Even if your family means well, I'm not trusting anyone. My aunt said that you received something in error and that she needs it right away. It's a matter of the utmost importance. To save her from being kept in jail for the rest of her life. Or hanged."

CHAPTER 22

AN ALARMING ARREST

HECTOR AND I HAD BEEN RIGHT! Miss Marianne had been the one to hide the letter in my notebook.

"What could you possibly have that matters so much?" said Rose. "If you'll give it to me, I'll take it on to her."

I found myself shaking my head. I would not pass along the letter to anyone, not even Rose Eversham. Perhaps Rose was only pretending not to know what she was asking for? She had not been ruled out entirely as a conspirator to the murder. Look how she'd transformed from a mournful damsel into a clear-eyed fighter in a matter of seconds!

"I feel," I said, "as if . . . I'm the guardian. Of the . . . *thing* that I have. I'll come with you to the police station. I'll give it to her myself."

"I suppose . . ." Rose looked uncertain. "But we must go at once."

She made the announcement as she swung open the drawing room door. "Aggie is coming with me to visit my aunt. Now, before poor Auntie M. believes that she has been abandoned."

Mummy and Grannie Jane were on the settee, their heads bent close, reading together from the evening *Torquay Voice*. As we came in, they startled and shuffled the newspaper untidily shut. Their expressions were remarkably like those of children with fists full of purloined sugar lumps.

"You have the evening news," said Rose.

Mummy and Grannie Jane coughed at precisely the same moment.

"Come, dearie, sit down," said Grannie. "This will be a bit of a shock."

I could read the words in bold print from across the room:

MERMAID ROOM MURDER
DANCING MISTRESS IN CUSTODY
FOR HEINOUS CRIME
by Augustus C. Fibbley

"In custody?" said Rose. "Does that mean arrested?"

"It does," said Grannie Jane.

Rose sat with a bump in Papa's chair. "Will you read it to me please?"

She sounded bossy enough that Mummy raised her eyebrows, but nevertheless straightened the pages and cleared her throat. Grannie Jane picked up her knitting and began a new row, the needles *click-clicking* an accompaniment.

"The investigation into the death-by-poison of Mrs. Irma Eversham Saturday last has reached a possible conclusion with the arrest this afternoon of the victim's spinster sister-in-law, Miss Marianne Eversham. She was dragged from the kitchen—"

"Dragged?" said Rose. "She wasn't *dragged*, except perhaps in spirit. She walked quite sedately, considering the circumstances."

"Yes, dear, you were there. She walked sedately *from the kitchen*," said Mummy.

". . . of the EverMore Villa, the home she inherited from her brother, the late Captain Giles Eversham, husband of the victim. The culprit's removal was witnessed by her niece, Miss Rose Eversham, who was too distressed to comment."

"I never *stopped* commenting to the police," said Rose. "But when that sneaking newshound showed up, I refused to say a word!"

"The gruesome crime scene on Union Street," Mummy continued to read,

> "was interrupted by the arrival of a number of Miss Marianne Eversham's dance students a short time after the victim's brutal demise in the Mermaid Room dance studio. Miss Agatha Caroline Morton, a twelve-year-old neighbor of the Eversham villa on Barton Road, was first on the scene."

Shame draped itself around me like a cloak. Every moment was further proof that I should never have spoken to Mr. Augustus Fibbley.

> "She described the body in accurate detail, matching the report released by the police. Miss Morton is a familiar of the heir to the victim's fortune, Miss Rose Eversham, seventeen. As previously reported, Miss Morton attempted to lay blame for the murder elsewhere than on her dance instructress. When interviewed at her home, Miss Morton suggested that the police were not following the correct path. Will this be a case where an innocent can see what—"

Mummy broke off reading to stare at me. "When were you interviewed in your home? How is it possible that a journalist is permitted to speak to a child without a chaperone?"

I flinched. "I'm not a child," I muttered, but it was no defense in the face of three pairs of glaring eyes.

"Where was Charlotte?"

"It was only a moment," I said. "Mr. Fibbley appeared at the garden gate. He was very polite. Leonard spoke to him as well." Here I was bending the truth in another direction. "Naturally Mr. Fibbley wished to hear the observations of an eyewitness."

"Agatha," said Mummy. "This is most incorrect."

"I'm sorry, Rose," I said.

Mr. Fibbley had made me feel observant and important. But then he'd twisted the words around to suit himself.

"Even Tony liked him." I tugged on Tony's silky ears. "And eventually stopped baying like a wolf."

"Don't apologize," said Rose. "You're the only person who has said that you believe Auntie M. to be innocent, and there it is in the *Torquay Voice*! I appreciate your faith."

"Do go on," she said to Mummy. "I must leave to see my aunt, but please keep reading while I find my hat."

The whole room seemed to sigh with relief after that. I'd done grievous harm to Rose, but here she was

221

rescuing me once more, this time from the trembling upset I could hear in Mummy's voice as she kept reading.

". . . a case where an innocent can see what is not visible to her elders? Miss Rose Eversham has been romantically linked to Mr. Roderick Fusswell, son of the Royal Victoria Hotel manager, Mr. Curtis Fusswell."

"You weren't wearing a hat," I said. "No hat, no gloves, no handbag. You were too upset to think about such things, I expect."

But Rose was staring at Mummy. "What was that?" she said. "The bit about Roddy Fusswell?"

Grannie Jane's needles paused in their clicking, as Mummy went on.

"Mr. Fusswell identified himself as fiancé to the—"

"Fiancé!" said Rose. "Conceited pig! I would *never*!"

This was good news. If she wouldn't marry him, she would not seek his help in killing her mother. One of those alliances of love that I was learning to understand.

". . . fiancé to the young heiress, and announced his intention of protecting her from further anguish.

222

"The victim 'was an unpleasant old carp,' he said. 'I'm surprised it took so long for someone to top her. She was asking for something like this to happen.' Before today's arrest of Miss Marianne Eversham, Mr. Fusswell expressed surprise that her guilt was not obvious to the police. 'A female without the guidance of a man is not to be trusted,' he said in an interview. 'She already owns the house, which is too heavy a responsibility for any woman. I can't help but wonder, what is she after now? If it's Rose's inheritance, she'll have to go through me!'"

Rose's hands were clamped over her mouth, as if she might be sick. "How dare he?" she cried. "Is there anything more?"

Mummy carried on.

"Miss Rose Eversham has not made a statement. No trial date has yet been set, but according to an anonymous source in the constabulary, Miss Rose may be required to testify against her aunt."

A series of loud knocks on the front door made us all jump.

"Heavens!" cried Mummy. "Has word gone out that we're as deaf as stones at Groveland?"

"I'll answer it." I hurried to the hallway.

A man's silhouette shadowed the narrow window next to the front door.

Would a killer knock? I thought not, and opened the door.

Mr. Roddy Fusswell stood on the step, his hat sitting crookedly and his face shiny with damp in the lamplight. I peered around him, into the night. Had Hector remained stoically on his quarry's tail, and was he now lurking nearby? Outside it was fully dark, slivers of rain flashing in the light cast by our hallway chandelier.

"I'm looking for Rose Eversham." Roddy Fusswell nudged the door further open, assuming an invitation that I had not made. "The maid over there"—he tipped his head in the direction of the EverMore villa—"said I might find her here."

I tried again to look past him, without being too conspicuous. No visible pale face or green eyes.

"Hello?" Roddy Fusswell rapped his knuckles on the open door. His yellow leather gloves barely softened the sharp raps next to my ear. "Tell Rose I want to speak with her, will you?"

Inside, with more light, Roddy Fusswell looked at me more closely. "Oh," he said. "It's you. This is where you live?"

I scowled at him and he scowled back.

"You've stirred up a cauldron full of trouble today, you and your insufferable grandmother, telling lies to that reporter, making me look bad in front of Rose."

I was insulted enough that I forgot to be shy. "You seem perfectly able to make yourself look bad, Mr. Fusswell. And my grandmother is not—"

"Is Rose here? It's very important." He had removed his coat and held it, dripping, at arm's length, as if I were going to take it and hang it up. I did not. He grunted softly and tossed it over the newel post at the bottom of the stairs.

"Where will I find her?" He plonked his hat on the hat stand.

Did Rose want to be found by a possible murderer? After what he'd said in the newspaper?

"Wait here," I said. "I'll ask whether she cares for a visitor."

Mr. Fusswell narrowed his eyes at me. "You cheeky little—"

I turned my back, feeling taller with every step. Before slipping into the drawing room, I saw him pause at the hallway mirror to smooth his caterpillian mustache.

CHAPTER 23

A BUMPY RIDE

"No," said Rose. "Send him away. I would rather meet an unwashed ogre in an underground cavern."

Goodness, was I to say that to his face?

And then Sally burst into the drawing room, flustered and pink-cheeked. "Sorry, ma'am. But Leonard has come back, ma'am. Mr. Standfast left his case behind, here in the drawing room, and Leonard's to fetch it. It's needed at the . . . at the jail, ma'am."

Leonard stood behind her, mopping his face with his cap. And then Mr. Roddy Fusswell pushed him aside, and pushed Sally too, striding into the room as if he were king of the world.

"Rose," he said.

"What are you doing here?" cried Rose. "Go away!"

"Listen to me," he said.

"I will not," said Rose.

"That smirking shrimp of a reporter made a mash of my words." Rose tried to duck around him.

"We can take Mr. Standfast's case," I said. "We're going to see Miss Marianne now."

"The *innocent* Miss Marianne," said Rose, glaring at Roddy Fusswell. "Would that be the case in question?" She pointed to a sturdy leather box with a worn handle sitting beside the chair that Mr. Standfast had used.

"That's it," said Grannie Jane. "The poor man—I expect it holds all the documents pertaining to your family's history, Rose dear. Not something to be mislaid." Being nearest, she stooped to pick it up.

"Let me help," said Leonard, from the doorway.

"I'll take that." Roddy Fusswell's long arm reached in front of Grannie Jane and clutched the handle.

Rose yelped like a puppy whose paw had been stepped upon. "Let go this instant!" She tried to wrest the case from his grasp, nearly toppling Grannie at the same time. Leonard was somehow part of the muddle, too, and neatly caught Grannie before she went over.

"STOP THIS AT ONCE!" Mummy stamped her foot in a most un-Mummy-like way.

The grandfather clock ticked loudly in the sudden quiet before Rose gave the case a sharp tug and won her prize.

"Thank you," she said. "Mrs. Morton? I am borrowing your daughter for a mission of mercy. Leonard, we'll meet you outside in a moment."

Rose, so bold! She had not asked permission, but had informed my mother of the plan. Leonard hesitated and then withdrew.

I tried to follow Rose's lead. "Leonard is driving anyway," I said. "We'll be looked after."

"Rose," said Roddy Fusswell.

Rose raised her hand. "I am too angry to listen to you just now. Please do not speak to me."

My chest swelled in admiration. How able she was!

Rose clamped the case between her calves and jammed her arms into the sleeves of her jacket. "Have you got . . . what's needed, Aggie?"

The letter from Fair Play! I did not! "I'll just fetch my . . ." I slid into the hallway to retrieve the all-important paper from inside my skate. But where were my skates? I'd dropped them on the floor by the stairs when I'd come in.

"Miss!" Someone was hissing at me.

"Sally! Did you move my skates?"

"In the closet, miss. I tidied them out of the way. But, miss!"

I swished aside coats to find my skates in their bulky case, lying atop the row of overshoes.

"Miss! Listen, please! There's a boy—"

The first skate was empty. I crammed my hand into the other one, but it was empty too. I swung around and scrabbled on the hall carpet to see if the letter had fallen out.

"Miss?"

"Sally! There was a . . . a paper! Inside my skate." My nose began to tingle, a sure sign that tears were next. "You must help me find it!"

"This one, miss?" Sally pulled a crumpled—but familiar and, oh, so beautiful—folded page from the pocket of her apron. "I were taking it down for the kitchen fire, miss. Here you go."

I snatched the letter and shoved it into the pocket of my dress. I plucked my coat from its hook and pulled on my beret.

"But, miss! I've been trying to tell you! There's a boy in the kitchen, and he's—"

I sprang upright. "You mean Hector?"

"He's dripping wet, miss. Ever so consternated, what with his shoes having got so waterlogged. We've given him a cup of broth and dry socks, but he wanted me to ask you: what happens next?"

I leaned against the wall, muddling the buttons on my coat.

What happens next?

The suspect had wrestled with the lovely heiress for possession of a case full of incriminating evidence. Where would his next move take him? The intrepid refugee, hardened by the difficulties of his escape from oppression, was determined to follow wherever he must, through rain or snow or dark of night. The devoted sleuth would accompany the heiress in her pursuit of the family honor, taking her—

"Miss Aggie? Most urgent, he says."

"Tell him the Caterpillar is on the move. Tell him I've gone with Rose to the police station, but he should stick with the Caterpillar. Have you got that, Sally?"

Sally wrinkled her nose, and went through to the kitchen shaking her head.

Rose came out of the drawing room, with Mr. Fusswell and Mummy as close behind as baby ducks.

"There you are," said Rose.

"Rose," said Roddy Fusswell.

"Rose, dear," said Mummy.

"Listen to me," said Roddy.

"I don't understand," said Mummy, "why you feel it necessary that Agatha accompany—"

"Mummy, yes!" I said. "I've promised! Rose needs company. You'd never wish me to break a promise!"

"Rose," said Roddy again.

Rose ignored him and spoke to Mummy. "Mrs. Morton," she said. "Aggie is a favorite of my aunt. She will be the ideal companion."

"But to a prison?" Mummy had a familiar wobble in her voice.

"Prison?" said Roddy Fusswell.

The door to the kitchen passage opened and Leonard poked his head through.

"It's not right for a girl to visit a prison unaccompanied!" said Roddy Fusswell. "I insist on—"

"Which is why Aggie is coming with me," said Rose. "Leonard, would you assist Mr. Fusswell with his coat? He'll be leaving shortly."

"Er, yes, miss." Leonard scooped up the coat from where Roddy had draped it on the newel post. I offered his hat from the stand.

"Give me that!" Roddy jammed the hat on his head. He snarled at Leonard to move off, that he could put on his own blinking coat.

Mummy was at risk of wringing her hands into rags, but I resolved not to be deterred in my mission. I kissed her.

Leonard turned to Rose, but kept his eyes on the floor. "The horse and cart are waiting, miss. Mr. Standfast was most urgent in his request."

"We'll come now," said Rose. "Mrs. Morton, you've been most kind. I'm sorry you're being left with . . ." She tipped her head toward Roddy Fusswell, who had made no effort to put on his coat but was brooding in a corner of the foyer.

"Take an umbrella." Mummy offered Papa's large black one from the stand by the door and Rose thanked her.

"Do watch out for Agatha," said Mummy.

"Are we all set?" asked Rose in a whisper. "You've got . . . ?"

I nodded. We stepped out into the night.

"Where's my blasted glove?" said Roddy Fusswell, as the door closed.

Rose began to giggle. "We've escaped!" she cried.

Leonard helped us into the cart.

"Hold this." Rose handed over Mr. Standfast's case. "I'll just get the umbrella up. I didn't think about your cart not having a roof!"

"Let me take the case," said Leonard.

"No, thank you, Leonard," said Rose. "We'll look after it."

"The gent asked most particular that I bring it."

"Goodness, this case is causing full-fledged battles in Torquay this evening," said Rose. "You *are* bringing it safe and sound, Leonard. With me attached."

"Just drive!" I said. "Rose's aunt is waiting in a prison cell for a crime she did not commit!"

Leonard shook the reins and Belle began to walk.

Our good cheer faded. A steady breeze was bringing in fog even all these hills away from the sea. Rose wrestled with the umbrella, fighting to hold it at an angle that would protect us from the rain.

"Even a brolly conspires to make life difficult," she muttered, and then was silent for several minutes as Belle clopped carefully over slick cobblestones.

When Rose spoke again, I cupped a hand behind my ear to show that I could not hear.

Rose raised her voice. "She may have wished my mother dead a hundred times, but she never would have killed her. Aunt Marianne is a gentle soul—except on the topic of the vote! It was my mother who carried bitterness in her heart."

She put a hand on Leonard's shoulder. "Even you can vouch for that, can you not? I saw you with her on The Strand last week, both scowling like spoiled children."

"Leonard?" I said. "Why did you have cause to speak to Rose's mother in the high street?"

"I didn't." Leonard flicked the switch against Belle's backside, and glanced around. "She bumped into me outside the post office. She tread on my toe."

"Is that what happened?" said Rose. "I was inside, posting a letter. I didn't see a collision, only her scolding you and you barking back. Good for him, I thought. About time she was made to drink a bit of her own medicine."

I gasped and Rose went silent. How horribly close to the fact of things.

"That's not w-w-what I—" Rose said. "Forgive me. That was thoughtless."

She went on, more quietly, "Mama was in a foul mood afterward, about strange young men getting in the way. A bit extreme, now that Leonard has explained." Rose's voice caught, and I knew she was crying. "So many sour encounters!" she said. "All these years of living with Auntie M., and never a kind word . . ."

How miserable breakfast must have been at EverMore, I thought.

After a few more damp and silent minutes, we arrived at the police station.

"Thank you, Leonard." Rose closed the umbrella and laid it on the seat.

"I can carry the case for you, miss," said Leonard.

"Don't be a silly," said Rose. "I'm perfectly capable. Find a sheltered place to wait. We shan't be *too* long. I shouldn't think they'll let us linger." We clambered down to the pavement and hurried inside.

"Dodging raindrops," said Rose, laughing, switching Mr. Standfast's case from one hand to the other.

An officer sat behind a desk, brass buttons straining to keep his jacket closed over his tummy. A nameplate by his elbow announced his name as Constable Lloyd Rushton. The man who had embarrassed Hector, I realized.

"Your Mr. Standfast is gone to supper," he told us.

"Up at the Crown and Cushion is where I recommended. Only one of you at a time is allowed in to see the prisoner. Dangerous villain like her, eh?" He grinned.

"That is not the slightest bit funny," said Rose.

"You go ahead," I said.

"No," said Rose. "She's wanting whatever it is that you've brought. You go first. I'll find Mr. Standfast." She leaned over and kissed my cheek. "Let's see if we can bring her home tonight."

The officer sighed and heaved himself up. He motioned for me to come along. More than a little nervous, I waved good-bye to Rose and followed the constable's wide navy-blue backside down a narrow corridor.

CHAPTER 24

A PAINFUL CONFESSION

I HELD MY BREATH, intent on believing the words that churned inside my head. *I will not be afraid. I will not be afraid. I will not . . .*

The constable stopped at a door covered with chipped brown paint. He gave the knob a hefty wrench and it squealed open. We seemed to be looking straight into a black velvet curtain. He unhooked a torch from where it hung on a nail inside the door. He pressed a button on its side and it lit up like magic. It was the same sort of torch used by Constable Beck on his night patrol, dull silver with a strong beam that illuminated a steep set of stairs leading down into a pit of darkness. *A cellar of gloom. An impenetrable night.* Apparently they were keeping poor Miss Marianne in a dungeon!

By the time we reached the bottom step my hand was covered in grime from the banister. Enough lamps burned down here to see without the torch, but the ceiling was so low that I could have touched it with an outstretched arm. The smell was like old socks in vinegar. An officer sat on a wooden chair chipping at a piece of soap with a knife. Miss Marianne, separated by a wall of iron bars, perched on a stool with her back to the guard.

The constable who had brought me this far spoke to the other fellow. "You might as well come have your tea break, Smithers. The prisoner's not going anywhere. And neither is the girlie. Unless she wants to fight the rats on her way out."

Rats? He was teasing. Wasn't he?

"Aggie?" Miss Marianne stood as the two policemen shuffled back up the steps. Her face was gray-hued, the blood gone from her lips. Her hazel eyes, usually sparkling, were dull and wary. And her hair! Usually she wore a tidy dancer's knot at the nape of her neck. She may have spent the afternoon tearing at it with both hands, the way it straggled out like unkempt straw. A place like this was designed to scare a person to bits, and it worked. What words of comfort could I invent?

"My dear child." Miss Marianne touched my fingertips through the bars.

"I . . . I've brought your letter." I passed the folded paper.

"It isn't mine." She unfolded the page and tilted it toward the weak gas jet in a corner of her cell. When she looked at me again, her eyes were moist.

"I know you didn't kill her!" I cried. "You never would."

"Thank you, Aggie, for saying that." Miss Marianne squeezed her eyes shut, causing tears to roll down her pale cheeks. "*'Is this a secret you can live with?'*" she read, the letter shaking in her hand. "I did not write this, nor was it meant for me to read. The envelope was addressed to Rose. But Irma didn't like Rose to receive letters from strangers. She opened it herself—and felt entirely justified, since she had saved her daughter from seeing such a thing."

I held my breath as Miss Marianne leaned against the bars as close as she could get to where I stood.

"They might end our visit at any time," said Miss Marianne. "And you deserve to know . . ."

Another minute passed while I watched resolve and indecision take turns upon her face. Finally, as if diving into a cold lake from which there would be no easy exit, she began.

"I believe," she said, "that this letter was written by someone I lost long ago. I think my own child killed Irma as the result of a terrible mistake."

She did not wait for me to collect my wits, which now were scattered on the floor. She had jumped into the water and would swim with no rest until she reached the other side.

"Long ago, I had a sweetheart."

A sweetheart!

"His name was Otis Connor. He was a horseman in the Royal Guard, though he thought one day he'd like to be a veterinary doctor. My brother, Giles, Rose's father, was thankfully pleased with my choice. Our parents were dead, and Giles was all the family left to me. It mattered, you see, even more then than it does now. A woman is rarely trusted to decide the path of her own life."

I nodded, as if I heard confessions of love every day. But my heart was skipping beats.

"Otis and I were to be married. I had a gorgeous dress, which had been my mother's—"

"But the wedding never happened?" I said. And then cursed myself for interrupting. A person will hear far more by listening than by talking. Grannie Jane had taught me that.

Miss Marianne peered at me in the dim light. "Your mother will not thank me for telling you these things. But . . . Otis and I . . . We loved each other dearly. We became as close as people who are married, do you understand?"

What Miss Marianne was saying fell into the cloudy region of grown-up life to do with love. Why my sister had married James, and what servants shushed about, why Charlotte went pink in the presence of Constable Beck, and why Mummy mourned Papa so woefully.

"Otis . . . ," Miss Marianne's voice was a little thicker, "belonged to a regiment of the army that went suddenly to the Sudan to squelch a rebellion. Before our wedding day. After he'd gone, I discovered that I was to have a baby. I wrote to him at once. Though we had not planned for a family so soon, I believed the news would bring him joy while away fighting. Within a few days I received a telegram that he had been killed in a battle at Khartoum."

Tears sprang to my eyes. "Oh no! So sad!"

How inadequate were words! *Sad*, for a whole life gone, and another changed forever. *Two* lives changed, because there'd been a baby to consider.

The baby in the letter belonged to Miss Marianne!

She wiped her eyes. "Let me tell you a bit more," she said. "I have thought of nothing else, of how this dreadful mistake occurred. My brother, Giles, had just been married to Irma. He knew that losing Otis had broken my heart, but he was dismayed about the baby. It is not good news to have a baby outside a marriage. The world does not look upon you kindly."

She closed her eyes again, her voice low and a little hurried. Giles had offered to adopt the baby, she said. He and Irma would raise it as their own child. Such a relief!

Her brother's suggestion meant that she would not lose the child entirely.

"Rose is your baby?" I said.

"No." Miss Marianne shook her head. "Not Rose."

The ending was not so simple as that.

Irma Eversham's opinion was firm and furious. No child born of a sinful union would be welcome in her family, and she certainly would not adopt such an outcast! She threatened Giles with ending their marriage and Marianne with ruin by unforgivable scandal.

I remembered the whispering ladies next to the cakes at the visitation for Irma Eversham. Wouldn't they faint dead away if they knew the truth?

Giles was torn apart, Miss Marianne said. He wanted to help his sister, but how could he go to war against his bride? Miss Marianne speedily resolved that she did not want her baby raised by such a heartless woman. She and her brother agreed that he should find a home far away to take the child, and so he did, settling matters with the help of his solicitor so that Miss Marianne did not know where her baby's home would be. She traveled to a village in the Lake District for her confinement. She never even looked into the infant's eyes before he was whisked away by the nurses. Her brother, Giles, paid a monthly allowance for his care.

Life continued as it had before Otis Connor had come into Miss Marianne's world. She resigned herself to being the Captain's spinster sister and remained living in the house where she'd grown up, though now she was the guest of her brother's new wife, the critical and bad-tempered Irma. A year later, baby Rose had been born, bringing renewed joy to her auntie's spirit, but also a reminder of her harrowing loss.

Miss Marianne stopped talking. She fetched a tin cup from the floor next to the cot. She pointed to a bucket of murky water beside the guard's chair where I might fill it up.

"And you never knew what happened to your . . . baby boy?"

I had not missed Miss Marianne's revelation. *He was whisked away by the nurses before he ever looked into his mother's eyes.* By now her baby boy was nearly a man, a year older than Rose.

"We did not speak of him again," said Miss Marianne. "The solicitor placed him with parents wanting to adopt a child. Even Giles did not know where the boy was raised, and never told Irma that he paid an allowance all those years. She'd have hated me more—and what if she found a way to put a stop to it? I wanted the child looked after, safe . . . and beloved. When he reached eighteen, the payments would end." Her voice broke. "We would never meet him," she whispered. "Nor celebrate those birthdays with him."

I bit my lip, sharing the weight of Miss Marianne's unbearable sorrow. My Papa would not have another birthday. For those of us left behind, his day in March would be one of loss instead of celebration.

"And then my brother died," said Miss Marianne.

All this awful remembering! She took a sip of water and hurried on. Irma had been livid to discover after her husband's death that he had been paying for Marianne's shameful mistake all these years. The Captain's will made no provision for the boy beyond a very small legacy. Irma instructed the solicitor to inform the family that payments had ceased a few months early because of Giles's death.

I did not like to say it, but, "This is where the confusion began, is it not?"

"It must be." Miss Marianne's voice was hollow, as if creeping up from a deep hole. She raised her hand, still holding the letter from Fair Play. "I think this was written by my son. He does not know the circumstances of his birth. His words suggest that he believes himself to be Rose's brother, that Giles was his father and not just an uncle. That Irma was his mother, not I."

"That's what he means about inheriting," I said.

"Yes."

"But Rose never read it," I said. "She didn't have a chance to make things right. If Mrs. Eversham hadn't stolen the letter, she would likely still be alive." And if

Miss Marianne had not ripped the letter from the dying woman's clasp and hidden it, if she had told the facts to the police about her baby, she might not be in this jail cell.

"Rose does not know the truth," said Miss Marianne. "I never told her. It was a secret that Irma and I meant to take to our graves."

A chill prickled my neck, as if a ghost were breathing ice my way.

"That is exactly what she did," I said.

"And so I shall not," said Miss Marianne. "How wretched that my own son—" She broke off, too choked by tears to finish the unsayable sentence.

One thing was now certain. Roddy Fusswell was not Miss Marianne's son and not the killer. The Fusswell family was well-known in Torquay. Roddy had lived here—at the Royal Victoria Hotel—the whole of his life, not hidden in some distant town, adopted by parents that no one knew. I should be looking for a stranger. My fists tightened around the bars of the cell, as if I might squeeze them to cinders. My mind flew to the pale, smirking face of Mr. Augustus Fibbley, his raspy voice and cocksure manner. When had *he* moved to town? And where had he come from?

"Can you tell me what happened on Saturday?" I said. Had Mr. Fibbley's visit overlapped with Mrs. Eversham? Had he gone into the pantry for any reason?

"When Irma appeared, so distraught, I feared that some great harm had befallen Rose. The studio was buzzing, as you know, but Irma thought her news so urgent that she did not wait to discuss it privately. She said that she was guarding her daughter's life from the shame I'd cursed her with, that the letter amounted to blackmail, and we must go at once to the police. Her face was bright red, the letter trembling in her hand."

"Who else was there?" I asked.

"The reverend had been up and down the stairs with two volunteers for half the morning, and they were carrying out the last of those boxes when Irma came, and several armloads besides. Roddy Fusswell took the tea urn and the cups, but he missed the sugar bowl sitting in the pantry waiting to be washed. Your garden boy came to fetch the floral arrangements. The reporter chap came by to find the case for his spectacles, which had been dropped under a chair."

I caught my breath. "When exactly did Mr. Fibbley come?" I said. "Do you remember?"

"He . . . well, let me think a moment. He held the door for Mr. Fusswell, so he was coming in as . . . But was that the first trip down the stairs, or . . . ?"

My mind was skipping about, uncovering further facts. Augustus Fibbley worked for the *Torquay Voice*! Fair Play had used letters cut from the pages of a newspaper!

"Miss Marianne," I said. "Do you suppose—?"

A sudden burst of footsteps thudded on the stairs.

"What the devil's going on?" Mr. Standfast appeared from the darkened stairwell. "I've been waiting over at the Crown and Cushion, eating a rather stringy chop. I sent that boy for my valise more than an hour ago, and he still hasn't come back!"

"But Rose has your case, sir." A wave of apprehension swept up my arms like a rash. "I came down here to see Miss Marianne, and Rose was going straight away to find you!"

"Have a look about for her, would you, Miss Morton?" said the lawyer. "I have a great deal to discuss here with Miss Eversham and my papers would be very useful."

I said good-bye to Miss Marianne, but did not wish her a peaceful night as that seemed like wasted words. She waved the letter, a small white flag, to say her thanks. I set my feet upon the steps with an aching heart and a shiver of worry. If Rose had not gone to meet Mr. Standfast, wherever could she be?

CHAPTER 25

A BOLD ACCUSATION

THE CROWN AND CUSHION was only a few streets away. Even I knew where it was, though I'd never been inside, as it was full of men drinking pints of ale and using coarse language. How could Rose have got lost between here and there?

I pushed against the heavy door at the top of the stairs and nearly tumbled into the corridor. My hands were filthy and I had a suspicion that I wore cobwebs in my hair. Poor Miss Marianne, having to *sleep* here! I wiped my hands on my coat and considered where I might begin to look for Rose.

But who should be standing by the desk—*leaning* on it with one casual hand—but the man who had been in my thoughts moments earlier. He thwacked a hat against his leg, spraying droplets of rain all over the tiled floor.

"Well, well. My lucky day!" said Mr. Fibbley, in that odd, croaky voice. My spell in the cellar had left me chilled and clammy. This was no one's lucky day. Rose's mother was dead. Miss Marianne was in a dungeon, possibly in the company of rats. And suspect number one stood before me, face bright with cheer.

"Here I am . . ." The reporter propped his hat on the desk and flicked open his notebook. "Chatting with the amiable Constable Rushton, waiting to speak with the Mermaid Room Murderess, and who should appear but Miss Agatha Morton, the indomitable mystery queen. How is it that you beat me to the scene every time? Not bad for a twelve-year-old. Are you trying to take my job?"

My voice had disappeared down my throat. How dare he be nonchalant and jolly? He had likely mixed mouse poison into a sugar bowl. At the very least, he had written rubbish in the newspaper for all the world to read.

Rose's words came to mind.

"I am too angry to listen to you just now," I said. "Please do not speak to me." I heard Mummy *tsk*ing. That sounded too rude, even if he were a poisoner. "Until perhaps next week," I added.

Mr. Fibbley tossed back his head and laughed, showing off immaculate white teeth. "Waiting a week in the news business is not a viable option," he said. "You are clever enough to understand that. I need today's truth today."

"Today's *truth*?" My heart thumped. "Today's truth is that Miss Marianne Eversham is not guilty of murdering her sister-in-law! You've already got that wrong. And I think you know it!"

Mr. Fibbley raised an eyebrow, high above the gold rim of his spectacles. He had rather nice eyes, I noticed in surprise, though I only looked into them for half a moment before directing my gaze downward. Could a murderer have nice eyes? And was there any resemblance between Mr. Fibbley and the woebegone prisoner in the cell below?

"I am most curious to hear your opinion on the matter, Miss Morton. If your dance teacher is not guilty, then who has performed this heinous act?"

Who indeed? Was he attempting to misdirect my suspicions? Could I perhaps . . . Might I lead him into an accidental admission of his guilt? I would not begin with the subject of murder, but tackle instead his irresponsible journalism . . .

"You implied in your report that I accused Mr. Fusswell," I said. "I admit that he is fairly loathsome, but he is not a killer. What you wrote has injured his reputation, and presented me as a silly girl."

"Fairly loathsome," repeated Mr. Fibbley. "May I quote you on that?"

"No," I said. "You make a show of caring what people say, but what gets published is entirely unrelated to the truth, despite your claims."

"Did I write down something you did not say?"

Blood pounded so noisily in my ears that I had difficulty remembering exactly.

"You twisted my intentions."

"Did I?" said Mr. Fibbley.

"I did not say that Roddy Fusswell murdered her, or suggest that he brought the poison with him!"

"Did you not?"

"Stop it!" I stamped my foot, just as Mummy had earlier. I stomped it again because it felt good. "What really matters is that Rose's mother is dead. And that Miss Marianne did not kill her!"

"Have you considered the notion that Rose herself is the most suspicious of anyone?"

Of course I had. Not so long ago, I had contemplated the possibility—with some sympathy—that Rose had sent her mother to the grave. But Miss Marianne's sad tale had confirmed her niece's innocence.

"It wasn't Rose," I said. "The killer was a man."

Mr. Fibbley jerked to attention, his fingers deftly opening the notebook and readying the pencil.

"What makes you think that?" he said.

"A man recently arrived in Torquay and not well known." It turned out not to be so difficult to look a killer in the eye, now that I was fired up. (And with a constable sitting across the room, inattentive as he was.) "A man of about your age."

Mr. Fibbley examined me with a hard stare.

And then began to laugh!

"Are you accusing me of murder?"

With blazing eyes, Mr. Fibbley stepped toward me, a smile on his lips. Was he dangerous? Armed with a pistol? Hiding a dagger?

I stepped back a pace, and looked over at the desk sergeant, who was chomping on an apple and paying no attention to the deadly drama playing out before him. Should I scream? The main door opened with a loud bang. Wind whistled in, along with a most welcome face.

"Hector!" I ducked around the reporter and raced to greet my friend. "Goodness, you're wet."

Hector stood in the doorway, blinking, as if surprised to enter a room holding light and people. His hair and jacket, his short trousers and stockings were all as wet as if he'd pulled them on straight from a washing tub.

"Oi!" called the officer from behind the desk. "Close the door like a good lad, won't you? Devil of a night out there."

Hector pushed the door shut and began to shake.

"M-m-my cap is lost." His plastered-down hair made it look as if his head had been dipped in ink. His shoes made a slurping sound as he stepped toward me. I knew, from my own misadventure last night, exactly how awful that felt.

"Poor Hector," I said. "Such a lot has happened. You're lucky I'm still here." Mr. Fibbley was lurking too close by. "Where is your . . . quarry?"

"The Caterpillar goes to the hotel," said Hector, "pausing to kick some fishing nets along the way. He sits in the bar to drink the whiskey. I am watching from the terrace. One glass of whiskey, then another, and then another. I believe he is intoxicated and not a threat this night. So, I come to find you."

"Roddy Fusswell is not the killer," I whispered. "You have been following the wrong man."

"The wrong man?" Hector's gloomy look darkened. His lips were the color of spring violets. "You know this?" He removed his jacket and jiggled it, causing a small rainstorm.

"She thinks *I* am the killer," said Mr. Fibbley, suddenly at my elbow.

"You, sir?" Hector looked at me.

"I have acquired . . . a *heap* of new information." I took Hector's hand and guided him behind one of the columns that held up a dark and distant ceiling. Mr. Fibbley followed us.

252

"If you're accusing me of murder," he said, "I have every right to know the reasons you—"

"Please to tell me *something*," said Hector. "I am most curious."

"I don't want to speak while *he* is listening," I said. "He has a very bad habit of taking a person's words and twisting them into—"

Hector led me to the very center of the police station foyer.

"Speak quietly," he said. "The man will become dizzy trying to tread on our tails."

I bent my head next to Hector's and murmured as efficiently as I could. "The baby in the letter belonged to Miss Marianne, but she never knew him after the first minute of his life. She couldn't keep him because she wasn't married. The baby was sent away, adopted, and the Captain provided money for support. Mrs. Eversham was furious about the baby. The letter was written to Rose, but Rose never saw it because her mother—*Oh!*"

I had forgotten for a few minutes about Rose. "Rose was meant to be here, but—"

Mr. Fibbley was again hovering close by, though I felt certain that he could not have heard my rapid report to Hector.

"If you do not permit me to consult with my associate," I told him, "I shall have no choice but to report you at once to the officer."

"Why are you waiting?" said the reporter. "I'll make it easy and do it for you."

He pretended to address the man across the room, speaking in a squeaky whisper. "Oh, constable? This little girl thinks I'm the Mermaid Room killer. And she surely knows what she's talking about, because she writes poems and has a vivid imagination."

Hector stopped blowing on his fingers to give me a sympathetic smile. "His manner is sarcastic, but from what you tell to me so far, there is not the necessary evidence to make such a grave accusation."

"You haven't heard everything yet," I said. "I have *almost* the necessary evidence." I glared at Mr. Fibbley. "And why don't you say you're innocent? Or anything else to dissuade me?"

"I know two things that you don't know," said Mr. Fibbley.

I turned my back on him and spoke rapidly to Hector.

"I have just delivered a document to Miss Marianne in her jail cell that confirms that the killer was a young man *not* from Torquay, who—"

"What document?" Mr. Fibbley propped open his notebook on my shoulder! "How did it come into your possession?"

254

"What two things?" said Hector. "Why do you not assist in clearing your own name?"

"Am I obliged to defend myself to children?" said Mr. Fibbley.

"Why do you always answer a question with a question?" I wished to thump him on the head.

"Do I?" said Mr. Fibbley, smiling.

"I remind you," said Hector. "A woman is come to a most unpleasant end."

"A convincing point," said Mr. Fibbley. "Here is my first defense. I have never, to my knowledge, met Mrs. Eversham. Why would I want her dead?"

"Another question," I muttered, but had the answer ready. "The document identifies the killer as a man, and also suggests very strongly that he is *unknown to the victim*. So, Mr. Clever Boots, you are not yet in the clear. You have a second item?"

"I do," said Mr. Fibbley.

"And it is?"

He looked at me and then to Hector and then back to me, as if not certain that this was the audience for his next words.

He cleared his throat, and when his voice came, it was softer. "I ask that this revelation remain in your pockets," he said. "Can I trust you?"

"But of course," said Hector.

"I suppose," I said. Was this another trick? The grave calm of his look told me it was not, that foolery had no place in this admission.

"I am not the man you're looking for," said Mr. Fibbley. "Because I am not a man at all."

CHAPTER 26

A SURREPTITIOUS UNMASKING

I GASPED. Mr. Augustus Fibbley was not a man?

"Remarkable." Hector gazed at Mr. Fibbley with what looked like admiration. "You make a most convincing gentleman."

I peered more closely. Smooth face, nice eyes . . . I made a blurting noise, and quickly manufactured a cough to cover my confusion. I'd been blind to so many clues! The raspy voice, the pretty lashes, the whiskerless cheeks and chin. But if she was a woman, why was she dressed like a man? How long had she dressed this way? What was her real name? Did anyone else know the truth? Did simply everyone have a secret?

"You do realize," said Mr. Fibbley (*Miss* Fibbley?), "your silence is essential? The masquerade protects my livelihood. As a woman, I would be relegated to reports on church suppers and tips for growing better dahlias. As a man, I can write the stories that people want to read, like *murder!*" She grinned and raised her eyebrows, assuming my understanding of such an equation.

I thought of Mr. Standfast saying that women could not be lawyers. And here was Mr. Fibbley saying the same about crime reporters. I had not paid attention to such things in the small world of Mummy and Grannie and me. But for now there was a far more pressing matter at hand . . . If Mr. Fibbley was a woman, she was not Miss Marianne's baby—and not the killer. If Mr. Fibbley was not the killer, *then who was?*

"Oi, girl!" My head shot up, and Mr. Fibbley's did the same next to me—something I would not have remarked two minutes ago.

Constable Rushton waved from behind the desk. "Miss Morton, isn't it?"

"Yes, sir?"

A second voice interrupted. "How did you get in here?"

Another policeman, older and even rounder than his colleague, had come into the lobby through one of the paneled doors that lined the back wall. His boot heels clicked as he strode across the tiles to confront Mr. Fibbley.

Miss Fibbley!

How would I remember what name to call her, without making trouble? It was best, I thought, if I did not try. She was dressed as a he and wanted to be known as a he. If I allowed myself to think of him . . . her . . . as a woman, I might reveal the truth in error. Until I knew a reason to expose him, he would continue as *Mister* Fibbley as far as I cared.

"I've spoken to you once already today, young man. No journalists inside the police station."

The reporter looked over at the fellow behind the desk, who had been quite chummy earlier, but now pretended not to see him.

"We don't want your kind in here," said the new one. "Off with you!" He pointed at the door, his arm as rigid as a signpost.

Mr. Fibbley pushed up his glasses and tried to smile. "Guilty as charged," he said. "A journalist inside your station. Who knows what I might write about that?" He stuffed his notebook into the pocket of his jacket and slunk toward the door, pausing to grin at me.

"I'm not going far," he said. "Just a turn or two around the block for some fresh air. There is plenty more to this story, and I intend to dig out every dark little secret."

The senior officer closed the door behind him.

"Miss Morton?" said Constable Rushton.

Hector touched my arm and tipped his head toward the policeman who was calling my name.

"I am going off duty now," said Constable Rushton. "Sergeant Cornell is taking over. But I've been tending this for your friend, Miss Eversham." He opened a cupboard behind the desk. "She left it in my care," he said. "Too heavy for a lass to be lugging about in the rain."

He was holding Mr. Standfast's valise.

"Where did she go?"

He shrugged. "Will you take it or not?"

The man was pulling on his overcoat.

"Yes, yes," I said. "Did she leave a message for me? It's just that . . . we're meant to be . . . do you know when she'll be back?"

"No," he said. "She asked could she leave it for a bit and off she went. Not to fret. A girl that age, head in the clouds. Went to meet a boy, I'll wager."

"She did not," I said. I did not like his smirk.

"She went to find the lawyer," I said to Hector, as we sat with the case on the bench between us. "They missed each other in the dark. We'll go look in a moment, but . . ." The temptation to pry buzzed loudly in my ears.

Hector patted the lid. "Is it locked?"

"Dare we?" I whispered.

"How can we not?" said Hector.

"Keep watch," I said. "Mr. Standfast is talking with

Miss Marianne in the dungeon. We should probably take it to him . . . But what harm could a few more minutes cause? You whistle if that door opens." I lifted one latch and then the other. Ever so gently, I raised the lid of the case half an inch.

Not locked.

"Mummy will faint dead away if I'm arrested for rifling private documents."

"Do so rapidement," said Hector. "I will divert the guard." He strolled across the marble floor.

"I am begging pardon," I heard him ask. "I am having the question for how to being a policeman?" His accent had suddenly become thicker, part of his disguise. Most people imagined that a boy who could not speak English was likely short of brain friction.

Well, ha! Brave and clever Hector!

And here was I, afraid to open a box. I took a deep breath, imagining the satisfaction of finding another clue ahead of Augustus-the-trickster-Fibbley!

Up went the lid.

Right on top were two thick envelopes, each labeled with a curving black script: *Last Will and Testament of Captain Giles Eversham* and *Last Will and Testament of Irma Millicent Eversham.*

As curious as I was to know the contents, it felt that opening a lady's will would be like cracking open her coffin.

I shuffled those envelopes aside. The next document was a list, a record of pounds sterling lined up with particular dates, but without names or other details. Below that was a collection of letters, held together at the top with a pin.

I glanced up. Hector was still deep in conversation with the officer. How long would his silly questions keep the man occupied?

Hurry, Aggie.

The door to the cellar was still shut. I ducked my head back down and began to read the first page, a letter dated four months earlier.

Dear Mr. Standfast,

Thank you for your letter of Friday last. Also your note when my wife passed on to her Heavenly Rest in February. I am sorry to hear of the Captain's passing. He was good to my boy. The allowance was a big help here on the farm. Our son is grown up strong and handsome, but he's a young man of his own mind now, wants to be away from home. I thank you on his behalf for the Captain's bequest.

Most sincerely,

My heart just about stopped when I came to the signature:

Cable!

"What do you have?"

I jumped, pinching my fingers as I slammed down the lid.

"*Oww!*"

Only Hector, thank goodness!

I snapped shut the latches and stood up to whisper, as closely to his ear as I could get.

"I know who wrote the anonymous letter. I horribly, awfully, dreadfully, believe that he is also the killer. I haven't told you Miss Marianne's whole story, because of Mr. Fibbley being nosy, and now . . . well, I looked . . . I spied . . . just a glimpse really, but all of it has collided, and—"

"I do not follow," said Hector. "We jump from Mr. Roddy Fusswell to Mr. Augustus Fibbley and now . . . somewhere else?"

"Roddy could never have been the killer because he has two parents of his own, you see? And he grew up in Torquay, so he couldn't be the baby, and the baby is the killer!"

"The killer does not have a family?" said Hector. "It is a baby cast out without attachment?"

"He was adopted," I said. "There's no time to explain everything. But it's not Roddy, and it's not Mr. Fibbley either, because he's not a *mister* at all!"

Hector tapped the valise. "You find something that tells you—"

"I'm worried about Rose," I said. "She left the case—"

"The case into which your nose is poking?" said Hector.

"She went to find Mr. Standfast, but he came back without seeing her. So where is she?"

"Rose is gone."

"What do you mean *gone*?"

"I am running here from watching Roddy Fusswell," said Hector. "Your horse Belle is trotting on the harbor road toward the Royal Victoria Hotel. I am, for a moment, elated. A ride, perhaps! But the fog churns like steam from a kettle. I jump to one side, unnoticed as a small beetle. Rose Eversham is sitting behind Mr. Leonard, asleep maybe, with eyes shut."

Hector slumped his shoulders and let his head drop crookedly to one side. "I think to myself, she is woeful from seeing her aunt in this dismal location."

"But that was ages ago!" I cried. "We must find her at once!"

"What is the worry?" said Hector. "She is in a cozy bed by now, is she not? Just as I would like to be."

"No!" I cried. "She is *not* at home in a cozy bed. She is with Leonard. And Leonard Cable is the killer."

CHAPTER 27

A TROUBLESOME DISAGREEMENT

LEONARD.

Leonard was Miss Marianne's baby.

"Leonard wrote the letter to Rose. He used letters cut from the newspapers heaped in his shed. He rolls them up and burns them in a bucket to keep warm."

"He is not the only person to have newspapers," said Hector.

"He is the only person whose father . . . or guardian . . . or whatever he is . . . A man with the same last name wrote a letter to the lawyer!" I rattled the handle on Mr. Standfast's case. "He is the only person to have received an allowance from Rose's father every month for all of his life!"

Hector looked as gobsmacked as I felt.

"I don't know exactly what turned him into a murderer," I said. "Or why he wrote the letter, or where Rose has gone, but I think I know what happened on Saturday morning."

Hector blinked. "On Saturday he visits the Mermaid Room to collect the flower vases, yes?"

"Yes, and he finds Mrs. Irma Eversham is in a tizzy, waving the letter that he wrote to Rose! She is furious at Miss Marianne for having a baby eighteen years ago without being married. For having *him*! But Leonard didn't realize . . ." Threads of the puzzle flew in from several directions at once, tangling themselves together, too knotted to make sense of in this moment. Leonard didn't know that Miss Marianne was his mother. He must have believed that he belonged to Irma and Captain Eversham, and that he might inherit some of the Captain's wealth. That's why he wrote the letter, to appeal to Rose directly, brother to sister.

I explained that to Hector. "But then he arrived at the dance studio and there was Mrs. Eversham in a furious snit about his very private letter."

"He fears that he will suffer from the wrath of this woman," said Hector.

"Miss Marianne offered her sister-in-law a cup of tea," I guessed. "To calm her down. Maybe Leonard was in the pantry, getting water? Pouring it out from the flowers? Mrs.

Eversham is alarming him. He thinks any minute she will call for the police and tell them lies as she has threatened."

"He wishes to stop her."

"The pantry has VerminRid," I said. "Washing-up powder, cocoa, lemon biscuits, all together on a little shelf."

"He makes a mixture," said Hector. "Perhaps he is intending sickness only. Just that she stops shouting."

"The hotel sugar bowl is there from the night before," I said. "Roddy has rinsed the teacups and put them away. The kettle is on the hob . . ."

"Leonard is a conjurer," said Hector. "Mixing poison into a bowl of sugar is no trouble to someone who extracts the sixpence from behind my ear!"

"But it all went terribly wrong," I said. "Mrs. Eversham died. Danger is closing in. He feels trapped. Rose knows he argued with her mother, but not the reason. Maybe he just wanted to talk to Rose, but what if . . ." I hurried toward the door, feeling for my gloves in the pockets of my coat. "What if she needs help? We've got to save her!"

"No, no," said Hector, shaking his head. "It is not for us to face a murderer," he said. "We are perhaps more clever than the police but we are not as strong. Let us speak with the inspector or with Constable Beck. Or summon Mr. Standfast from the jail cell. We will tell them of your suspicions and—"

"NO!" I wrenched the door open. "They think we're children! Rose could *die* before they believe us. Are you coming or not?"

Hector shook his head and turned toward the sergeant, who now was dozing behind the desk. Too much time had already blown by! I barreled out into the foggy night.

Outside the police station, I hurried downhill toward the harbor. Two minutes later, I stopped running, already persuaded that Hector may have been right. I could see nothing at all before me. A dank, drizzly fog obscured every familiar building along the road. My long curls drooped, my coat was gilded with silvery drops, my skirt and stockings clung to my legs like damp compresses.

I trailed my hand along the rain-slick walls of the buildings, meeting window frames and door gaps, trusting that I would eventually edge my way to the waterfront. My breath caught when I heard the clip-clop of a horse's hooves and the ring of wheels on cobbles. But Belle's harness had no jingling bells, so it was not the cart that I hoped to meet.

Though I was moving slowly, my mind began to race. How had Leonard persuaded Rose to leave without me? Where did she think she was being driven? Had he played a trick to purchase her cooperation? When did she realize that she was alone with the man who had killed her mother?

I'd thought Leonard to be my friend but had not seen beyond his disguise, those genial brown eyes. He'd hidden so much hurt, and this disguise I understood. I hid my grief for Papa and my shyness every day, pretending to be braver and more eloquent than I knew myself to be. And Hector, whether he liked it or not, was forced to become a new person in a whole different language! Everyone, I supposed, had pieces to hide or to offer as we dared, or did not dare, to face other people.

And as for people in disguise—I stumbled off the curb, and stumbled again stepping back onto it—Mr. Fibbley! A woman!

I should have known when I noticed those eyelashes. No, I should have known the moment Tony began to bark. Dear, clever Tony, trying to protect his mistress from mysterious strangers. Mysterious women. How bold to chop off her hair! What would she look like with long hair, properly up, the way my sister wore hers? Did she wear a dress when she visited her mother, with a lace collar and a cameo brooch at her throat? I supposed that Hector and I would never see her that way. Her revelation must be our well-kept secret.

My breath came raggedly as I paused to wipe my face, my gloves no better than wet flannels. The fingertips were blackened from trailing through grime on the walls that led me here. I peeled them off and flung them into the gutter.

269

Tony must be pining for me, waiting for an ear-scratch before bed. Mummy would be worried too, at how long we were. Grannie perhaps would soothe her, but be wondering also. They believed me to be with Rose, after all. What harm could come? If they knew the truth! That I was stumbling along a darkened street, trying to find Rose in time to save her life . . .

Hector was right. I should never have set out alone.

But here I finally was, arrived on The Strand. I could smell fish and the briny tang of the sea itself. Boats creaked as they strained against wet ropes, water slapped against pilings. The fog was thicker by the water. I made myself stand still for a moment. Long enough to hear my own breath, and then the lonely cry of a seagull. Questions swarmed in a frightening cluster, blowing away all logic. If only Hector were here! But panic would not help. Hector would ask one question at a time and answer it sensibly before moving to the next. I preferred to invent stories, to make up what people might say to each other, to try out more than one path toward an ending.

Perhaps if I used both methods at once? I could be the inspector asking questions, and then I'd answer as myself.

"Thank you for assisting us, Miss Morton." I aimed for a gruff detecting voice, but it came out breathless with my hurrying. "Where are you going?"

"To the Royal Victoria Hotel."

"And why do you suppooose . . . ."—the inspector's voice lingered on the word—"that was their destination?"

I saw a faint yellow glow nearby, and then another a few yards farther on. The lamps along the harborside promenade! I found the railing and moved forward, watching for the next pale light.

"Miss Morton?"

The hateful answer to why Leonard was taking Rose toward the hotel crawled out from the cobwebbiest corner of my mind.

"Because," I whispered, "Leonard wants people to think that Roddy Fusswell is the killer. If Rose is hurt near the hotel, Roddy will be blamed."

"Hurt?"

Or killed. I could not bring myself to say it aloud, even in a fictional conversation. But I knew that I was right.

CHAPTER 28

A LONELY SCREAM

HECTOR AND I HAD TOLD Leonard on Saturday afternoon about the murder. We'd told *him* about the murder *he* had committed! We'd asked him to bury the rabbit, and told him about Mrs. Eversham, while already he was scheming! Leonard told us, bold as brass, that Roddy was being particular about packing up the teacups. He diverted our attention from the very first minute—just like a conjurer!

Why had I not seen this before? Logical answer: because I liked Leonard and never imagined deceit. Or *evil*.

Oof! I tripped over what turned out to be a whopping great coil of rope. Then, *bump!* The railing took a sharp left turn and I'd hit the corner full on. Here the street turned from running around the harbor to climbing the hill toward the hotel.

Please let me find Rose!

"But *why*? *Why* does kind and handsome Leonard dislike Mrs. Eversham so much that he wanted to kill her?"

I did not know for certain. Hector and I had guessed that he was afraid of the harm her fury might cause. But now I wondered . . . If he believed she was his mother and had cast him away—first as an infant and again this week—must he not hold fury too? And hurt beyond bearing? Only Leonard could tell us that.

I was stilled by a thought, hand to my lips. Perhaps it should be Leonard's voice I summoned instead of the inspector's, to learn his truth, from behind his eyes. Could I do that? The villains trounced by Sherlock Holmes were not given much to say for themselves. No book I'd ever read was narrated by a murderer. But killers, I imagined, carried more than their share of sorrow. Why else would they be so reckless with the hearts of others?

A noise, very nearby. I stopped, dead still. An odd, snuffling noise, then a creak and a scrape—as if something heavy were shifting over cobbles . . .

"Rose?"

Might she be muffled by a gag?

"ROSE?" I hadn't meant to shout. But what if—

And then, a snort.

A real, live, horsey snort!

"Belle?"

A soft whinny in response.

"Belle!" I lunged forward and bumped smack into Belle's wet and wonderful flank.

"Dear Belle, I've found you!" A giddy laugh escaped. I'd got to the right place. "If only you could tell me where to find Rose!"

She must be nearby. With her captor. Tears bubbled up on top of the laughter. I was only *nearly* to Rose and didn't know where to go next. The fog choked the world under a woolly blanket.

I draped an arm as high up as I could over Belle's back and bumped my forehead against the horse's side. Once, twice, three times. What happens next?

Leonard, where have you taken her?

Belle stood quietly, occasionally lifting and dropping a hoof.

Where would *I* go to scare someone silly?

Somewhere isolated. Somewhere that felt like a trap.

The killer, cornered by his own wicked deeds, imagined that he had one last chance to cast the blame elsewhere. Ignoring the girl's frightened pleading, he forced her out of the cart and . . . and . . . prodded her down the slippery stone path to the small, protected beach at the bottom of a scary ridge of rock . . .

I knew exactly where they were. The Royal Victoria Hotel sat on a cliff overlooking the Ladies Bathing Cove and the sea beyond. Where better to pretend that the victim had been pushed over the edge by the son of the hotel manager? What better place to construct another crime scene?

It was a bit of a scrabble in the dark, to clamber down the slippery, pebbly slope, but my new certainty drove me to the water's edge without hesitation. The sea rumbled steadily behind a curtain of near-white mist. Of the whole huge ocean I could see only a pearly ribbon of foam tumbling against the shoreline. I wanted desperately to call out a warning to Rose, but that would have alerted Leonard that I was stalking him.

How had he got Rose this far? Had he knocked her senseless? When Hector saw her slumped in the cart, had she been dead? I paused to wipe my face and realized how loudly my boots had been crunching on the stones. Standing still, I listened hard.

Waves scraped the stones. A seagull called. Another seagull answered. And then, a scream.

I crouched to untie my laces. I slid out of my boots and moved softly in stockinged feet, a boot on each hand like monstrous paws. Mummy would go into fits if she could see! I side-stepped a boulder and felt squishy spikes of seaweed through my stockings. I was too wet to care.

Wait, what was that noise?

I closed my eyes to hear better.

Voices. Yes, truly, voices! One low and one higher, angry—but *alive*! An odd blur of notes, as if the speakers had swallowed fog and their words turned to billowy mist.

Until another choked cry.

I wrenched the boots off my hands and flung them away. I skittered across the beach but lost my sense of direction at once. The fog had wrapped me inside a cloud. Very close by, someone else's footsteps crunched on sand, scaring a whimper from my throat. Not a fine sleuthing moment. The footsteps went quiet. Could one small whimper end up killing a person?

Then *oomph*! A shove sent me to the ground. My shoulder and cheek hit the gravelly beach with a scraping crash. Before I could catch my breath, arms snatched me up, as my right leg buckled in pain. I stumbled forward, prodded by mean knuckles poking into my back. The assailant's other hand clamped over my face, damp fingers squashing my nose and jamming my mouth shut. I tried to bite him, but he held on tight, pushing me roughly over several yards of the stony ground until he shook me to a stop.

"Up," he said.

What did he mean?

"Up."

I lifted a foot—and found a step. I lifted the other foot, and met a second step.

"Leonard," I whispered. "Don't hurt me."

"If you'd just left things alone," he muttered.

I opened my eyes and found a door two inches from my face. A wooden door, painted the color of a robin's egg. His arm reached across to open it, hurling me through in one swift, unfriendly action.

"Leonard!" I cried. The door slammed shut. I pounced on the handle but he had managed to make it secure. Was he leaning against it? Was there a lock? I began to shriek.

"Don't do this! Let me out!! Where is Rose? Leonard? Can you hear me?"

His answer was a hard smash against the outside handle of the door. He'd used a rock or some other heavy thing to disable the latch.

I knew now where I was. Inside a bathing hut.

I had been inside a bathing hut every week of every summer of my life. On the outside it was brightly painted, the striped roof a banner for summer pleasures. The wheels were as tall as my shoulders, built for rolling into the waves. But inside, on a foggy night in October, I was surrounded by the darkest dark I'd ever known. It was small, I knew that much. All four walls were only just beyond the reach of my stretched-wide arms.

The floor lurched. I was knocked from my feet and landed on my bottom. The hut was moving.

"Leonard, stop!" I hollered. "I don't like this."

Another pitching lurch. I heard the wheels grinding as I bounced over the shingle beach. Where was he taking me?

Then quite a different feeling. I knew it at once, from the many warm, delicious summer afternoons I'd spent in this cove. The moment when the bathing hut leaves the beach and rolls into the sea. Too heavy to float, but the water took some of the weight, holding the tiny house like a child in arms, rocking ever so slightly. And the water—cold seawater—swirled in through the bottom slats like the contents of a spilled bucket on the kitchen floor.

"Don't leave me here!"

I heard splashing as he waded away. He was well past listening, no longer the Leonard I'd thought I knew. The old Leonard would never have pushed me about or stuck me in a locked box. Out there somewhere, Rose had screamed. What had he done to her? Was she drowned? In the frigid water?

The girl's hair floated up around a face as pale as cold ashes, but no less beautiful in death . . .

Or was she, too, trapped in a hut? Awaiting the incoming tide.

The sea whooshed up through the cracks of the floor, subsided, and whooshed again. Bathing huts were not built to be watertight, only to ease ladies' entry into the waves and to protect our modesty from the prying gaze of uncouth men.

I was up to my ankles in seawater, as icy as melted snow. Waves in October, especially after a rainstorm, are insistent and swollen. Several rushed in every minute, tipping the hut back and then forward as they gurgled out again. But not all gurgled out. I was standing in more water each time, though I knew the tide could not be coming in so quickly as that. The hut was rolling deeper with each wave.

I hurled myself against the door, wishing it to tear wide open like a paper screen. Alas, it was as hard as one would expect from a wooden door. My shoulder, already sore from colliding with the ground, throbbed in outrage. I sank to the floor, tears creeping into my eyes, but then dragged myself upright, wetter than ever.

Whoosh! Another wave wrapped my clothing about me like clammy seaweed. I was tilted backward, my ankles immersed and then my knees. The wave receded, and the hut tipped forward, emptying the flood back into the sea. I shifted my weight with each ebb and flow, as if learning to stand in a rowboat.

My knees bumped against the small slatted bench that was meant for sitting upon when adjusting one's woolly swim-stockings. I climbed to stand upon it, and stretched to see whether I could reach the window. My fingers touched the lip of the opening, but even if I'd had the agility of a monkey to hoist myself up, my body could never squeeze through.

I heard Hector's voice in my head. *We are perhaps more clever than the police but we are not as strong.* I could never rescue Rose by myself! I could scarcely push the sopping hair from my face. If Charlotte were here, she'd smooth away my hair and wrap me in a sun-baked towel. And no doubt remind me that if she had accompanied us to town, I would not be in such a predicament. Only I could get myself out of the icy puddle I'd landed in.

Think, Aggie, think!

I squeezed my eyes shut and imagined being warm— being *too* warm, as often happened on a humid afternoon in July. Charlotte and I walked all the way from Groveland, through the town, around the harbor and finally to the Ladies Bathing Cove. I tried to conjure up bright heat and sticky perspiration, the tickling anticipation of arriving on the beach with the sea waiting. I imagined hopping up the wooden steps right behind Charlotte, into the dim and suffocating hut, changing into my bathing costume as speedily as ever I could. And then, as soon as slowpoke Charlotte was ready too, I would . . . *unhook the fastener that opened the shuttered doors facing the sea!*

Silly goose! Silly, shivering and waiting-to-be-drowned goose! I'd been trying to think how to get through the door, when the opposite side of the hut was designed to open up like a picture window for the very purpose of inviting bathers to enter the sea!

I smacked my hands against the middle of the wall, just above my own height. Yes! A hook was attached on one side, sunk into a metal loop on the other. My tug freed the hook. Easy as pie, as Mrs. Corner would say— though my definition of easy would certainly not be making a pie. Eating pie, perhaps?

I'd missed supper! Hunger, on top of all the other miseries! I'd think about pie to keep my strength up. As the hut pitched again, the unhooked shutter doors creaked open to reveal the night. The pulling tide, thank goodness, was still below the doorstep. I sent a small word of thanks to the Heavens. These few minutes of being trapped had seemed like hours. Outside my prison, the fog had begun to disperse, now swirling instead of merely lying over the world like thick dust. *Bam!* The shutters slapped shut as the hut tipped backward with another flood of water around my calves.

On a shining summer day, the shutters would be fixed in place by the sturdy and muscular Russian Betty, guardian of the lady bathers. She'd then pull the hut into the surf and assist young ladies in making a genteel entry into the waves. Charlotte took an age to edge her way down the steps, but I liked to stand on the threshold and plunge in with a splash.

A plunge would not be so fun tonight. The sky was black. The water was black—and churning and frigid. But

I could not hesitate another moment. I tugged off my sodden, woolly jacket, now as heavy as the sheep it had come from. My skirt should probably come off as well, so as not to impede my motion in the water, but my fingers were too numb to succeed with buttons.

The next wave came in.

I hauled myself up to the ledge.

"Blackberry pie," I said, a prayer.

And jumped.

CHAPTER 29

A MORBID FLOTSAM

NOTHING HAD EVER BEEN colder or wetter than the water
that night.

Or harder to move through.

I felt as if I'd swallowed a tack as shock pierced my
chest. My skirt knotted around my legs, not letting me
kick as I knew I must. A wave flipped me all the way over,
making me swallow half the sea before I fought my way
back to the surface. My feet scrabbled to touch down just
as the undertow dragged away the stones beneath. I was
dunked again by the next swell. I tried to scream, *Mummy!*
But salty foam filled my mouth. I clamped my teeth into
my lip to keep from drinking more.

I'd be ready for the next wave, just watch. I'd be a boat,
that's what. I'd float instead of sink.

And so I did. I rode the surface of the water as it carried me toward the shore—not so very far after all—to a clumsy arrival on my hands and knees. I dragged myself across the stones, out of the churning water and finally to rest, lying flat, the warmth of my tears most welcome on my cold, cold face.

The relief was fleeting. My cheek, scraped and stinging, pressed into the rough grit of the beach. With enormous effort I turned my head, imagining the other cheek would find a feather pillow instead of bumpy gravel.

Something lay on the sand just a few feet away. Something bigger than me, dark and motionless.

Not something. Some*one.*

Someone's body.

Rose.

Though barely able to turn my head a few seconds earlier, I now crawled like a beetle across the pebbled beach. She lay on her back, arms flung wide. Oh, please, not greeting angels.

"Rose!"

Not so much as a shiver.

"Rose?"

I was not gentle, pushing tangled hair from her face and

roughly patting her cheeks. Bruising showed on her neck and shoulder beneath the torn collar and sleeve of her coat.

No, please, *no*. Could he have been so cruel?

"Please, Rose, *please*, open your eyes!"

I remembered Nurse Welles, the silent woman who had tended Papa, reaching for his wrist each time she approached the bedside. Would I recognize a pulse if I found one? I lifted Rose's arm, but my hand was too numb to feel anything useful. I put two fingers in my mouth and sucked hard, willing the warmth to come.

The steady clatter of water turning over pebbles was broken by a new sound, a very faint cry. Not from the unmoving girl beside me. Could Leonard be returning to finish me off?

The frightened girl, huddled and frozen, lifted her head and strained to listen, knowing that readiness could decide her fate. She cast about for a weapon and found a stone, heavy and slick with seawater, perhaps deadly if it needed to be.

I shivered and cast it away, holding instead to Rose's arm. "Oh, do wake up!"

Again, a cry, closer now.

"Aggie-eeee!"

My name! In more than one voice.

"Here," I croaked.

Waves crashed, stones slid and grated. My little voice was not enough, about as noisy as a toad call. I pushed

285

myself to standing and held my hands beside my mouth as I'd seen men do when they hollered on a cricket pitch.

"Here!" I cried. "HERE! We need HELP!" Rose did not stir. "HEL-L-L-LP!!"

"Ahoy!" someone called.

"We're coming!" A different voice.

"Keep calling! Where are you?"

"Aggie-eeee!"

"I'm heeere! We're heeere, near the water! HELP US PLEASE!"

Footsteps. Friendly, wonderful footsteps, crunching down the path and across the beach. Torch beams danced on the sand and several dark shapes emerged from leftover wisps of fog. Night clouds swirled, revealing suddenly the pale glow of the moon to light the dreadful scene.

Hector came first. "Ma chère amie!" he cried.

He threw his arms around me and then pulled hastily back.

"Ugh," he said. "Wet."

I would have laughed, because *wet* could not begin to describe how wet I was, but, "Rose," I said. "I don't know if she's alive or dead."

"Blankets!" Hector shouted. "We need many blankets."

"What are you wearing?" I said. "You look ridiculous."

"I am clothed in the cricket uniform of the Torquay police. I have many cozy layers." He shrugged off the outermost jersey and held it out to me. I pointed to Rose, and Hector draped her still figure with his meager offering.

A man's voice had taken up the call. "Blankets! Beck! Fetch blankets!"

"And a doctor!" cried Hector.

"And a doctor!" The voice belonged to Inspector Locke, standing suddenly right next to me.

"Yes, sir," called someone from farther up the path.

The inspector took one look at me and removed his Ulster overcoat. He draped it across my shoulders and did up the top button. I was encased from neck to toe in a sudden warmth so welcome that I happily ignored the stench of bay rum cologne coming from the collar.

The inspector knelt with a finger on the side of Rose's neck and then put his head on her chest.

Hector took my hands and began vigorously to rub them with his own.

"Has Leonard been caught?" I said. "He was just here. They should be looking for him. He put me inside . . ."

I pointed at the bathing hut. From here, it looked to be rocking gently in the moonlight. How different a place could seem, from only a few waves away!

"He might have killed me. With Rose he really tried!"

Please, please, *please* let Rose be all right.

"No Leonard yet," said Hector.

"I was wrongheaded," I said. "I should have listened to you. He got away because it was only me."

"Perhaps he is not so far," said Hector.

"You rescued me," I said.

"You rescued Rose."

But had I? Hot pricks of pain shot through my fingers and up my arms, as the massage began to work.

"We have a pulse," said Inspector Locke.

A pulse!

Tears flooded my eyes as I pulled away from Hector. I wanted to see her breathing, but there was such a knot of policemen crowding around that I could not get close.

"Get her off the ground," ordered the inspector, "and into a warm bed at once." The officers churned the sand as they turned about, wondering how to carry her.

"The medic hasn't come yet," one of them said. "We haven't got a stretcher."

"No useful footprints," murmured Hector. "Sherlock Holmes would be most disappointed."

"We don't need deduction," I said. "We already know who was on the beach." On the beach and then gone.

"The hotel has beds," I said, trying to get the inspector's attention. "Take Rose up there." I pointed to lights that earlier had not penetrated the fog, but now shone through a hundred panes of glass.

"I know you'd like to be helpful," said the inspector,

"but you've done enough, I think. Will someone remove these children?" he called out. "I want the guardians informed. They do not belong at a crime scene."

"But I'm part of the crime!" I protested. "Leonard pushed me into the hut and left me there! The sea was pouring in! You must find him! May we not watch for a little—"

"No," said Inspector Locke. He tapped one of his constables. "Get these two home to their warm, wee cots. We'll take their statements tomorrow."

"The girl may need to see the medic, sir," murmured the constable. "There's blood."

"Blood?" I said. "I've got blood?"

Hector touched his own cheek to show where I could find my injury. My fingertips came away dotted with blood.

"Then get her tended to!" commanded the inspector.

"Yes, sir."

But no one produced a bandage or paid us a scrap of attention. The police had other worries for the moment.

"Is Belle still here, at the top of the path?" I said. "With the cart?"

"Yes, Belle is here," said Hector. "The villain must be attempting to escape on his two legs only."

"How far do you suppose he could have run by now?" I lifted the hem of my borrowed coat so as not to drag it across the wet sand. "And who will drive us home?"

"This I do not know." Hector crouched to examine something. "Inspector Locke!" he called. "Come to look, please! Here is evidence."

I peered over his shoulder, but was firmly pushed to one side by an eager constable.

"What is it?" said the inspector.

"The boy is right," said the constable, peering down. "It looks like a man's glove. Yellow. Posh. Dropped in flight, I'd say."

"You'd be saying in error," I said. Where had I got the nerve to sass a constable? "That glove belongs to Mr. Roddy Fusswell."

CHAPTER 30

A RED HERRING

INSPECTOR LOCKE EYED ME with a flicker of interest. "You recognize this glove, Miss Morton?"

"Yes, sir. Mr. Roddy Fusswell was wearing it when he visited my home earlier this evening. When it came time for him to leave, one of the pair was misplaced. He was in a right sulk about it."

I held his gaze, astounded at how well my mouth was working. "Those are the facts, sir. I believe that Leonard Cable stole it from our front hallway and dropped it here for the purpose of incriminating another man."

Rose and I had giggled while Roddy whined about losing his silly yellow glove. We'd fled to what we thought was the safety of the pony cart. And there Leonard had stood, hands behind his back, appearing to wait respect-fully to drive us into town.

Oh, Leonard . . . My breath felt like lint in my chest. *Were you always wicked?*

Inspector Locke ordered one of his men to put the glove in a burlap sack. "We'll check to see if it's a match," he said, "but for now, I'd like to get the victim to a hospital."

"Sir!" I said. "Have you not enough men to look for Leonard as well? He murdered Mrs. Eversham and tried to strangle Rose." I felt my voice get small. "And me," I said. "He hurt me too. He cannot have got far."

The inspector put his hands on my shoulders—that were newly broad and sturdy under his coat. "You've had a fright, Miss Morton. But now you must put your trust in the Torquay constabulary. Get off the beach. We will arrange for a ride home."

I looked over to where Rose was surrounded by men with torches. I sent a wish across the wind, *Please be well again.*

Hector and I hobbled slowly up the path holding hands.

"Thank you for coming, Hector."

"You make also a good decision," he said. "You are correct that time will not wait for the rescue of Miss Rose. We are the cunning foxes, you and I, two halves of the best resolution, no?"

"How did you make them listen to you?" I asked. "A foreign boy must be considered even less reliable than an English girl."

"After my regrettable enthusiasm for powdered sugar as a weapon, the police believe me to be a nincompoop," he said. "This is the correct pronunciation? Nincompoop?"

"Yes," I said.

"I persist because of my concern for you and for Rose. Sergeant Cornell, he is most discourteous. Then up from the jail cell comes Mr. Standfast who receives his valise with great relief. I say to him the words you say to me, *the baby is Leonard Cable, the gardener and driver for Mrs. Morton.* This lights a firecracker, much activity occurs, *kaBOOM!*" Hector's hands fluttered to show an explosion.

At the top of the path, dear, patient Belle whinnied and I neighed happily back. Hector climbed onto the cart where I joined him after giving the horse a good long pat.

"Alas." Hector lifted one foot and then the other, inspecting the once-shiny leather, now battered and torn. "My new shoes."

"Poor Hector," I said. "You were so proud of them."

"One thing this night is making clear to me," he said. "I am a thinker, and not built so much for the heroic action."

"I don't think anyone sets out to be a hero," I said.

"Perhaps not," agreed Hector. "But a hero must face danger, and this I do not like."

"A hero sometimes faces danger," I said. "Like a dragon-slayer or a nurse in a jungle hospital. But don't you think a hero might also be a person who does what no one else wants to do?"

Two officers trotted past, scattering stones from under their heavy boots. They carried a canvas stretcher rolled on two poles, and disappeared down the path to the beach.

"That's borrowed from beside the hotel swimming pool," said a voice I knew too well. "For old ladies who faint." Florence Fusswell materialized out of the darkness. She gave me an amazed and steady look, taking in the mass of sopping hair and Inspector Locke's enormous coat.

"Are *you* one of the girls who was attacked?"

I nodded, pushing back my hair with the coat cuff that dangled over my fingers.

"Are you . . . *harmed*?" said Florence.

"A few scratches," I said. "And my clothes are soggy. The inspector loaned me his coat."

"A constable came panting into the lobby saying two girls were hurt," said Florence. "I never imagined it might be someone I know! How thrilling! You look terrible."

Before I could find an answer, Florence hurried away back up the hill, as her brother arrived with a steel flask.

"Hot drink, for Rose," he said. "It's rum with honey, so I shan't offer you any. You did well, though, finding Rose, I will say that. We've telephoned to the hospital.

Medics have been dispatched. One of the constables insisted that I make a telephone call to your home. Your grandmother was not pleased to hear from me." He loosened the cap of the flask and tightened it again. "But your family has been informed of your safety and your whereabouts. I believe a constable will assist in getting you safely home."

"Thank you," I said.

"When I leave Roddy Fusswell, he is drunk," whispered Hector. "Now he is king of the rescue operation."

A braggart and a bully, but not a killer. I should have been clever enough to realize that *he* wasn't clever enough, nor the least bit brave. Just like Grannie's Bertie Cummings.

My biggest worry at breakfast had been that Mummy would discover I'd been out riding a bicycle last night. And now . . . there'd be no hiding the frightful story of this evening's adventure if she'd heard already from Roddy Fusswell. Constable Beck would no doubt tell his version to Charlotte. I was in for a shower of trouble.

"I am begging your pardon," said Hector. "Does anyone know where the villain might be?"

Roddy Fusswell glared at him. "The workings of the constabulary are no business of the foreign element."

"The foreign element?" I nearly spat. "The *foreign* element happens to be the reason the constabulary arrived in time to rescue Rose!"

Hector began to protest, but a clamoring bell announced the arrival of a carriage from the hospital. At the same moment, the inspector and several other policemen emerged from the shadowed path to the beach. The two men holding the stretcher poles were not sure-footed in the dark. My stomach turned over as Rose tipped awkwardly to one side.

"Steady on, there!" shouted Roddy Fusswell. "You'll have her overboard!"

"Move!" Inspector Locke barked so abruptly that Roddy tripped over his own feet trying to get out of the way.

Hector and I watched from our perch as the stretcher slid with a bump into the medical wagon. We pinched each other when Roddy Fusswell tried to insist on climbing in with her, only to be rejected by the attendants. He moved sulkily away, unscrewed the cap of the flask and took a long drink.

Just as the ambulance doors were fastened, Mr. Gus Fibbley came trotting up the hill.

"We meet again." He doffed his brown hat to Hector and me. His spectacles were slightly steamed over, the only sign that he'd been hurrying or breathing hard.

"What the devil are you doing here?" said Inspector Locke. "You've got a nose like a damnable bloodhound!"

Mr. Fibbley grinned. "Yes, sir," he said. "I see a police horse galloping past and am compelled to chase it. What can you tell me about the connection between

Miss Marianne Eversham and . . . And whoever is inside that medical wagon, needing emergency care?"

"Can't tell you a thing," said the inspector. "And unless you want to join the lady in the jail cell, you'll put yourself a long way out of my sight. Only thing worse than children is a reporter. We've still got a killer on the loose!" He marched off to bellow instructions at his men. I climbed to the ground with Hector right behind me.

"*Psst!*" I said to Mr. Fibbley.

He leaned down a little.

"I know who is going to hospital," I whispered.

"Well?" said Mr. Fibbley.

"I know everything that happened here tonight."

He looked at me more closely, taking in the outsized overcoat, the bedraggled hair, my injured face and general dampness.

"But I do not want to be misquoted," I said. "It's my story and I want it right."

"First an accusation of murder," said Mr. Fibbley, "and now blackmail?"

I shook my head. "I am merely setting the terms for our interview. For now, I'll tell you who was in the ambulance. Tomorrow, you can come and hear the rest. Or at least the parts that are not other people's secrets."

Mr. Fibbley removed his spectacles and polished the glass with great care, using a corner of his dotted necktie.

"You'll be doing my job in about ten years," he said. "And by then you may be allowed to wear a skirt even for murders."

"Trousers look to be a good deal more practical," I said.

"The best thing about men's clothing," said Mr. Fibbley, "is no corsets. In my opinion, that small particularity explains a good deal about society itself. It's extraordinary how different the world looks when a person can breathe."

"Miss Marianne says exactly the same thing," I said. "Perhaps that is why she dances. I don't wear a corset yet. I'm tall, but not . . . you know . . ."

"My advice," said Mr. Fibbley, "is to avoid—"

I could trust him. Her. "It's Rose," I said. "Rose Eversham has been taken for medical care, following an assault."

"And where is the perpetrator?" he asked. "*Who* is the perpetrator?"

Inspector Locke was here again, interrupting before I could think of what to say. "Did you not hear me?" he said. "This young lady will not speak to a reporter until she is accompanied by an adult member of her family. If you're lucky, it won't be the grandmother. Now, go!"

Mr. Fibbley jammed his spectacles back on and set out at a run, on the tail of the hospital wagon. Was he right? Might I be a writer someday, hurtling down the road in pursuit of a story?

"I'll have my coat now, if you please," said the inspector, looming over me. "It may be an endless night, looking for this scoundrel." He lifted the coat from my shoulders along with its envelope of warmth. "You can use one of the blankets."

He pointed to the police wagon. Hector hurried over to fetch a gray wool blanket with TORQUAY STATION embroidered across one end.

"Don't touch that nasty thing!" Florence was back. "I've brought you some of *my* clothes." She handed me a bundle. "You're bigger than I am, but I did the best I could."

Tears of grateful surprise sprang to my eyes. I clutched the offered clothing and stepped behind Belle to make use of it. Florence held the blanket as a curtain while I wrestled my wet things off. Was it more absurd that I was nearly naked on a public road or that I was pulling on a skirt and sweater belonging to Florence Fusswell? On no single morning could a person wake up confident about what might happen that day. Was it God in Heaven who had an eccentric sense of humor? Or the nature of humans to be entirely unpredictable?

Florence's skirt came only just below my knees and I could pull up the stockings hardly high enough to cover anything with decency, but it was all better than what I'd had before. Florence kept chattering on the other side of the blanket.

"Your feet could never fit into my shoes. They're custom-made from Italian leather. I brought my mother's Wellington boots instead. And her Persian lamb jacket, though she'll be furious. But how often does a person have the opportunity to loan one's clothing to a nearly murdered, fatherless waif? Lavinia will *die* of envy."

I knew I must look hideous, but I was dry, making these possibly the best garments I had ever worn.

"Oi!" A shout from up near the hotel. I flung aside the blanket and stepped out from my hiding spot.

"Sodding villain! Stay put!"

"Let me go!"

An angry scuffle and more shouts.

"Hey! Stop! You there! STOP!"

CHAPTER 31

AN UGLY MOMENT

SOMEONE HURTLED DOWN the road from the Royal Victoria Hotel, going so fast on the hill that he staggered a little. Another someone chased him, the beam of a torch bouncing from cobbles to tree branches with every pump of his arms. It was Leonard who ran in front, we could see him now, hair flying, with a scratched face and wild eyes. I shivered and shrank back behind Belle.

"Hold up!" It was Constable Beck who chased Leonard. "You! Stop!"

Hector leapt directly into Leonard's path and raised his hands as if to snatch him. I saw the look on Leonard's face as he nimbly swerved out of the way. He was fueled by demons and no mere boy would thwart his escape. I jumped from the shadows and thrust out a large Wellington boot. Leonard tumbled, grunting, to the ground. Constable Beck thundered up and threw himself upon his quarry. Runner and captor lay panting in a heap.

Leonard's mouth twisted in pain. I had to remind myself that he did not deserve pity. And yet . . . why did my heart feel sore? A friend had turned out to not be a friend. He'd locked me in a leaking vessel on an icy sea and not heeded my cries for help.

"Bravo, Aggie!" Hector's normally sleek hair was ruffled and his pale cheeks flushed.

"Bravo to you," I said. "You sent him my way. An action hero after all!"

"Man down!" cried Constable Beck. Leonard squirmed and kicked, but the policeman was bigger and kept him pinned.

Two more officers leapt forward, letting Constable Beck roll out of the way as they yanked Leonard to his feet and gripped him tightly between them.

I could not bear to watch and yet could not look away. The demon of a few minutes ago was gone. It was a boy I saw now, with a bruised face and bloodied nose. A boy who tended flowers and did magic tricks and fed Tony nubs of sausage.

A boy who had killed a woman in a most horrible fashion.

"I'm sorry, Miss Aggie. It all went wrong."

I could scarcely hear his voice.

"I wanted her to get sick, that's all, to stop her calling the coppers on me. I was going to talk to Miss Rose, only then it was too late. She was telling me lies and I got mad, I didn't mean . . ." He tried to wipe his bloody nose on his shoulder but the constables held him too tightly.

"I didn't want to hurt you, only—"

"Only you did," I said. "And Rose too. You hurt everyone, Leonard."

He took in a hollow-sounding breath and began to cry.

Inspector Locke dug in the pockets of his coat for a pair of handcuffs and snapped them into place. Leonard yelped as the metal at his wrists was used to pull him away. His teary eyes met mine for one moment more, but I thought only of Rose, lying on the stretcher. The officers shoved Leonard into the police wagon and climbed in to flank him. Hector's hand found mine, a small, warm comfort in the wet, black night.

"Constable Beck." The inspector clapped the young officer's shoulder. "I commend you heartily for your courage and speed. You've run the villain to ground!"

Constable Beck's left eye was swollen nearly shut, his face sweaty and smeared with dirt.

He saluted. "Sir!"

As soon as the inspector turned away, I saw Beck grin like a birthday boy.

"Constable Beck," I said.

He smiled crookedly beneath his puffy eye. "You have broken a promise," he said. "Last evening you vowed to leave policing to the police. But here you are again, wandering about in the dark, improperly dressed and jumping into the path of wanted criminals! For which I must heartily thank you," he said.

"I don't think it will happen again," I told him.

Constable Beck offered his hand. I shook it and so did Hector. We shared a look, Hector and I. After all our deductions and daring and drenchings, it did not seem quite fair that Constable Beck should be the only hero. I supposed that being children we were overlooked, though I felt we deserved small medals at the very least. Nonetheless, we gave a good show of congratulations, for we were mightily relieved to have the escapade at its end.

I wished suddenly with all my heart to be tucked into my bed, with Charlotte bringing me a cup of hot milk, and Tony snuffling at my feet. How would I get home? And what about Hector? Had the charitable Mrs. Teasdale even noticed that her little immigrant was not inside the vicarage?

The hoofbeats and wheel rumble of another vehicle came up the road from town, a lantern swaying wildly from the driver's seat.

"Hello?" A woman's voice. "Hello?"

The person holding the reins was struggling to keep the horse moving uphill in a steady line.

Good Heavens! "Mummy!"

"Darling one!"

I recognized Star Lady, the horse belonging to old Mr. Herman who lived two houses along, on Bertram Road. Next to Mummy on the wagon seat was Charlotte, holding the lantern aloft and looking positively white with fear.

"Whoa!" Mummy pulled so sharply on the reins that she and Charlotte were jolted backward with the sudden stop.

"Your mother is a new driver?" asked Hector.

"She has scarcely left our house since Papa died," I said. "I've never seen her drive a horse!"

But Mummy had done it. After an evening of ever-growing anxiety, with Grannie Jane and Charlotte stoking the fire and pacing the drawing room in turns, Groveland had received a dire telephone call from Roddy Fusswell at the Royal Victoria Hotel.

"I needn't relate all the ruckus that followed," said Mummy. "Because all's well that ends well. I drove the cart myself! And here *you* are, sweet pea, safe and sound. Come along, we'll have you home in two shakes of a lamb's tail."

"But Hector—?"

"Hector, too, for Heaven's sake. He'll stay with us. We left word at the vicarage on the way here. Up you get. Sally will have the fires blazing by the time we get home."

Despite Mummy's feat in driving all the way here, Inspector Locke asked for a volunteer from the constabulary to manage the return journey. Constable Beck hastily shot up his arm and had his foot on the carriage step in an instant. Another officer would follow us with Belle. I knew that Charlotte's face was as pink as raspberry pudding, though it was too dark to see anything really.

"Oh, Charlotte," whispered the handsome constable, pushing her hat askew with his nuzzling.

"Oh, Morris," she murmured in return. "To think that we met because a kindly confectioner tumbled to the floor."

"And our alliance continued because a stout lady drank mouse poison with her tea and died a horrible death."

"So romantic," she breathed.

"Even your Miss Aggie helped us along," said Morris. "Her misbehavior allowed us more cause to meet."

"Yes," sighed Charlotte. "All is forgiven."

Hector and I sat under a fur rug on either side of Mummy, leaning in for warmth. We both were lulled to sleep before ever arriving at Groveland, and learned at breakfast that we'd been carried inside by Constable Beck.

VILLAIN APPREHENDED IN MERMAID ROOM MURDER!
SECOND VICTIM THREATENED IN BATHING COVE DRAMA

by Augustus C. Fibbley

The greatest excitement was occasioned late on Tuesday at the Ladies Bathing Cove near Torquay Harbour. From careful inquiries pursued by this reporter, we are able to present many authentic particulars for the edification of our readers. This commotion displaces the arrest yesterday of the pitiful lady who was confined in error for many hours. Miss Marianne Eversham has been released and returned to her residence on Bertram Road.

As rumors have declared throughout the town, the Mermaid Room Killer has indeed been apprehended. His name is Leonard Cable and a more heartless fiend has rarely been encountered. He is recently arrived in Torquay, employed as a gardener, and not well known in the village, though he impressed some with his comely appearance and steady work habits. But Leonard Cable was all deceit. Not content with the cunning murder–by–poison of Mrs. Irma Eversham, Cable yesterday evening abducted her daughter, Miss Rose Eversham, and removed her to the isolation of Cove Beach with harmful intent. There he revealed his purpose and the grievous error of his motive. Believing Rose Eversham to be his sister, and Irma Eversham their shared mother, Leonard Cable was driven mad by greed, expecting to inherit some portion of the late Captain Eversham's fortune. Alas, his heinous actions were founded on a deluded relationship and caused nothing but harm and sorrow.

Miss Rose was insensible upon arrival at the hospital but had rallied by morning, despite a lump on her head and cruel bruising to her neck and shoulders where the villain clutched and shook her in his frenzy. She will not be disfigured by her misadventure. Also injured in the evening's incident was Miss Agatha Morton, the twelve–year–old dance student who discovered the body of Mrs. Irma Eversham last Saturday morning. Miss

Morton's persistence in asking questions resulted in cracking open the investigation, alas, too late for Rose Eversham's safety. The intrepid child pursued the killer and his hapless victim through the foggy night and was trapped in a sea-soaked bathing hut by the pitiless Mr. Cable. Belgian visitor Hector Perot also played a part in rallying assistance from the constabulary.

Six officers of the law, under the direction of Inspector H. Locke, were involved in the rescue of Miss Rose Eversham and in the subsequent pursuit of the crafty criminal. Receiving special commendation was Constable Morris Beck, who tackled the monster to the ground and held him until other officers could assist in the arrest.

The prisoner betrayed much agitation about his person when removed into custody. His step was unsteady as he approached the bar, his clothing disheveled and his countenance that of a savage. Mr. Ableman, Justice of the Peace, addressed the prisoner, "You stand committed to Dartmoor Prison to take your trial for Wilful Murder." The prisoner was then removed from the bar. In response to a question put forth by this reporter in the courthouse corridor, the suspect said, "It was all a mistake. I'm so very sorry." Perhaps remorse is valued in the eyes of God, but it offers little comfort to Irma Eversham or her family.

CHAPTER 32

A FINAL EXPLANATION

A VERY PALE ROSE sat in Papa's chair. An embroidered scarf around her neck covered what I imagined—even six days later—to be livid marks of a brutal attack. *Violet shadows of a cruel encounter. Smears of berry juice upon an ivory tea cloth. Splashings of blood on a snowy field.*

Outside the windows, a bruise-colored sky turned from twilight to autumn night. Earlier, Tony and I had rolled my hoop in the drive and felt the snap of coming winter. Here in the drawing room, the fire was roaring. Best of all, Marjorie had come home for a few days to see for herself that all of us were safe and sound. She sat beside Rose on the ottoman with me nestled under her arm and Tony splayed on the carpet before us. Mummy was here, Grannie Jane and Charlotte, and also Hector.

Miss Marianne remained at home in bed with a dreadful chest cold, the result of her ordeal in the dungeon.

She may have been coughing, but I believed her malady went deeper still, that her heart had cracked right down the middle and then again cross-wise. Poor Miss Marianne had lost her sweetheart, her brother, and then her son . . . for the second time. She'd lost her sister-in-law, which was perhaps not the greatest sorrow, but they'd been related for half a lifetime, and that must count for something. Not least of all, Miss Marianne had nearly lost her beloved Rose! The folly of Leonard's single error, approaching the wrong woman as his mother, had unwrapped heartache for all of us. Such weight in Miss Marianne's chest might easily be mistaken for bronchitis.

This was my first encounter with Rose since the awful vision on the stretcher. I longed to ask a thousand questions, but knew it was kinder to let her tell the tale in her own time. Hector I'd seen every day. As soon as school was finished he came straight to Groveland and worked on his assignments while I read beside him at the library table. Grannie Jane and Mummy agreed that he was quite the most polite boy they'd ever met, and excellent advertising for befriending a foreigner.

He hopped up now to hold open the door for Sally coming with the heavily laden tea trolley. Pea soup with buttery croutons. A giant wedge of cheddar and honey for dipping it in. Ham sandwiches with cress from the green-house, picked by Mummy.

"Cook says to remind you, Miss Aggie, there's, alas, no blackberries this time of year, but she's done an apple, since you made such a noise about pie." Next to the pie were ramekins of chocolate pudding and a plate of bourbon biscuits. Tony went begging from one knee to the next. Though he was scolded often, I was not the only one to succumb.

Cook also knew by now that Hector preferred drinking what he called chocolat instead of tea. *Shock-o-la* was my name for it, really just cocoa but twice as thick.

"I suppose they never have sweets at the vicarage?" I poked Hector. "The way you're tucking in?"

"How is the old Reverend Teabag?" said Marjorie.

Hector licked his spoon. "The minister is at all times kindly, but his wife, she thinks I am deaf. Also, she is most untidy."

"Heavens," said Mummy. "If tidiness is your ideal, you've got the wrong friend in Aggie."

"I am not untidy," I objected. "I merely surround myself with a plethora of possibilities."

Grannie Jane was alone in her laughter, but that was enough for me.

"Well, Rose?" said Marjorie, when Sally had wheeled away the tea things. "Will you tell us about your darkest hour? Or is it too much to dwell on the idea that Leonard wanted you dead?"

"I do not think he wished me dead," said Rose slowly. Her voice was weak, as if she were recovering from an ailment of the tonsils. "What he wanted was for me to be his sister, to have Mother greet him as her long-lost son. We each tried to tell him it wasn't so, but he thought we were lying, trying to shun him." She paused to sip her tea. "As he talked and stormed down there on the beach, the truth of the error leapt out of the dark, stopping my breath with its simplicity." Rose wiped a tear from the corner of her eye.

"If only," she said. "If only I'd known the secret burden that Auntie M. carried. And if only I had seen the letter addressed to me."

"I didn't know the letter was yours!" I said. "I was trying to find out quietly, so as not to alarm anyone."

"Yes, I know," said Rose. "Just that if I'd been home to collect the post, there might have been a happy ending! Instead, Leonard did terrible things, far past forgiveness. One mistake piled on the next until he could see no way out. The way he *shook* me when I tried to explain what I'd just guessed . . ." Her fingers strayed to her shoulders, where Leonard's fury had left its mark.

"But how did it all start?" said Grannie. Her ball of wool rolled off her knee and across the floor. Hector and

I both pounced but Hector won, and wound it up before handing it back.

"Leonard's mother, Mrs. Cable, preferred him not to know that he was adopted," said Rose. "Nor about the allowance. She was afraid he would feel unloved, knowing he'd been given away, or imagine that she cared only because she was paid to do so."

"A shocking thing to learn when he was grown," said Mummy. "That he was not who he'd believed himself to be."

"When Mrs. Cable died," said Rose, "her husband finally told the whole story. After that, Leonard could not rest. Snooping through papers, he identified my father as the source of the allowance. From that moment, he burned to meet the man he guessed to be his father."

Rose sipped her tea. I knew it must be cold by now and poured more fresh from the pot under the crocheted cozy.

"Mr. Cable received a letter from the solicitor, announcing my father's death and enclosing a small legacy of thirty pounds. That thirty pounds set Leonard off, a hint of what else might belong to him, and enough to pay for his travels to find out. He soon said good-bye to the Cable farm and made his way to Torquay."

Rose closed her eyes and rested her head against the back of the chair. "I suppose it's easier to talk about this with Auntie M. not here," she said. "My mother never forgave my aunt for shaming the family by having a baby. Imagine her shock when that baby turned up to haunt her."

I glanced at Grannie, who was steadily knitting, and Mummy, staring at the half-eaten biscuit in her hand. Neither of them would have chosen to discuss a baby's origins with Hector and me in the room.

But here we were.

"After many weeks in Torquay," said Hector, "Leonard is finding the courage. He stops Mrs. Eversham beside the post office. With much longing he tells her, I am your son. And she rebuffs him."

"She called him filth," said Rose, "and did not even tell him the truth, I assume because she preferred to keep hidden any hint of scandal that would tarnish the Eversham name."

"And on Friday evening," said Hector, very quietly, "your mother is again making the threat, is she not?"

"Leonard delivered the flowers for the concert," I said. "He was standing right there when you and your mother came through the door."

"She must have recognized him," said Rose. "She said . . . remember? She said that any young man who dared to approach her daughter would be imprisoned on a charge of attempting to assault her."

"I thought she was being mean to Roddy Fusswell," I said.

"So did we all," said Rose. "It was *so* embarrassing!"

"Instead she is warning Leonard," said Hector. "Reminding him that she means to do him harm."

"And again the next morning," I said, remembering Miss Marianne's description of the minutes before the murder. "When Mrs. Eversham read the letter, she wanted to go straight to the police. Her threat was her own death sentence."

"Poor Auntie M.," said Rose. "If only he'd said those words to her! She would have a son and I a cousin, without prison bars between us."

"Mrs. Cable died," I said. "He must have missed her. And he was not content on the farm. He was looking for a new family."

But he'd ended up sleeping in a cold shed in a stranger's garden looking up at the warm, pink lights of the window where he believed his sister to be sleeping. That might make a person lose his reason, mightn't it?

"It is not perhaps only a matter of money," said Hector. "Being without a home, it is very difficult, the wishing to belong somewhere."

Tears scalded my eyes. When I blinked them away, I saw that everyone else was pink-eyed too. Tony rested his nose on Hector's knee. My sorrow was for Rose being an orphan, for Miss Marianne losing so much, for Hector being far from his family, and for Papa, whom I would never see again.

"Hector, dear," said Marjorie.

"Madame?"

"When does your family expect to make the journey from Belgium?"

"They hope to come in the spring, madame."

"I wonder whether you would consider spending Christmas with all of us at Owl Park? It will be my first holiday as mistress there, and I intend to make it awfully jolly. We have a skating pond and a wonderful cook and a fireplace in every room . . . What do you think?"

I clapped my hands. "Oh *do* say yes, Hector!"

Hector appeared to be speechless. He gazed at Marjorie with something that looked like adoration.

"*Yes!*" he said. "I will very much like to come."

Marjorie laughed and shook his offered hand. "Well, then. It's settled. You shall have an old-fashioned English Yuletide with roasted chestnuts and carol singers and figgy pudding. And I promise there will be no dead bodies, unless poor old Father Christmas drinks too much eggnog and knocks himself stupid on the hearth!"

"Do not make such a promise," I said. "Bodies can show up anywhere."

AUTHOR'S NOTE

ONE OF THE MOST EXCITING MOMENTS of my reading life was discovering that the author of the book I'd just finished (at the age of twelve) had written several dozen other books waiting on the library shelf! Oh, lucky me! Hours and hours more of mayhem and murder!

Agatha Christie—after William Shakespeare—is the second best-selling author in history. It would be hard to find a reading adult who has not heard of her, as more than two billion copies of her books have been sold around the world in over 100 languages. Of course there were more stories!

As an adult, I became curious . . . What made Agatha an expert on betrayal, suspicion and wickedness? What sort of family and community had populated her childhood? What kind of books did she like to read? And from what seeds of inspiration did she conjure up her two famous detectives, Hercule Poirot and Miss Jane Marple? When Tara Walker at Tundra Books "casually" asked whether Agatha Christie might be a good model for a child sleuth, my heart jumped on the spot. And what if she had a best friend? I thought. A clever boy with an accent . . .

A single comment, after a life of being a mystery fan, led me to write this entirely fictional story, featuring the made-up character of Aggie Morton. I did lots of research about what the world was like in 1902 when Agatha Christie was twelve years old. I read her autobiography, as well as some of her favorite childhood books and a couple of biographies. I visited her hometown, spied the view from her hill, walked the streets she walked, leaned on the railing overlooking the harbor. Certain details of Aggie Morton's nature and circumstances overlap with those of Agatha Christie's youth, but her adventures are my own creation.

The famous crime writer grew up in Torquay, England, in a house named Ashfield, many hills up from the harbor. She lived with her parents, a series of beloved pets, and a few devoted servants. Her brother, Monty, and sister, Madge, were ten and eleven years older than she was and moved away when Agatha was still a child. Her young life was happy and secure until her father died when she was eleven. The family's sadness was immense, but Agatha continued to be surrounded by people who cared about her. One of her grandmothers, a wise and humorous woman, came often to visit. Agatha was extremely shy and much preferred solving puzzles and reading books to interacting with real people. She ceremoniously buried her dead pets and often chose the graveyard as a destination for her walks. She played with neighbor children, and had many imaginary companions, but she never met a

Belgian boy named Hector, nor did she discover a corpse or pursue a killer.

Agatha Christie was in her twenties when World War One began. Many thousands of Belgians sought temporary asylum in England when the Germans occupied their homeland. When Agatha later began to write mysteries, she dipped into her own memory of these refugees to create her famous sleuth. I have given her a friendship with Hector Perot a few years earlier than that.

It was no surprise to the Victorians that people from other countries were eager to come to glorious England, but newcomers then (as now, all over the world) were often greeted with suspicion or condescension, even by the well-intentioned. With the status of outsiders and the common label of "foreigner," refugees, or immigrants like Hector, ached to be safe and welcome in their new home. By using authentically thoughtless language—that we might consider unacceptable today—I hoped to emphasize the loneliness of a boy far from family and familiar surroundings.

As a writer, I know that ideas sit for a long time in the cobwebbed corners of the brain. A chance encounter, an odd phrase, a funny incident, a half-heard conversation . . . the observations of an ordinary day are jotted down, photographed, recalled—or misremembered—and take on new shapes weeks or years later as part of a made-up story.

Some of the challenge and much of the fun in writing *The Body under the Piano* was placing such seeds in the path of my heroine. A chance encounter could be reinvented as the excuse for an alibi, the half-heard murmurs a lesson in eavesdropping. That odd phrase might inspire a book title. I like to imagine that my Aggie Morton will grow up to become a writer herself one day.

SOURCES

I HAVE READ AND LISTENED to more mysteries than I could ever name, each one contributing to my stash of tropes and trickery. I cannot claim to have read every story ever written by Agatha Christie, but I've given it a good try!

Alongside Christie's novels, and innumerable websites and movies about murder and Victorian England, here is a selection of other books used for research:

Christie, Agatha. *An Autobiography*. London: Collins, 1977.

Curran, John, ed. *Agatha Christie's Complete Secret Notebooks*. Glasgow: HarperCollins, 2016.

Doyle, Arthur Conan. *The Complete Sherlock Holmes*. London: Longman, 1979.

Farjeon, Eleanor. *A Nursery in the Nineties*. London: V. Gollancz, 1935.

Flanders, Judith. *Inside the Victorian Home: A Portrait of Domestic Life in Victorian England*. New York: W.W. Norton, 2004.

Flanders, Judith. *The Invention of Murder: How the Victorians Revelled in Death and Detection and Created Modern Crime*. London: HarperPress, 2011.

Fry, Stephen, John Woolf, and Nick Baker. *Stephen Fry's Victorian Secrets*. Read by Stephen Fry. Audible Studios, 2018. Audiobook.

Hochschild, Adam. *King Leopold's Ghost: A Story of Greed, Terror, and Heroism in Colonial Africa*. Boston: Houghton Mifflin, 1998.

Thompson, Laura. *Agatha Christie: An English Mystery*. London: Headline Review, 2007.

ACKNOWLEDGMENTS

THANK YOU to Tara Walker, Margot Blankier and Shana Hayes for an elevated editorial process, a balance between delighted applause and scrupulous attention to detail.

Thank you to my steadfast agent, Ethan Ellenberg, and to the loyal support team at Tundra Books.

Thank you to Isabelle Follath for the gorgeous cover and witty portrait gallery, as well as the dozens of clever spot drawings throughout. Your pictures are everything I hoped for.

Thank you to my wise and wonderful early readers and story consultants, Judy Blundell, Hadley Dyer, Sarah Ellis, Vicki Grant, Deb Heiligman, Margo Rabb, Martha Slaughter, Natalie Standiford and Rebecca Stead. You offered insight, brutal truths, and love.

Thank you to my darling daughters.

And thank you to Agatha Christie for a thousand hours of reading pleasure and the inspiration for Hector Perot and Aggie Morton.

More adventure,

more mystery,

more murder . . .

COMING SOON IN THE NEXT

AGGIE MORTON
MYSTERY QUEEN